BEN

CORA ROSE

To Charity VanHuss. I left the poop just for you.

CHAPTER ONE

BEN

"Why do you look so tired?" Vikki asks, leaning over the reception counter and eyeing me with severity. Those light blue eyes miss nothing. For being an old lady, she sure has keen eyesight. Like a hawk in search of a meal. But she's not wrong. I am tired. I work a lot to help offset the cost of college. My dad is helping me, but he can't be expected to pay for it all. That's why I have this job at the senior living facility and the one at my dad's automotive shop where he and his two best friends build and refurbish old cars and motorcycles.

I mean, that job is a no-brainer. All that mechanic eye-candy can't go ignored.

"I'm not tired," I say, biting back a yawn. If she only knew *why* I was almost nodding off on the job, she would riot. She'd honestly probably get a kick out of it. She and Martha are the biggest perverts. And don't get me started on their new friend Norma. She's secretly the biggest nympho on the planet.

I shudder thinking of them having sex but then feel bad. No one can be a bigger slut than me.

You'll see.

"You look like you've just gotten out of a sex marathon," Martha says behind me, making me jump. "That's what Vikki was trying to say. You look oversexed."

"I don't think that's a thing," I say, and Vikki cackles, as does Norma who appears at her side.

"I don't think so either, dear. There is no such thing."

I smile at her and then shoo the three of them away. They ignore me, but they do eventually amble off out of the lobby, whispering to each other. And by whisper, I mean they're shouting their theories about me to one another. Everyone in the room can hear what they're saying, and I sigh, staring down at my phone and seeing the missed texts from two men.

Two men who are utterly exhausting me and yet, I can't stay away.

I should, but I can't. I fucking can't.

Quickly, I type back a response and then smile widely at the young woman who enters the building. Bethany. She comes to visit her grandmother regularly, and we're on a first-name basis.

"How are you managing the Wild West in here?"

"Oh god, your grandma is the culprit. You know that right? She tried sneaking out of here this morning."

Bethany rolls her eyes. "God, where was she going?"

"Said she was going to try out for a burlesque show in Vegas."

"Oh lord, no. She cannot do that with her back and ankles. But I swear, she has these ideas in her head, and I can't convince her otherwise."

I smile widely at her, and she smiles back.

"I'll have a talk with her. Don't worry. Though it won't help at all though, and next week she will be trying to escape again."

"God help us all," I say, and she laughs, throwing me a wave before disappearing down the hallway.

I watch her go and my mind turns back to those two men who are waiting for my response. If anyone knew what I was doing in my free time, they'd kick me to the curb. They'd disown me. I'd be the sexual pariah.

Quiet little Ben who works at a senior home with the old men and women, who bakes snacks on the weekends for his friends, who helps his dad mow the lawn when he can...

Sweet, helpful little Ben who is so kind and thoughtful.

If they only knew. If they only knew what I did behind closed doors.

I press my fists into my tired eyes and sigh.

Not like I have any intention of stopping.

No siree. Not a chance in hell.

I won't stop until they make me.

———

I'm the sluttiest slut, I think as Cash grabs on to my hair and fucks into my mouth. He has a big cock, a tattooed one that slides down my throat roughly every time he thrusts forward. I'm on my knees with my hand down my pants, jerking my own dick as he fucks my throat relentlessly.

I groan, my chin and forearm wet with my own saliva as I stroke him with my free hand. Even though I'm a deep-throat whore, I still can't fit this big dick all the way in.

I glance up and watch as Cash stares down at me with those dark eyes, those long lashes hooded. Shit, he's hot. A gay guy's wet dream. I can't believe he's letting me do this, that he's been letting me suck his dick. I must be that good. God, if my dad found out I was on my knees for his best friend, he'd be so disappointed.

It's the filthiest secret I have. But I can't stop. I can't.

I'm the horniest fucker on the planet.

No one would guess it. Meek, quiet little Ben. But fuck, I want all the dick. *All the time.*

No more thinking of my dad. No, I'm focusing on Cash and his big tattooed cock. It has a black and red dragon slithering down its length—a rather impressive cum-breathing dragon.

"Your mouth, *shit,*" Cash rasps as his legs start to shake. "Shit, Ben."

The way he says my name, the smell of him, the taste. I could do this all day, just cockwarm his dick until he gets hard again. He hasn't fucked my ass yet, but I'm ready when he is. I don't want to pressure him though. I'm not quite sure he's gay—more like questioning. Like I was saying, the fact he's fucking my mouth right now is a miracle.

But then again, the way I can swallow him without gagging is quite the thing.

"Gonna come," he moans and my hand works my cock faster. God, I love the taste of him, and just knowing he's forbidden makes this so much hotter.

My balls draw up as I peer up once more and see his handsome face staring down at me. That day-old scruff lining his strong jaw and his mussed hair. My length swells and as soon as the taste of his release hits my tongue, I explode in my pants. Just endless streams of it as I shake and groan, swallowing down as much of his cum as I can. It's a lot, just wave after wave, as if he's been holding it all in for me.

When I finally come down from the high of my orgasm, I slump forward, my forehead resting against his hairy thigh. It scratches my shaved skin and I sigh, loving the feel of it against me.

I let his softening dick fall from my mouth and take large gulping breaths. I know I look wrecked, my cheeks splotchy, my nose running, my mouth puffy and red, but I don't fucking care. I am addicted to this. To this feeling of danger and lust.

And I know where I'm going after this. I know I shouldn't, but I can't help myself.

And like hell I'm giving it up any time soon. Maybe that makes me a bad, selfish son, but hell, I've done everything in my life the right way. Everything. I've always done what everyone's asked of me, never complained, always complied. I'm so tired of being selfless. It all came to a head several weeks ago when I snapped. When I unzipped Cash's jeans and slid his dick into my mouth.

For the first time in my life, I decided to take what I wanted, bit by bit.

And I want more. More of all of this.

"You okay?" Cash asks, looking slightly concerned at how wrecked I look. But he doesn't get it. I love the pain of it, love the feel of being ruined. I'd be ruined *all day long* if I could. Just a hole to be filled over and over.

"I'm fine," I say as I push myself up and swipe at my mouth. My eyes meet his dark ones as he zips up his pants and buttons them.

He runs a shaking hand through his hair, looking slightly guilty. He knows who I am, and he knows what his friendship means to my dad. And yet, I've been sucking his dick for weeks. It started out slowly, a drunken night where his cock ended up in my mouth after he drove me home from work and I asked him in for a drink. He was upset about a recent breakup with a long-term girlfriend, and I was happy to help him forget.

Come inside and relax.

Fingers and thighs brushing.

Sighs and groans.

Stripes of cum marking the inside of my mouth.

And I thought for sure it would end there, that my choking, moaning blow job would scare him away. I was so damn worried that my dream come true would be dashed, but it happened again. I ended up back at his place a few days later and made sure that he wanted it again.

And again.

Nearly every day now. Sometimes twice when he can get me alone.

My hole clenches in excitement, and I mentally talk it down. Cash isn't ready for that. Not yet. But I know where I'm going right after this —who I'm gonna see that will take care of my needy hole.

Ford.

I'm gonna go straight to his place and take it right up the ass.

Yep, I'm addicted to my dad's best friends. The three of them have been co-owners of the shop for at least fifteen years, and they've been friends for even longer. I've always thought Cash and Ford were hot, for as long as I've known I like men. But I was just a kid before, and they never spared me a second glance. It wasn't until recently, now that I'm grown, that I finally decided to see if I could get what I've always wanted.

God, I'm going to hell when I die. Just straight on down. But it doesn't stop me. It only excites me more. I'd probably fuck Lucifer at this point. That's just who I seem to be—a guy who will fuck into eternity.

I question myself sometimes. Am I doing this to fill some gaping hole in my life? Sex has always been good, but something about them has made it different. Perhaps it's because they've been a part of my life for so long. Perhaps there is some loneliness that I don't want to deal with.

Fuck knows. That's for a therapist to look at in the future. The only gaping hole I want to think about is my ass when Ford is finished with it.

"You want to stay for dinner?" Cash asks, and my heart clenches in my chest. Because, no. I can't stay. I've already made plans with his best friend. Those are the rules I have. I never stay. I might be fucking them both, unbeknownst to them, but I still feel slightly guilty. This is just sex, pure and simple. And they know it. This is not exclusive. I've told them that explicitly, and they both stared at me like I'd lost my mind.

Maybe I have lost it, but I cannot and will not fall in love with either of them.

That's not possible...not an option. For many reasons.

"I can't. I have other plans," I say, and Cash runs a hand down his face. It's always the same answer. I have plans. Plans that involve school, or work...or Ford.

And the same goes when I'm with Ford. He wants me to stay the night, wants to hold me, but I push him away. *I'm tired. I can't.* And then I leave.

It's a wonder they keep coming around with how little I'm giving them in return.

The sex must be amazing in their eyes.

"Alright. See you at work tomorrow?" Cash asks, and I nod, walking to the bathroom to clean myself up the best I can. I need to start pulling my cock out of my jeans when I jerk myself, but sometimes the heaviness of his dick in my mouth makes me lose all reason. I usually regret it afterward and will have to stop at home to clean up before going to Ford's. As much as the thought of meeting with him covered in my own jizz, with someone else's in my belly turns me on, it seems almost like a betrayal of sorts.

I mean, let's be real. It is, but this one tiny boundary makes me feel a little better about myself.

When I come out of the bathroom, Cash is leaning against the door. He towers over me—big, muscled, and tattooed. His arms bulge and his thighs bunch under his jeans. He's so fucking sexy. Hairy. Manly. I don't know what he sees in me—a twenty-one-year-old with admittedly questionable taste in clothing and a timid personality. But I guess it's working for him.

And Ford.

It's working for both of them.

We are *insatiable*.

Imagine what it would be like to have them at the same time, I think but then quickly push that thought away. No. That won't ever happen. Never. It's just a horny guy's dream. I need to set that aside and never think of it again.

"Text me when you get home safely," he says softly, and I peer up at him, biting my bottom lip. I want to kiss him, to run my tongue along the insides of his mouth, but I told myself I wouldn't do that either. This is just sex. Kissing gives me all the feels.

Feels are something I can't afford right now. I'm already walking a thin line. So kissing is off the table.

"Yeah, I will," I say, reaching down and grabbing my book bag. I have one more semester left in college, and then I'm done. And it can't come soon enough. I'm ready for it all to be over so I can just relax. Relax and enjoy my life. Maybe I'll move away and start somewhere new where I can soothe my broken heart.

Because that's what's gonna happen at the end of this.

I'm going to be broken when it all comes to a head.

I can't have my dad finding out. He'd see who I really am.

Who his friends are.

Everything would come crumbling down around us all.

I scoot past him and head to the front door, Cash following along behind me. Reaching around me, he opens the door, the musky smell of him making my cock twitch in my pants. God, I want to fall to my knees and suck him all over again. It's becoming a problem.

"Bye, Ben," he says lowly, and I give him a small wave before jogging down the steps to my car. As soon as I'm inside, I pull out my phone and see the missed messages from Ford. Fuck, he's been waiting. I'm gonna get it so good from him for being late.

I glance once more at the doorway Cash lingers in and think that it was so fucking worth it.

———

"Where were you?" Ford asks, making me squeal in surprise as I trudge up the steps to my small apartment. He's waiting at the top of the stairs, near my door. Shit. I wanted time to shower and clean up before I met him, to wash away the evidence of where I just was.

And since when does Ford come to my place? That's too fucking risky.

"Why are you here?" I ask softly, unlocking my apartment door and pushing it open. I live on the same property as my dad, in a small apartment over the detached garage, so Ford showing up and hanging out with me would arouse major suspicion.

"I was with your dad having a drink. He and Avery took a night ride. We're fine," he says as he follows me into my place. And instead of feeling ashamed that I was just with someone else—his best friend, no less—I feel excited. Thrilled. Nervous that he might discover it. That it might all implode.

But Ford doesn't seem to notice as he reaches out and eagerly pulls my shirt over my head, tossing it to the ground before twisting me around and roughly unbuttoning my pants. Oh, he doesn't like to be kept waiting. He's always so impatient, so urgent. Where Cash is more quiet and steadfast, Ford has the manic energy that I wish I could have. He's the energy in the room, the zing of excitement.

His hands tug my pants down as he pushes me forward, my body falling onto the bed, my ass sticking out, still cloaked in my boxer briefs. If he reaches his hand around the front, he'll notice that I'm wet, that I came in my pants just fifteen minutes ago. But he doesn't. He's too impatient.

"Look at that ass," he murmurs as he tugs my underwear down, and I hear the clink of his belt buckle as it falls to the floor. "Gonna wreck it." Then the rip of a condom wrapper pierces the silence.

"You good?" he asks as I feel cool lube slide down my crack right before his fingers push inside of me.

I gasp, feeling myself immediately accept him. I love it, love feeling full down there. Love the stretch and sting of a cock as it pushes into me.

"Always," I moan softly as Ford works his fingers inside of me. One, two, three. I want him to fist me. Want him to stick his whole goddamn hand up me, but I'll take it slow. He does what he wants, when he wants. And I love it. Love the suspense, the thrill. I never know what he's gonna do to me. Never know what he has planned.

But no matter what, I'm here for it.

The shuffle of feet moving forward has me arching back and when I feel the tip of his sheathed cock press against my waiting hole, I take him in. Take it all. Just a swift thrust of his hips and he's balls deep. A unified groan surrounds the space between us and then it turns into panting as Ford leans down and bites at my shoulder.

"Fuck, your ass is so goddamn needy," he rasps and then thrusts again, taking it slow at first, but then ramping up the tempo. My cock is hard between my legs, bouncing with each fuck, and I try to temper my moans, but I can't. I can't stop the sounds from exiting my mouth. They're needy and feral and disgusting and yet, there's no way to hold them in. Not when Ford's dick is stretching me out. It's long, thick, and hard. And I take all of it, every inch. In and out it goes, hard and punishing. But it's when he shifts forward and pulls me up so I'm standing that I feel my cock drip endlessly. I'm impaled on him fully now, just unable to move or think. I'm just a hole now—a sore, aching hole that is being rutted into until I feel the choppy thrusts of Ford behind me.

"Fuck, your ass is good. I want to fuck it all night. Just stay inside of it and fill it over and over."

I want that too. Want it so bad. I want Cash and Ford to take turns having me all night long, but I don't say that. Just hold those devious thoughts in as he thrusts into me over and over.

"I want your cock to come first. I want to feel it explode untouched," he says and then bends me back down, thrusting his hips back and forth as he takes me even harder. The bed hits the wall, my eyes crossing from the sheer pleasure of it, and as if on command, my balls draw up and a pained cry leaves me as I erupt across the sheets.

Ford groans at the feeling of my ass clenching around him, and I feel him pound into me faster and faster until he finally unloads into the condom, falling against me and biting his way across my shoulders.

"Damn," he murmurs, and all I can do is swallow and nod.

He doesn't pull out right away, just holds himself inside of me, and I let him, bearing the heavy weight of his body behind me. We're sweaty from our exertion and the musk of sex fills the air. If my dad were to come in, he'd smell it. He'd know what we'd done.

When he finally pulls out, I collapse onto the bed with weak knees, utterly satiated from coming twice in the past hour. To be honest, I'm young. I could do so much more than this. I could literally go all day. My libido is through the roof, but for now, I take it as it comes. And it comes a lot. And so do I.

Ford pulls the condom off, tosses it in the trash bin, and flops down on the bed next to me, his lips tilted up in a mischievous smile. Cash and Ford look similar in many ways—tattoos lining their skin, dark hair, dark eyes, and scruffy jaws. They're even almost the same age. Cash is forty-two and Ford is thirty-eight, and even for their ages, they're in shape. I could spend hours tracing the lines of the muscle ridges in their abdomens. But here is where they differ. Where Cash is more stoic, Ford is more excitable. A perfect yin and yang. And I'm the holes in between.

God, I need therapy.

But hell, the way my body feels right now, used and satiated, I figure this is the best medicine. Sex therapy.

"You can't stay," I say, trying to keep my tone as nice as possible. "My dad could come home any minute."

Ford's smile slips and he turns on his side to really look at me, his big dick hanging limply between us. My lips are dry, and I wet them, trying to curb this insatiable hunger I have for these men, but failing miserably. I'd let him fuck me again, right now if I could. I so would let him in again. I've never felt this obsessed with anyone before, and here I am, torn between the two of them.

"Yeah, yeah. I know. Don't worry," Ford says and then cocks his head, taking me in. I know what he sees—my thin body, flushed cheeks, and my mussed brown, just-been-fucked hair. "But I want to fuck you again before I leave. So don't make me go yet. I'm not done."

I bite back a moan, unable to say no. Of course he can fuck me again. Of course he can, but he shouldn't.

"We really shouldn't," I say, not really meaning it.

Even as I say it, my cock is hardening between my legs. It's insatiable, greedy—has a mind of its own.

"Yeah, well, give an old guy a second to get hard again. Then I'm gonna fuck you nice and slow. Then I'll leave. Like you want me to."

I nod, already trying not to rut against the mattress. But failing miserably after Ford reaches down and starts to fuck more lube into me with his fingers. He gets all four in me, twisting, hitting my prostate with each thrust, making me whine.

"There it is. You want my whole fist, don't you, you greedy little fucker," he says and I nod, whimpering at the sensation of being stretched once more. Oh god, I need help. I need someone to tell me this insatiable need I have is normal.

"But you know what I really want? I want you raw. I want to feel that ass take me with nothing between us."

I want that too. I want it all, but we can't. I need to be safe. I'm fucking two men without them knowing. I can't do that to them. That would just be utterly selfish.

"Can't," I moan as he straddles my hips from behind, his cock sliding between my cheeks, searching for my hole. My face is turned into the mattress, and I feel Ford's stubble brush against my neck as he puts on a new condom and sinks into me.

"One fucking day, Ben. I'm gonna have you every way I want. Whenever I want."

I cry out as he thrusts all the way in and fucks me slowly. I lose track of time, just feeling the drag of him moving in and out of me, feeling the way our skin sticks and slides together. And once again, he doesn't come until I do, the orgasm barreling through me almost painful this time. Only then does he let himself come, leaving me wrung out and sleepy. I have quite possibly had too much sex.

Pfft.

There's no such thing.

"You really need to leave," I say when he pulls out of me and flops down next to me, but my eyes are closing. So fucking tired and relaxed. Heaven. Fucked senseless is heaven.

"Yeah, I know," Ford murmurs, his finger tracing the pout of my lips.

And that's the last thing I hear before I am catapulted into a dark dreamless sleep.

CHAPTER TWO

BEN

When I wake the next morning, I note that Ford is gone. And while a part of me is thankful that he didn't stay while I was passed out, a small part of me is disappointed that he left. But then again, I'm doing this to myself. I made a choice when I first let them take me in the most inappropriate of ways, that I couldn't let anything go any further than this.

Sex. That's all it is.

Just a lot of sex.

No feelings involved.

I run a hand down my face and stare up at the ceiling just as my phone pings.

I grab it and see Cash's name appear on the screen.

CASH:

Meet me before work?

My heart pounds a little faster in my chest. I totally shouldn't, but I so am. I quickly get up and shower, brushing my teeth and pulling on some clean clothes. Locking the front door, I run down the steps of my garage apartment, my backpack flung across my back.

"Hey," my dad calls out, and I skid to a stop, feeling guilt plow through me. Yeah, I'm having the best sex of my life, but with that comes the guilt of knowing what I'm doing to my dad.

I don't think he'd be cool with it if he found out.

Yeah, I'm pretty sure he wouldn't be happy with me or his two friends.

I refuse to be the reason they part ways, but at the same time, I can't stop.

The sluttiest selfish slut on the planet.

"Where you off to?" my dad asks, running a hand down his unshaven face. He's big and muscular too. Very similar to Ford and Cash. I don't know how he's my dad. If it wasn't for that ancestry test we had done, I'd think I wasn't his son. But I am. When I look in the mirror, I see her. I'm a carbon copy of my mother. The same slim stature, same skin tone. My messy brown hair and mousy brown eyes are all her. Really, when I look at myself, I don't see anything special, but I have to have something going for me to grab two men like Ford and Cash.

I had no idea they were even a possibility until it happened. And now I'm loath to give it up.

Not yet.

Not quite yet.

"Just heading out to meet a friend before work," I lie and my dad nods, giving me an awkward wave before disappearing back into his garage.

God, he's lonely. Ever since my mom died when I was a baby, he's focused solely on work and raising me. He's dated, but it was few and far between. I should be a better son and spend more time with him, but right now, I'm stretched thin.

And so is my ass.

Stretched and aching.

The best feeling, I think as I stride to my car and slide in. I know my dad hates that I drive this. It's a basic Honda Accord with far too many miles. *You're giving me a bad name*, he teased, but I like this car. I don't feel comfortable driving a wily muscle car. I'd rather just be in my little beater that gets me where I need to go. One day, after I graduate, I'll look for an upgrade. Maybe a newer model.

My mouth quirks a smile, remembering how my car bugs both Cash and Ford. They've both made comments about it to me on separate occasions.

But this is mine, and I'm gonna hold on to it for as long as I can.

When I make it to Cash's small house on the other side of town, I hurriedly get out and jog up the steps to rap on the door.

Seconds later, the door swings open and there he is—shirtless and in gray sweatpants. I stare at the intricate, colorful tattoos on his broad chest and arms, and my mouth instantly goes dry.

"We have thirty minutes," I say as I enter and the door shuts behind me.

Cash folds his arms across his chest and eyes me, that gaze raking down my abdomen to my legs before moving back up again.

I feel my entire body tremble just from him looking at me. God, I need more. I need him to fuck me.

"Come on," he says and turns toward his bedroom. I'm shocked, never having been in there before. Usually, I end up on my knees in the kitchen or on the rug in the den, but never in his room.

As soon as I enter, I take it in. Everything is masculine just like him. Dark wood and light gray sheets, an overflowing hamper in the corner, and then Cash standing in the midst of it.

"You in a rush?" he asks as I set my bag down on the floor and shift on my feet.

"Not really. I just have to get into the shop and get some filing done before class. You know my dad's ridiculously unorganized. It's gonna take ages to clean that mess up."

He nods and then takes a step toward me. I move to kneel, but he stops me.

"No. Not yet. Clothes off."

The way he commands me makes my entire body light up. Oh god, I've never been naked with him before, and now he wants to see me.

"You sure?" I ask, and he nods.

"I'm fucking sure. Show me."

Swallowing, I pull my t-shirt over my head, feeling a little insecure about my lack of defined muscle, but Cash doesn't seem to care. He just stares at me, his eyes roving over my chest and then landing on my waist when I start to remove my pants and boxer briefs.

As soon as I'm naked, my hard cock jutting out before me, Cash runs a hand across the stubble on his jaw.

He likes what he sees, I know he does. I can tell by the way his pupils dilate, by the way his cock grows down his thigh. He's probably trying to process it. First, the blow jobs, and now this. He doesn't know what to make of me or why his body's responding to a man.

God, the fact that I'm the reason for this man's sexual awakening turns me on even more. Boring Ben, and yet here I am, making Cash's dick hard.

"Turn around," he says gruffly, and I do as he says, spinning slowly, letting him take a good look at me. His breath comes out a little stuttered, and I peer over my shoulder, my eyes meeting his stare.

"You gonna fuck me?" I ask softly, and Cash moves toward me, his hands encircling my waist.

"You'd like that, wouldn't you?"

"Yeah," I say, and it's not a lie. I really would like it. Like it a whole hell of a lot. Just the thought of it makes my cock leak in anticipation.

But instead of bending me over, he reaches around my front and grabs on to my cock, pumping it slowly in his hand. He's never touched me before like this. It's always been me on my knees, my clothes on. And holy fuck, my entire body zings with pleasure at the sensation, the feel, the way it looks to have his large ringed, tattooed hand wrapped around me.

"Shit," I moan as I arch up into him, my head falling back against his shoulder. "I'm not gonna last."

He tightens his grip on me, his other hand sliding down my hip and cupping my balls. His lips are tucked into my neck as he slides his hard bulge against my ass.

It's too much, too fucking much. The only thing that would make it better is if Ford was here with him. My fantasy would then be complete.

The stubble on Cash's jaw abrades my own as he breathes against my skin, jerking me. "You come. You come and then suck my cock."

I let out a low moan as he thrusts up against me and his hand slides down my length. I'm close. So fucking close to falling over the edge.

You'd think I would be tired of it by now, but I've always had such a high sex drive and it's only heightened by the fact the two men of my dreams are taking me.

Over and over.

My cum shoots from my cock as I let out a strained gasp and moan. Cash watches it all, his solid body still behind me. And then he lifts his sticky hand to my mouth.

"Suck," he says, and I do, my tongue slipping out to clean each of his fingers. I don't even balk at it—just do as he says. I'll do anything he says.

When his hands are wet with my spit and clean of my cum, he runs it down the crease of my ass, encircling my hole. Just once, but it's enough to have my mind spiraling out of control.

Fuck. Me.

But he doesn't. He removes his hand, spins me, and pushes me to my knees. I go willingly, pulling his sweatpants down and wasting no time in taking his cock to the back of my throat.

He moans above me, his hand fisting my hair while he uses me, thrusting in and out of my open mouth frantically until he spills into me. I swallow as much as I can and then sink back onto my haunches, my chest heaving, my dick half hard from just having him in my mouth.

It's a bit of a problem, I admit. But then again, I've never been more sexually satisfied than I am now.

"I need to go," I manage to say between gulping breaths. Cash just stares down at me and then reaches a hand out, pulling me to my wobbly feet.

"You're gonna eat breakfast with me first."

He doesn't even ask, just commands, and I really fucking like that. I shouldn't, but I do. He pulls me into his kitchen completely naked and grabs something from the warmer. Then he sits on a kitchen chair and pulls me onto his lap.

"I'm gonna watch you eat this and then you can go."

"I can't," I say, but my fingers are already unwrapping the breakfast burrito.

Cash scoffs. "You don't eat enough."

It's true. I've been so stressed that I don't make enough time to take care of myself. And with all the cardio I get from fucking these two guys every day, I really should be putting more calories into me so I can keep up with them.

I bite into the burrito and my tastebuds light up. This is fucking good, and within a matter of minutes, I've polished off half of it.

"I can't eat anymore," I groan, feeling my stomach bulge from the amount of food I just put in it.

Cash takes it from my hand and sets it aside.

"Good. Next time you'll eat more of it."

I nod and then lean my head back against his shoulder. I shouldn't linger. But he feels nice beneath me—that big strong body, the way one of his hands is pressed against my abdomen and the other on my bare thigh. It's not forgotten that I'm naked against him, can feel the heat of his bare chest against my back, his half-hard cock pressed against my ass crack.

"I need to leave," I say and yet make no move to leave. Just a few more minutes.

"You could stay for a bit longer," he tells me, his finger tracing circles on my leg, slowly moving up toward my groin. I feel the drag of it through my entire body. I want him again. I want him all the time.

As if reading my mind, he grabs on to my cock once more and works me over the edge in a matter of minutes, leaving my head reeling and my entire body shaking with relief from the orgasm he pumped out of me.

God, this won't ever get old.

"Come over after class," he tells me, and I shake my head, gulping down air.

"I can't."

I can't because I have plans with Ford after class.

Jesus. I'm so fucked up. It's unhinged, and yet I can't stop. Won't stop.

I know I should probably pick between Ford and Cash, but I can't. I can't fucking pick. They're both perfect in their own ways.

I need them both right now.

I need them both for forever.

"I have to get to work," I say, pushing myself up and walking with wobbly knees to the bedroom where my clothes are. Cash is leaning against the doorframe, watching me dress, and I feel like I'm on display.

My cum is everywhere in this house. On his floor, in the kitchen, on his hand. Oh my god. I've marked my territory like a dog.

As soon as I'm dressed, I head to the front door, turning my gaze over my shoulder and catching Cash eyeing me.

"Tomorrow?" he asks, and I nod. Because hell, there's no way I'm not showing up for another round of whatever that was. I want his hands on me again.

"Thanks for breakfast."

"Always," he says, and I stumble outside, the cool air hitting my face and making my warm, overheated skin positively burn.

"Goddamnit," I murmur as I walk to my car, feeling wrung out and satiated. I could go for a long nap. A really long one. Curled up in Ford's lap. Or Cash's. Or both.

For fuck's sake, I think as I start my rickety car. I need to get a grip. I need to get a grip on something other than my dick.

I pull out of his driveway and feel a pang in my heart.

I don't like leaving so quickly, don't like these walls between us, but it's the only way.

The only way this can work.

———

"So, how's it going juggling two men," my best friend, Tatum, asks. His pink hair sticks straight up, and I swear I don't know how he manages it. But he does. It's unreal. You'd think he spends hours on it, but I know him. He wakes up this way.

I stare at him and then focus back on my computer, trying to get ready for the lecture on urban sociology, which is a topic I am interested in, but I'm unable to focus. My ass hurts from not being filled. It's getting greedy. Just a hole that needs to have something in it at all times.

It's grown accustomed to this kind of life and now it's starting to have expectations. What will I do if they ever dump me? What if they find out what I've been up to and leave me?

It will be a sad time, for sure. I'm not sure I'll survive it.

I'll have to get two different butt plugs, name them Cash and Ford, and wear them when I'm feeling particularly lonely.

"It's going fine," I say and then peek over at Tatum who is wiggling in his seat, his pink lips pulled between his teeth. He has a stain on his shirt and a rip in his pants, but he's one of the smartest people I know. He's in his last year of college too, also studying to become a social worker. I plan on working with the elderly, and he plans on working in adoption.

We've become fast friends over the past few years from having so many classes together. I took to his fun, energetic personality and how open he is. And he took to me...well, I'm not sure why.

I wish I could be more like him at times, but I tend to be more reserved and afraid.

Afraid of so damn much. That's why this whole situation is so crazy. It's the single time I've been brave and just gone for something I want.

"Yeah, and how's your butthole?"

The way he asks this so candidly makes my face heat.

"Jesus, Tatum," I murmur, and then he smiles widely at me.

"What? No one heard, and listen, I am concerned. Is your hole okay? It's gotta take a beating."

It has but I don't tell him this. Instead, I just lean over and poke him. "It's fine. It closes like a Venus fly trap. Now mind your own business."

He chuckles lowly and then shakes his head. "You lucky duck."

I am lucky, but I also know that I'm a bit of a shit too. Honestly, I should tell them, should disclose that I'm fucking them both, but I'm not ready for it to be over. And I have a feeling that it would end as soon as one of them found out about the other.

Does that make me selfish?

Yeah, it does, but I never said I was a saint.

I'm a slut and a selfish one at that.

"You are," Tatum agrees, and I close my eyes.

"I said that out loud?"

"It's an issue, but one I love so very much."

I face forward as class begins, the two of us frantically typing up our notes and then exiting class an hour and a half later. As we walk out, Tatum nudges my arm with his.

"Come on, let's grab dinner and then you can go get your ass pounded."

I roll my eyes and sock him lightly in the arm. To be honest, seeing Cash and Ford earlier at the shop was atrocious.

I mean, watching the two of them together is hot enough—all dirty and oily and working with tools I can't even name. Most days, when I'm sitting at my desk, filing documents, I feel like I'm going to combust. Combine that with the healthy dose of guilt I feel every time I see my dad, and I feel worse.

Horny and sad.

A lame combination.

"Okay, yeah, I could use a little sustenance before tonight."

Tatum grins at me and pulls me toward the college cafeteria where people gather to eat and socialize. I've never been one to do any of that. I'm far too quiet.

"You do need a lot of carbs for all that cardio you're doing."

I silently agree. It is exhausting, but in the best way.

"So what's it gonna be?" he asks as he peruses the options. I go for what's cheapest and what won't leave me too full. A bowl of pasta and a bottle of water. Tatum, on the other hand, has loaded up his tray with an egregious amount of food. A burrito, a bowl of spaghetti, and some kind of yellow soup. Makes my stomach churn just looking at the combination, but Tatum always was a garbage disposal. How he stays so thin is beyond me. Maybe it's all the energy he has. He just burns it all off in his sleep.

"That soup is nasty."

"It does look a bit like baby diarrhea, so I am definitely intrigued."

A snort escapes me. "I swear to god. You're disgusting."

"I know. But all the people love me for it. The things I'm willing to do."

Oh, I know, but I don't want to hear it. My poor ears have already heard too much. Not that Tatum doesn't listen to me blather on about the predicament I've found myself in, but then again, I don't go into detail.

No, I keep all those details for when I'm alone in bed. So I can relive them over and over again.

And I do. They are on repeat.

"So, tell me about your dad. Has he found out yet?" Tatum asks, slurping on his poop soup.

"No, no way. God, he can't ever."

"Shame, but really, Dean is a hunk of man meat."

"Ew, no. Don't talk about my dad."

"Well, you're doing two dudes who are the same age. Don't judge me."

Yeah, he's right, I can't, but I can judge him for his choice in soup.

Quietly, I place a napkin over the top of his bowl, and he stares down at his covered soup.

"For real?"

"It's nasty. I can't watch another minute of you eating it."

He smiles, setting his spoon down and then picking up the burrito. "Fine. It wasn't even that good. Tasted like nut."

I don't even want to know what he's talking about, so I just dig into my pasta and finish it off, my mind a hundred places at once. It's so damn hard to focus when I'm juggling so much. There are times when I feel like I'm just going to crash and burn. Maybe one day I will, but the adrenaline of it has propelled me forward.

It propels me to Ford's place later that night, my entire body thrumming with need. I watched him at work, saw those thick thighs in those jeans, the way his hands flexed on the tools, and I knew I needed him.

And it couldn't come soon enough.

I trudge up the steps to Ford's house, taking note of the neatly trimmed bushes lining the walkway and the two wooden chairs on his front porch. He's sprawled in one, those thick thighs that propel him into me so roughly spread out before him.

He looks good, like sex. Like need. I need him on me, in me. All around me.

I let out a shaky breath, already ready for him to do what he wants to me.

"You're late," he says, and I nod and then shake my head. "You know I hate waiting for shit."

"Had some homework to catch up on."

He pushes himself up, and I bite back a groan. Fuck, he towers over me. He and Cash both do. I love how much bigger and stronger they are than me, how much more capable. They could easily lift me and throw me around a room.

Oh hell, I want that.

"You eat already?" he asks, and I nod, letting him lead me into the newly remodeled kitchen. The cabinet doors are dark wood and the counters are a lighter granite. I love it—sleek, masculine. And knowing that he did this all himself is so damn sexy to me. I'm sure Cash helped him too. The two of them working together in here.

Two best friends helping each other out.

I push that thought aside and look at Ford. He has a grape soda in his hand and he's sipping on it slowly. I just watch the way those lips move and feel my entire body shudder.

This is becoming quite the problem.

"You want a beer? Some wine?"

"I probably shouldn't." I can't because I need to drive, and if I drink I'll have to stay. And if I stay, things change.

Fuck, they can't change.

This can't ever be more than it is because of my dad.

And yet, when has that ever stopped me?

He sets the can down and cocks his head at me. "You look tired. Have you been sleeping?"

My shoulders stiffen at that, because does that mean he doesn't like how I look? I mean, that's entirely possible. I'm not the hottest guy out there. Ford could snatch anyone better than me.

"Doesn't mean shit other than you look exhausted. Come on," Ford says, probably noticing my discomfort and nods toward the bedroom. "I'll give you a massage."

Oh fuck, well, I can't let him do that for…reasons…ones I'm not quite sure I can even remember right now. I follow him down the hall, my legs carrying me to his room. The room where he's entered me far too many times, the mattress where he's shoved my face into the sheets as he plowed into me.

I stare at it, wetting my lips, watching as he makes the bedding up slightly so that I have an unrumpled place to lie down. He knows it's just gonna end up tangled and dirty within the hour.

That much I'm sure about. That much I can guarantee.

"Clothes off," he says, those dark eyes meeting mine. "All of them."

His voice drops an octave, and I feel goosebumps line my skin. I'm shivering and overheated at the same time. I'm defying nature.

My shirt comes off and then my pants and underwear. My hard cock bobs up against my stomach, and I watch as Ford runs a hand across his jaw. So similar to Cash. They're so fucking alike.

"Face down," he orders, and I walk toward the bed in silence, my hole already clenching around nothing—needing to be filled. It's so damn greedy. I swear my body is committing all of the seven deadliest sins being with these men, and I am loath to stop any of it from happening.

As soon as my body hits the mattress, Ford straddles my thighs, his large hands pressing into the muscles of my back, making moans slip from my lips at how good it feels. Everything with him feels so right.

"Hm, love the sounds you make," he murmurs as he works on my shoulders. "You sound like I'm fucking you."

I do. I sound like the slut I am when he's pounding into me. But I can't help it. Every part of him touching me now is making my balls draw up toward my groin and my cock leak profusely where it's pressed into the mattress.

Those hands move down my back, massaging my sore, angry muscles and forcing me to relax even further. When he gets to my ass, he kneads the globes of it gently, spreading my cheeks open so he can stare at me.

And I let him look. I'm caught between relaxed and incredibly turned on. It's a precarious place to be.

He shuffles a little down my legs until he's at my knees, and then I feel the warm breath of him on my skin, right against my crack.

Oh fuck, well, this is something he's never done to me before. Usually the fucking is frantic and with a time limit, but we don't have one right now. Right now, he can take all the time he wants.

His hands pull my ass cheeks apart, and I feel his wet tongue slide along me, licking over my hole and making it clench in anticipation.

He hums as he does it, licking up me once more and then swirling the tip of his tongue around my ass. I arch up, wanting more, wanting to be stuffed full, but he makes me wait. He's teasing me, tormenting me. And I love it.

He sucks on my rim over and over, waiting until I'm whining before he plunges his tongue inside of me.

I cry out, my fingers grabbing on to the sheets, bunching them as I feel his tongue strain forward, pushing as far into me as he can.

Oh fuck, *oh fuck*.

My hips grind against the mattress, my words a jumbled mess as he continues to eat me until I'm nearly panting in frustration. This is good, but it's not enough. I want more.

Need more.

His head lifts, and I feel the weight of him as he reaches over to his nightstand, pulling out a condom and some lube.

"I know you need more, you greedy little slut," he says that last word like it's a term of endearment. I hear the condom wrapper crumple and the cap of the lube snap open. When he pushes two fingers inside of me a second later, I take them without any problem, my hole already waiting and open for him.

"You taste good," he says softly as he fingers me, pushing as much lube into my hole as he can. It dribbles down my taint and onto the sheets below me.

"I should have you eat my ass next," he adds, and I wholeheartedly agree. I would so eat his ass any day.

Breakfast, lunch, and dinner.

I'd eat Cash's too. I'd take turns gorging myself on them. Like the glutton I am.

His fingers move from my hole, and I feel the tip of his sheathed cock press into me. He's big. Thicker than Cash, but not as long. Having the two of them together would be the perfect pairing. Thick and long, stretching me open together.

The traitorous thought nearly has me coming as he holds my hands over my head, pressing into me over and over. My legs are sprawled flat against the mattress, my hips unable to move as he ruts into me. The angle and position have my eyes nearly watering, but I love it. I crave it.

"You always take me so damn good," Ford groans as he nips and sucks at my neck. It's painful and delicious. "Always so fucking tight."

He thrusts into me, and I cry out, my mouth suddenly feeling empty.

I want to suck on something, want his fingers against my tongue as he ruts. I want another cock in my mouth.

I let myself envision it as he pounds me into the mattress, my dick already so full and throbbing, my balls pushed up as far as they can go. I'm not going to last. I'm going to come, going to mess up his sheets.

And I know Ford is only getting started. He's going to make me come twice, gonna make me see stars and pass out from all the orgasms. He's trying to make me stay, and I just might this one night.

He shifts above me, causing an unnatural groan to escape my mouth. And he likes it because he grunts, doing it again and again, making my throat nearly raw from the sounds it's making.

"Come. You come right fucking now."

The way his cock is dragging across my prostate doesn't make it hard to explode a minute later, my entire body trembling, my hole clenching around his cock as he continues to pound into me. I lay there, limp and messy, a satiated fuck toy as he continues to use my ass. And I love it, love that he takes me like this until I'm pushed over the edge again.

His hands loosen around my wrists and he drags his nails down my arm to my face, where he presses two fingers into my mouth. It's like he knows exactly what I need.

"Suck," he tells me, and I do. A sigh escapes me, feeling full and achy, feeling like I can finally relax.

"You like both of your holes being filled, don't you?" he asks as he pushes his fingers down the back of my throat. I nod, loving the dirty talk, feeling my dick already perking up from the thought of it. His hips are thrusting against me in tiny bursts, making me see stars. But it's when he shoves his fingers as far back as they can go and I'm forced to swallow that I feel my cock start to harden completely.

"There you go. You greedy little thing," he murmurs as he holds his fingers inside of me and continues to take me.

I moan, writhing beneath him, needing to come again. Needing it all over again.

"Look how lucky I am. To have you beneath me."

He has no idea. It's me who's lucky. I'm nothing compared to them.

He pulls his fingers from my throat, and I suck on the fingertips before he thrusts them back in and my eyes roll back into my head.

"Good boy," he says and continues to fuck both my holes until I'm panting, my entire body sweating. Our skin is slapping against each other as he works me over the edge expertly.

When I finally come again on a cry, I feel his body shudder above me, a low groan torn from his lips.

"Fuck," he says on a long exhale. "Fuck. It's so good every time."

His fingers slip from my mouth at the same time his cock slips from my body, and I suddenly feel fraught that it's over. The minutes and hours I have with Cash and Ford where I'm aching for release are always so good. But when I finally come for the last time, I realize it's over. And that I have to leave.

I have to crawl my way out of those moments, but I do it because it can't be more than what it is.

"Come here," Ford says, pulling my sweaty, aching body against his chest. I flop onto him, knowing that my cum-smeared abdomen and cock are going to get him messy, but he doesn't seem to mind. He just pulls me into his arms, and I let him.

"Good. You let me fucking hold you, Benjamin," he says, his hand running into my hair and tugging softly. "About damn time."

I don't say a word. My throat feels raw from crying out, from moaning. My entire body is limp. I can barely even swallow. It almost hurts to breathe.

"You can stay like this for just a bit, for a little while longer before you fuck off back home."

There's a hint of anger in his tone, and I hate it. So I softly kiss the skin of his chest nearest my lips, and I hear him shakily inhale. I've never kissed him before. It's a line neither of us have crossed, but he's holding me now. So I might as well let my lips linger.

"One day I'm gonna kiss that mouth too. This isn't just fucking around for me."

Well, shit. It is for me. I lift my head slightly and meet his dark stare.

"I need to leave," I say, and I watch as his lips turn down in a frown.

"Always fucking running. Fine. You can keep doing that, but one day I'm gonna catch you."

I feel my entire body tremble with that proclamation. I'm not sure what will happen if he catches me. I'm not sure I'm gonna want to run.

Fuck.

I pull away from his arms and stumble out of bed, pulling on my shirt with shaking hands as Ford sits up and watches me, his eyes following my every move.

"We need to tell your dad about us."

I freeze and feel the muscles in my already sore body bunch.

"No. We can't. This has to stay between us."

Ford smirks at me. "It will for now, because we aren't exclusive yet. But as soon as we are, he needs to know. He's my best friend, and I'm fucking his son."

Oh god.

With shaking legs, I pull my pants on and then run my hands through my messy hair. I should have cleaned myself up better because I'm sure I smell like sex. I can feel my mess drying on my skin. But at the same time, I love the feel of it on me, of knowing he's a part of me somehow.

"See you tomorrow," Ford says as I rush from the room, feeling my heart pounding through my chest.

Yeah, I know one day I'm gonna get caught, and yet that doesn't stop me from planning to meet up with him tomorrow.

I'm so doomed.

———

"What's that thing on your neck?" Martha asks, her eyes squinting behind her glasses. Her hair is bright orange today, and I know who had a hand in dying it. Last month it was bright purple.

My hand slaps up on my neck, and I shake my head, frantically grabbing my phone to see what she means. Ford better not have left a hickey last night.

"Looks like a bruise," Martha says with a wicked grin. "Or like you've been getting busy with someone."

I blanch as I open the camera on my phone and point it at my neck, seeing the small black and blue mark right below my ear.

Oh my god.

"You been naughty, Ben-Ben?" Martha asks with a waggle of her eyebrows as Vikki rounds the corner with their friend Lex at her side. "Vik, Lex, come see."

They crowd around the desk, and I feel my cheeks heating to epic proportions. I'm going to kill Ford. I can't believe he left me with this. I'm going to the shop later today, and Cash will definitely see it. He will wonder what the fuck I've been up to.

Oh god. My dad may see.

"Guys, this is bad."

Lex leans over the counter and pokes at it, making me lean away.

"What's bad about it? I love when William leaves marks on me. The sexiest sex on the planet..."

"Guys..." I say and then run a hand down my face as Martha and Vikki stare at me. "I'm... I need to find a way to cover it up."

"Oh, well, we can help you with that. But my dear boy, we need the tea first. Why is this so bad?" Martha asks.

"Yeah," Lex asks with an arched eyebrow. "Why is it so bad? What are you ashamed of?"

I stare at the three of them, and despite telling myself that it's none of their business, I blurt it out anyways. "I'm with two guys..."

Lex's eyebrows fly right up to his hairline while Vikki just waves her hand in disappointment.

"Two is child's play. I once had four at once."

A nervous laugh escapes my mouth. "Oh god, but you don't understand... they don't know, and I work with them at the shop."

Lex's eyebrows disappear into his hairline and he just gapes at me.

"Sweet, innocent Ben fucking two of his dad's best friends. Bravo."

He starts a slow clap and Vikki and Martha join in, looking mighty proud.

"Guys, this isn't... stop clapping," I hiss when I see other people start to stare. I don't need these old gossips getting ahold of this information. I'll never live it down. This senior living home is worse than a middle school.

"How is it? Two big men like that?" Lex asks.

I don't respond, just take a large sip of my water and close my eyes.

"I bet it's good."

"It is," I manage to say and then stare at them. "But really. Cover it up. I'm serious. Cash can't see this…"

"Of course he can't," Lex says, standing up and then adding, "Come by Vikki's room on the way out. She has this amazing concealer that her daughter sent her. We can slather some on before you leave. I won't even charge you… this gossip was worth more than gold."

I feel my shoulders sag in relief, hoping that Cash doesn't notice it when I arrive at work.

And he doesn't… initially. Lex did a good job in covering it up, but the concealer doesn't quite match my skin tone, and Cash eyes my neck far too many times that afternoon, despite my attempts to avoid him. But I make a dire mistake. I end up alone in the back room halfway through my shift, and he corners me. I should run, but his touch freezes me. His hand wraps around my neck, his thumb smearing the makeup right off.

His eyes darken as they land on the bruise, and I feel my entire body flame and start to melt into the floor. That possessive look, the anger behind his eyes. Oh fuck, I messed up. I really fucking did. If he ends this, I only have myself to blame.

Will I end up begging to keep him?

Can I bring myself to my knees?

I think I can.

"What's this?" he asks, his hand falling from my neck to his side.

I swallow roughly and look away. I can't admit it. I can't.

"Just a bruise," I lie, and Cash's eyes narrow.

"I'm not an idiot," he mutters.

I swallow and then meet his stare. "Cash, I never said we were exclusive. I told you that."

Oh god, he's not happy. And neither am I. If he gives me up after this, I wouldn't blame him.

"I know that," he says, and then he turns and stalks away. I feel my shoulders droop and my chest constrict. God, I'm such a fucking idiot. I should have known better. Should have called out sick until that bruise went away.

Quickly, I pull my phone out and snap a pic, sending it to Tatum. If anything, he will know how to calm me down.

He replies instantly.

TATUM:

Oh fuck. Did they see it?"

ME:

Cash did and he's upset.

TATUM:

Course he is, you goober.

Little does he know you're the sluttiest slut.

Tell him to join you and Ford next time.

I sigh, putting my phone back in my pocket and running a hand down my face. Yeah. Tatum was unhelpful. Don't know why I even bothered, even if his last suggestion is something I'd love to do.

My stomach grumbles, but the stress of this situation makes me more nauseous than anything. Eating right now will probably make me vomit. I'm not a stress eater. If anything, I tend to avoid food when I'm upset.

"You okay?" Ford asks, rounding the corner, a concerned look on his face. I just nod, slapping my hand over my neck and deciding I need to go the fuck home. Right now. I don't need Ford seeing this hickey and then putting two and two together when he notes Cash's mood. So I say nothing, just stride past him, grab my backpack sitting on my desk chair, and jog out to my car. My dad arches an eyebrow at me on my way out, but I don't say anything to him either. I just need to get the fuck away.

When I get inside my car, I lock the doors and allow myself a minute to breathe before starting the engine and nearly peeling out of the parking lot. I know my dad will probably try to ask me about what's going on when he arrives home, but I can't tell him.

I'm a terrible person.

Making my way across town, I find myself back at my apartment where I trudge up the stairs and into my small kitchen. My bag lands on the floor and then I shuffle to my room and flop onto my bed. I was supposed to head to Cash's later, but I'm almost sure that the invitation will be rescinded. Cash and Ford don't seem like guys who like to share. There's a difference between knowing we aren't exclusive and seeing evidence of it. I know for a fact that Cash was in a monogamous relationship for years before she left him for someone else. He probably wants monogamy. But this isn't a relationship, this isn't more than what it is because it can't be. My dad is a major reason, but also because I want them both. Equally. At the same time. But right now, the lines are getting blurred, and I don't know what the hell to do about it.

A frustrated groan escapes my mouth, and I pound at the pillow, feeling tears sting my eyes.

I got greedy and look what happened.

Pulling out my phone, I see that I've missed a call from Ford, but I just delete it and open my camera again, angling it down to my neck and brushing my fingers over the purple bruise sitting on my skin.

My cock perks up at the memory of Ford rutting into me, and I roll my eyes to the ceiling.

"You need to get your shit together," I mutter, more to my dick than to myself... hell, who am I kidding. I'm talking to myself too.

"You really need to get it together," I add, and then shut my phone off and toss it onto my pillow, slapping a hand over my face.

I can't run forever though. I have to go in to the shop tomorrow... and the next day. Maybe I'll just tell my dad I quit, that I can't help him anymore.

Maybe I'll just avoid Cash forever.

The thought of losing him makes my heart and stomach clench, and I roll onto my side, pulling my knees to my chest.

My eyes close, and I focus on what I can hear and feel, trying to push the anxiety out of my mind. It works just enough to let me fall into a restless sleep. Visions of Cash and Ford plague my mind, and then my mom's face suddenly appears... a face I don't even remember seeing, it's just a face from photographs.

Her usually smiling face bleeds into a frown, and dread fills me as I wake with a start.

I sit up in bed and press my hand against my chest, feeling my dead mother's disappointment from beyond the grave.

"Goddamnit," I say and then stand up, chugging some water and then stumbling into the shower.

It's when I step out of the steaming room, feeling only slightly better that a knock on my apartment door has me freezing.

It could be one of three people, I think as I pull on some sweats and a white t-shirt before opening the door and seeing my dad on the other side.

"Hey," I say, and my dad gives me an awkward wave.

"Avery said to give you space, but I just wanted to make sure you were okay."

Avery, my dad's new roommate and the guy who mans my dad's office at the shop. I've always liked him, and I like him even more right now. He obviously has my back.

"I'm fine," I say and then pull my shirt up over the hickey lining my skin. My dad's eyes fall to it and he arches an eyebrow.

"Guess it has something to do with that?"

His words linger between us, and I shrug, feeling so fucking guilty. Not that it's ever stopped me.

"Sort of," I say. Gotta keep it vague. I don't want to be the reason my dad stops talking to Cash or Ford. I don't want to ruin things more than I already have.

"Alright, well, I just want you to know I'm here... if you want to talk."

"Thanks, Dad," I say, and he shifts on his feet, looking awkward, so I pull him into a hug and we pat backs like men do before pulling apart.

"I'm going to take Avery on a ride, if you want to join us."

I don't know how he thinks I can join, I don't ride motorcycles. So, I just shake my head.

"I'm good. I'm going to go hang out with some friends."

My dad bobs his head and then pats the doorframe, the rings on his fingers knocking roughly onto the wood.

"Have fun."

And then he's turning and ambling off, his large frame carried down the stairs. And I watch him disappear, feeling like a shit son and an even worse person.

CHAPTER THREE

CASH

I shouldn't have cornered Ben and smeared that makeup off his neck, but once I saw the discoloration on his skin, I couldn't help myself. I had to know.

And now I do. He always told me this wasn't exclusive, but for some stupid reason, I figured it was anyways. Seems I'm a dumb fuck. Of course a young guy wouldn't want to be exclusive with an older man like me.

Fuck.

I scrub a hand down my face and grab a beer from my fridge, popping the top off and taking a long chug. I feel like I'm seventy fucking years old, not the forty-two-year-old guy I really am.

Maybe that's why Ben isn't interested in me. He's too fucking young. Should have never started anything with him in the first place. I don't even know if I'm gay.

But fuck, that mouth. The first time he wrapped it around me, I lost my mind. I soared to places I hadn't been in years. He awoke something inside of me... and now I have to squash it.

Unless I can learn to share.

And I've never been one to do that.

"Goddamnit," I murmur, setting my half-empty drink down on the counter and grabbing my keys. I need to go for a fucking ride and clear my head. Gonna figure this shit out.

The ride doesn't help, but when I arrive back home, Ben is waiting outside my house, looking sheepish. My motorcycle shuts off and I sit on it, my hands on the handlebars, feeling like I need to hold on to something. That bruise is still visible on his neck and my fingers tighten their grip. Jealousy surges through me, and I wonder who did it. Who the fuck is he playing with?

He lifts his hand in an awkward wave, and I see his dad in him in this moment.

Not an image I want right now.

Throwing my leg over the motorcycle, I shove the keys into my jeans pocket and stride over to him, my jaw clenching and unclenching the closer I get to him. I don't know what he's done to me, but I'm enamored with him. He's just so fucking pretty.

"Hi," Ben says as I approach, and I shove my hands into my pockets so I don't reach out for him. I really want to fucking touch him, even after all of this.

"You okay?" I ask, my voice a little too rough from underuse.

"I... I... You don't get to ask me that, Cash," he says, peeking up at me through those long lashes, the freckles on his nose standing out under the lamplight. "I should be the one asking you that."

"I'm fine," I grumble and then shift on my feet, my boots squeaking under my weight.

"Are you?" he asks softly and then runs a nervous hand across his neck, skimming over the bruise on his skin. My eyes are drawn to it for a second, and I look away.

"I'm fine... this was never exclusive."

Ben swallows, and I can hear it, the clicking of his throat. "I know but... I don't want this to end. Does that make me selfish?"

I stare at him and feel my chest start to crack right down the middle. He looks so fucking fragile in this moment, so fucking tired. Well, at least we have that in common.

"Come on. I'm not discussing this shit in the driveway."

I lead him up the steps and open the door for him, gesturing for him to go inside. He does, and I follow him, locking the door behind us.

Ben stops near the back of the couch and fiddles with a loose thread coming up from the fabric. I should buy a new one, but I never really got around to it. This place is just a temporary rental. It's not really *home*.

I haven't had a home in a long-ass time.

The place that feels more like a home to me is Ford's house. I helped him remodel his place, helped him paint and put up cabinets, helped him lay down flooring and set up the shed outside. His place feels just as much mine as it is his. He asked me to move in with him after my breakup with Claire, but I turned him down. Now, I'm wondering what I was thinking. If I was with him, I wouldn't be this fucking lonely.

"Want something to drink?" I ask, and Ben shakes his head before nodding.

"Sure, a water would be great."

I nod, moving past him to the fridge and pulling out a bottle of water and a beer for me.

Ben uncaps it and takes a small swig.

"Um," he begins and then shifts nervously on his feet. "Like I was saying, I'd like to continue this with you... I like you, Cash."

My heart thunders in my chest. "That so?" I ask as I flick the cap off my beer and take a long drink. What I really want to do is crash my lips to his and suck on his tongue, but who else has he been kissing? Oh god, what if he's letting that other man kiss him, but not me?

It bothers me more than it should.

"Yeah, that's so."

Our eyes clash, and I feel my cock twitch in my pants. But now's not the time. I'm surprised he even showed up here. When he left work, I was real fucking worried. About him and about me.

"How many guys you seeing?" I ask and then gulp down some more beer, trying to wash away the bile gathering in my throat.

Ben's eyes turn away, and he won't look at me when he says, "Just one."

My eyes narrow, and I clench my beer bottle hard.

"I see."

Ben's eyes slash to mine as he fiddles with the label on the water bottle. "If it's too much—I understand if you can't keep going."

"Never said that, did I?" I bite out and then chug the rest of my beer and set it roughly on the counter. I shouldn't be mad at him, but my mind is all twisty right now. I don't even know if I'm gay and yet, I'm obsessed with this guy.

My best friend's kid.

I was there before he was even born, and I held him when he was a baby. And yet, here I am.

I'm all sorts of fucked up, aren't I? The only thing that makes me feel better is that I never had these feelings for him until that night a few weeks ago.

And now I can't get him out of my head.

"How set are you on this other guy?" I ask, and Ben's cheeks flush.

"I'm not giving him up."

I nod and then run a hand through my hair. "That's your right. But I need time to think on if this is right for me. I don't share."

Ben nods and then he takes a step forward before stopping himself.

"I'm sorry, Cash."

"Don't be. You never lied to me about what this was, just didn't share what you were doing."

His eyes look a little wet as he glances at me. "I didn't."

"You eat?" I ask, noting how pale he looks.

"I'm not hungry," he says and then swipes at his eyes. "I should go. You have my number if you want to try this again."

I nod and watch as he leaves, his shoulders slightly slumped, and for a second, I think about calling him back to me—wrapping him up in my arms and holding him for a while.

But I don't. I need to think on this. Can I share him with someone else? Am I ready to get my heart wrecked? Because that's what will happen if I keep this up. I'm going to end up ruined. I'm already starting to feel a deeper pull in his direction. And I just got out of a long relationship and I feel a little battered and bruised. I'm too old for this shit.

I sit for a while in my drab living room before grabbing my keys once more. I need to see my best friend. Maybe he will have some fucking advice.

Before I take off, I message Ford and let him know I'm on the way. Don't even bother with much of a heads up. We're close, been through so much together, and he just gets me. Can see through all my shit. Maybe he will have some advice.

I haven't told him yet, haven't said I'm with a guy yet. Like hell I'm telling him who I'm with, but since he's bi, maybe he has some advice for a questioning guy.

"Hey, you fucker, I'm outside," Ford calls from his back porch as soon as I open the door to his house. I have a key to his place and he has one to mine. We exchanged them ages ago when we realized it just made everything easier.

"What are you doing?" I ask when I see Ford trying to move something heavy without help. "Should have called me earlier. I could have helped you with this."

I move toward him and huff a laugh when I see him rolling his eyes.

"Don't need no help," he says and then sighs when I help him lift a plank of wood and hold it up.

"Seems like you did. What are you building now?"

He always has some project going on. His kitchen was the most recent. I helped get that shit together. But Ford has some manic energy that he needs to burn at all hours. And usually I'm right there with him, helping him out.

"A shed."

"You already have a shed. What do you need this for?" I ask as he grabs his nail gun.

"It's gonna be a sex shed."

A surprised laugh escapes me and Ford grins stupidly at me.

"Gotcha."

"Yeah, well, you horny fucker. I wouldn't be surprised if you did something kinky like that."

Ford waggles his eyebrows at me, and I roll my eyes once more, helping him get the right side of the shed upright as he swipes a hand across his forehead. It's a cool night, but still, my best friend seems to have been out here a while working up a sweat.

"Come on, you can help me finish this after a drink."

He waves me inside, and I follow him, my eyes taking him in. He always was a bit smaller than me, but not by much. Those muscular arms and legs can out-lift me any day, but for some reason, I hold on to the bulk more.

"What do you want?" he asks and before I can answer, he hands me a beer.

I grab on to it, our fingers brushing slightly as I take it from his hand.

Ford pulls a grape soda from the fridge and pops the top, chugging half of it. A small burp escapes him when he's finished and then he swipes the back of his hand across his mouth.

"So, what's up?" he asks, stepping toward me. His hand settles gently on my face, his thumb brushing over a spot near the corner of my lips. "You got a bit of something there."

I let him wipe me up and then his hand drops to his side and he arches an eyebrow at me.

"You looked handsome with it there, but I thought nah, you'd wanna know. I'm not like you. I don't let things just linger in people's teeth without telling them."

I smile softly at that and then pull him into my side, inhaling the scent of him, like the outdoors and man.

He knocks his forehead against mine and then we walk toward the back porch once more, the two of us taking separate chairs, but he props his boots up onto my lap and I scoff.

"Get the fuck off me," I say, but don't make him move. I just relax a bit more into the chair and lay a hand on his ankle.

"So, what's up, Cash? You look extra serious today."

"Just had a bit of a revelation."

"And what revelation is that?" he asks, staring out at his half-finished shed.

I swallow some more beer and open my mouth to tell him, but nothing comes out. God, if I can't tell Ford, who can I tell?

"What? You okay?" he asks, and I shake my head, pressing my beer bottle to my cheek. The cold shocks me slightly, and I mutter.

"Been letting a guy suck me off."

Ford stares at me, blinking rapidly.

"Huh?"

"Been getting some head from a dude," I repeat, and Ford's feet hit the porch with a bang.

"You're fucking a man?"

"No," I shake my head. "That hasn't happened. Yet."

"Well, damn." A laugh escapes him and then he's moving his chair toward me until we're side by side. His hand comes out and grabs on to my arm. I can feel the heat of him and I shiver slightly.

"Didn't know you liked dick."

"Seems I like this one."

Ford's eyes widen. "No shit. Who is it?"

I shake my head. "Can't say."

"Ah, a secret. I can live with that. For a bit. Though I am curious who this guy is who enticed you to give men a shot."

"Yeah, seems I like it a whole lot. But..."

"But what?" Ford is practically on my lap now, his eyes boring into mine. I can make out the gold flecks in his dark eyes. Like Jupiter.

"But just found out he wasn't exclusive. I mean, he's seeing someone else."

Ford scoffs and then shakes his head. "Well, he's a fucker then."

"Yeah, but I don't think he is. It's not like he was leading me on—"

"Fuck him," Ford spits, starting to get angry. Love this about him. He's fiercely protective. Always has been.

"I like him though."

"Yeah, well he can go fuck himself anyways. If he doesn't see what an awesome guy you are."

I turn my gaze away and Ford grabs on to my chin gently, forcing me to meet his eyes.

"You. Are. Amazing."

I wet my lips and wrench my chin from his grasp, taking another gulp of beer. It slides down my throat easily, and I lean my head back.

"I need to figure out if I want to keep doing things with him even though we aren't exclusive."

Ford snorts. "It's something I'm open to, but you? Nah. That's not you, man. Never will be."

Yeah, and that's the problem. I love commitment. I went into this with the hope that it would last.

"Fuck. I'm screwed."

His hand reaches out and latches on to mine, squeezing it gently. I glance down and see our tattooed skin, the rings on our fingers almost identical, and something unfamiliar shifts in my chest.

"Nah, man. He just doesn't know what a gem he has in you."

I meet Ford's stare and a smile pulls my lips up. "You getting sappy on me?"

"Just love you."

I clear my throat and then knock his hand away. "Alright, you sap. Let's get this shed built and then you can massage my back for my troubles."

"Yeah, okay, old man. Fine."

We laugh as we move toward the half-built shed and get to work.

CHAPTER FOUR

FORD

"Oh yeah, right there," Cash groans as I work the muscles in his thick back. He lost his shirt a few minutes ago and is sprawled out on my bed. The same bed that Ben has been in over and over.

My cock hardens slightly as I lean down and put my elbows into it.

"God, you need a massage nightly," I grunt as I work on a knot right below his shoulder blade.

"I know."

"Jesus, these things are as big as baseballs."

I'm huffing and puffing, putting my back into it and Cash is grunting as well. This can't feel good. No way in hell he's enjoying this.

"Oh right there," he wheezes, and I nearly levitate off the bed with how hard I'm pressing into him. God, this fucker likes it rough. Whoever that poor soul is that he's fucking... well, I sure hope that ass is made of steel.

But wait, he's not fucking him. Just getting blowies.

Well, probably fucks his throat hard then.

The thought of it makes my entire body tingle.

"No more," Cash coughs, and I let up, letting my hands skate down his back, lightly massaging down his spine.

"Jesus," Cash grunts, and I sigh.

"Yeah, well, you're a stress case, man."

"Been a lot on my mind," he huffs and then he flips over, nearly knocking me off.

He's now underneath me, his barrel, tattooed chest moving up and down as I straddle his waist.

"Do you think I'm gay?" he asks me.

"I mean, this is a bit gay," I say and then grind down on him playfully.

He glowers up at me, his hands landing on my waist.

"Fuck off, Ford. For real, though. Am I?"

"I mean, probably bi, like me. If you like pussy and cock."

"Jesus."

"I mean, you like this guy's cock, right?"

He hesitates and then nods. "Touched it for the first time recently. I fucking liked it."

"'Course you did," I say, rolling off of him onto my stomach and leaning up on my elbow to stare down at him. Fuck, he's hot to look at. I mean, I've never gone there because he's my best friend, but I can admire how he looks. Platonically.

"You gonna fuck him? You know, if you decide to keep going?"

"Don't know. Anal kind of solidifies the gay thing, doesn't it?"

I smile at him and that intense stare bores into mine. "Kind of think you're already there, bro."

"Fuck."

"Yeah, fuck," I say as I sit up and pat his bare chest. "Come on. This is even gayer if we stay here in bed."

"But I like your bed."

Hopping off of it, I turn to face him. "Yeah, I know. Told you to come move in with me, but you're being a stubborn ass in that ratty rental across town. You could have a home here, Cash."

He sighs, sitting up, his abdominal muscles contracting as he does. Fuck, he's big. Bigger than me, and that's saying something.

"Yeah, but it's your place. I don't want to get comfortable and then end up having to find a new place. It's better this way."

He pulls his shirt on and then we make our way out of the bedroom. When I say that I wouldn't mind Cash moving in with me, I mean it. He's my best friend, well, apart from Dean, and I'd love for him to find a place to call home.

But then again, with his upbringing, I'm not surprised he's so fucking wary. I would be too. Not everyone can have parents like mine.

"Alright, so what are we doing the rest of the night? The shed is mostly up, you got your massage."

"Should probably go home."

I throw my arm around his shoulders and pull him into me. "Not a chance in hell. We are gonna order a snack, smoke some weed, and fall asleep in that bed you like so much."

Cash eyes me and then a small smile cracks his lips.

"Fine, you motherfucker."

I beam at him. Now that's what I'm talking about.

CHAPTER FIVE

BEN

Ford didn't message me last night and neither did Cash, so I'm thinking that whatever I had with both men is over. Perhaps they talked and they know about me, about what I've done. The thought has put me in a terrible mood.

"Um, why the gloom?" Tatum asks, flicking my ear softly. I'm waiting outside of class, my eyes stuck on the empty screen of my phone.

I glower at him, and his smile falls slightly.

"Oh shit, you look real bad. What happened?"

"They didn't message me today," I say, and Tatum's eyes widen.

"You haven't been fucked in twelve hours?" He sounds appalled and he should be. He should be so fucking upset.

Because I am. I don't know what to do with myself.

"Shit, that's bad. How's your butthole?" he hisses, and I slap at his chest.

"It's empty, you jerk."

"Of course it is. It doesn't know what to do with itself."

I stare at him and a laugh bubbles out of me at how utterly ridiculous this is.

"And I see you have a nice little mark on your neck."

I pull my scarf around my neck a little tighter. "God, don't remind me. This is what started it all."

"I know, you told me. In glaring detail last night."

I huff and then stuff my phone away when the professor walks by.

"It's fine. It will all be fine," I tell myself and Tatum, who bobs his head and then follows me into the classroom.

"It will be. It will all work out."

I'm not sure if I believe him. Especially when I end up at the shop after class and Cash and Ford are both there. Cash doesn't make eye contact with me and my heart drops in my chest. Ford looks a little wrecked too, his eyes bloodshot and his hair a mess. Something happened last night, and my stomach turns as I envision it.

Has my biggest fear come true and they talked about me?

"What's up with you two?" my dad asks his two friends, who look a little guilty.

Cash stands up and presses a hand to his temple. "It was Ford's idea."

I lean forward, trying to hear what's going on but also not wanting to look like I'm prying.

"What was?" my dad asks just as Avery, the office manager appears, wearing a skirt and army boots. He looks fucking hot, and I can't miss how my dad's eyes slide across his legs.

"We went a little crazy last night. Forgot we weren't twenty."

"And why wasn't I invited?" Dean asks, and Ford rolls his eyes and then winces.

"You were with Avery. Where you should be."

Avery blushes and then taps Dean on the shoulder. "Hate to break up the bromance but you have a phone call. Angry Myrtle has questions and I can't, Dean. I cannot or I will quit."

Dean's eyes soften, and he follows Avery back up the stairs where they disappear into the office.

Ford and Cash both watch them go and then both sets of eyes turn to me. I feel color bleed into my cheeks as I fumble with my pencil. It falls onto the ground, and I fall to my knees to grab it, hiding under my desk for a little too long.

God, I don't want to come out. I want to stay down here until they leave. But I can't. Literally. The desk is moved back two feet and I'm exposed, hunkering down, the pencil in my hand like a guilty child.

"Thought there was a trap door down there and you fell in," Ford says as Cash eyes me warily.

"I just—I got a bit distracted. Lots of dust under here…"

When they arch their eyebrows at me, I fling the pencil to my right, and they both turn to look at it sail across the garage.

I've lost my fucking mind.

"Why'd he throw the pencil?" Ford whispers, and Cash shrugs.

"Who fucking knows why he does the shit he does?"

It's laced with venom, and my heart sinks. This doesn't bode well for me.

"It slipped," I say defiantly and then march over to where the pencil is, bending over and grabbing it before standing up.

"I got it. You can stop staring," I say, feeling my hot cheeks flare to epic proportions.

"But you have a scarf on. Why do you have a scarf on?"

"I'm cold."

Ford arches an eyebrow and Cash cocks his head. He knows what's behind it. I'm surprised Ford hasn't noticed.

The two of them glance at each other and then meander back to work, their movements a little stunted. They got into something last night and for some reason, I hate that I wasn't involved, that I wasn't part of it.

But then again, what do I expect? For these men to be okay with sharing me?

No, that's not a fucking thing in the real world.

I keep my head down the rest of my shift. It's only a few hours, but I hate every minute of it. My mind swirls, wondering what they talked about, what they did together when I wasn't there. I know that it's silly, that there is no reason for me to feel this way. I didn't ask them to be exclusive and have no right to expect that of them either. But I do care. I feel like I've been left out, and it's all my fault.

I made this choice, and I have to live with it.

The clock ticks down, minute by minute until it's time for me to go. And without a word, I grab my things and trail outside, opening my car and getting inside. Cash and Ford didn't even say a word to me as I left.

They had to have talked about me, they must know what I've been doing. And now they're done.

My eyes sting as I start my car, and as I drive out of the lot, I see Cash and Ford standing at the open garage door, both of them watching me leave, their arms folded across their chests.

It's like a bad omen or something.

I force my gaze away and don't look back.

———

I'm moping. I can't help it. I went from insatiable sex for weeks on end to nothing for twenty-four hours and it's all my fault. No Cash, no Ford, and my dick feels like it's going to fall off. And my heart feels as if it is limping sadly along. I will probably be dead soon from lack of sex.

My ass feels empty, so does my mouth.

I'm just an empty shell.

I end up in a theater across town, munching on stale popcorn and watching a movie that is so terrible the chairs all around me are empty—save for a lonely old man in the front row.

He might be dead.

Oh god, I am watching a movie with a corpse.

I stare at the screen and then choke on a popcorn kernel. The man in the front row turns back and glowers at me.

So not dead. Maybe a zombie, however. The way his neck swiveled was eerie.

I should leave, this is just sad. I stay until the credits have stopped rolling and the lights go on.

The old zombie man gets up and ambles out, but not before farting on his way, leaving a terrible unearthly smell in his wake. I plug my nose and jog out, skidding to a stop outside and inhaling deeply. It's not even dark out. This day is endless. I don't know how to make it go any faster.

If it was last week, I'd be busy getting railed into the next day, but now I'm just a loser, ghosted by two men and left to deal with the stench of zombie farts.

I need to get a hobby. Maybe go on a date and cut my losses. Although, the last date I went on was with Colin, and I fell asleep. While he was mid-sentence.

How mortifying.

But maybe I should give it another shot. If Ford and Cash are done with me, then maybe I should branch out.

Try and find something healthy and boring.

God. I don't want that. I want something forbidden, something taboo.

I want Cash and Ford. At the same time.

I push the thought away and walk quickly to my car, pulling up my dating app as I go.

I'm distracted and not really feeling most of the men that appear on my screen, but I make a valiant effort. I eventually end up at Ford's place anyways. My car idles on the street, the evening sun setting behind the hills as I sit and stare. The door is closed, the light on, and I wonder what he's doing in there. Is he with Cash?

I glance around and see Cash's car parked opposite mine. I don't know what they're doing, but I'm obviously not invited. Not that I would be. I'm just a hole to be used. That's all I let myself be.

It's my fault.

I should go to the door to see what they're up to. Part of me wants to tiptoe to the window and peer through like a creep, but instead, I drive home. I'll spend the night staring at my wall and scrolling mycology posts on Reddit. Mushrooms are so fascinating and most look like dicks.

Dicks that I'm not getting anymore.

Avery's outside washing his car when I pull into the driveway and sit for far too long with my head on the steering wheel. "You okay?" he asks through my closed window. He probably thinks I died.

Me and zombie man can be soulmates in the afterlife.

I turn my head toward him and smile weakly.

"I'm fine."

"Get out of the car, man. You look too sad."

I sigh and get out as fast as I can, which is the pace of a snail.

"Jesus, do you normally move that slow?" Avery asks, his perfectly shaped brows rising. His long blond hair is pulled up into two buns on the top of his head, and I see black eyeliner and mascara on his eyes.

"I find the motivation to move my appendages lacking," I say, and Avery shakes his head, those buns bobbing back and forth.

"Come on. Your dad is out, let me make you a margarita and you can spill all the beans."

"Oh god. I can't tell you anything."

"Why not?" he asks, nudging my shoulder as we walk to the house. I haven't been in here for ages. I should visit with my dad more, but with my schedule, it's so damn hard to find time to do anything like socialize.

Unless that person is socializing with my asshole.

Then I make all the time in the world.

"Wow," I say, taking in the new throw pillows and the brightly painted wall. "You did this, didn't you?"

"Yeah, your dad just needed a pop of color in his life."

I glance at Avery with his bright purple tank and blue short-shorts and think that this is exactly what my dad needs. Everything in this house looks lighter, brighter. Even Avery brightens up the space.

"Anyways, what do you want? I can do a strawberry margarita or," he shuffles around in some cabinets, "I can totally do a lemon drop."

"Oh," I say, feeling slightly overwhelmed. "How about both?"

Avery smiles widely at me.

"Fabulous taste," he says and gets to work on making us both drinks. I sink down into a kitchen chair and watch him work, his lithe body moving back and forth, almost like he's dancing. When he's finally done, setting both drinks in front of me, he lowers himself down opposite me and waggles his eyebrows.

"So, Benjamin, what's the deal? Why were you having an existential crisis in that car of yours?"

I take a large gulp of margarita and then chase it with one of the lemon drop.

"I can't tell you details, but I can tell you that I'm in a bit of a pickle."

"Oh, I love pickles," Avery says, leaning his elbow on the table and taking a large sip of his drink.

"I do too."

"Especially when they're dick pickles."

I snort a laugh at that, and Avery smiles widely.

"So, who's pickle are you on?"

"Two pickles," I say, and Avery chokes on his drink.

"Two?"

I nod. "You cannot tell my dad."

He pretends to zip his lips and then smiles widely at me.

"Two. How is it?"

"Oh god. I mean, yes, two but not together, not yet, but... *oh hell*."

"Not yet?" Avery says, catching my slip.

I sigh and gulp some more lemon drop. "I wish."

"Oh, Benjamin. I know."

He makes the sign of the cross over his chest.

We continue drinking, and I open up slightly, telling him vague details about what my predicament is. I think I'm desperate to have someone to talk to, someone who doesn't joke constantly about my asshole, like Tatum. And Avery is a good listener.

"Oh, god, you do have a predicament," he says as he brings us our third set of drinks. My head is spinning slightly, and I lean my cheek down on my arm, peering up at a bleary Avery.

"I do. Told you. Two pickles. And one doesn't want me anymore. And I think the other one doesn't either. They don't want to stick their dick pickles in me."

"You know what you need to do?" Avery asks, waggling his finger around my face.

"What?"

"Communicate."

"Pfft," I snort and then let my eyes close. "What I really need is a straw. The cup is too far away."

"I know. Who made these? Not alcoholics," he says as he stands up and wobbles toward the kitchen, but he doesn't quite make it and slumps onto the ground.

I stare at him just as the front door opens and my dad walks through.

"Jesus," he says and moves toward Avery, staring down at him. Avery is sprawled out on the floor, his arms askew, his eyes closed.

"Hello, handsome man. What's your name?" Avery slurs, and I snort a laugh as my dad sighs and bends down, picking Avery up easily and carrying him to his room. I watch them go, watch as Avery nestles his head into my dad's neck and seems to inhale.

I wish I had a man to inhale, wish I'd inhaled either Cash or Ford once more before it all ended. But I didn't and now I'm all alone.

"I've got Ben, Dean," a voice says behind me, and I turn to see Cash and Ford looming in the doorway, and I almost melt.

My two pickles, I think as they approach. Big sexy pickles.

"Shit, he's drunk," Ford says, and Cash nods as he moves behind me and picks me up, jostling me slightly until I'm fully in his arms.

"So strong," I say, my vision blurring as Cash shakes his head, equal parts disappointment and humor.

"You're both so strong. Big muscles."

I need to keep my lips sealed, I think as they walk me out the door. I can't drunkenly tell them my secrets. I pull my lips between my teeth as Cash walks me up the stairs to my garage apartment and sets me on my mattress. My shoes are pulled off and then my socks. I want them to undress me completely. Want to be sprawled out for them both to see.

I stare up at them, the two of them looming over the foot of my bed, looking so big and imposing. God, what I wouldn't give for them to crawl up and touch me, to have both sets of hands on my stomach, my chest, my cock.

My hand sneaks down to my dick which is hardening in my pants, and I give it a squeeze. Oh god, I'm horny. It's been two long days of nothing and I'm despondent.

"Shit," I hear Ford murmur and then I feel my hand being pulled away from my dick.

I let out a whimper and Cash and Ford shift around me.

"Guess he's horny when he's drunk," I hear Cash say, and Ford snorts. They both should know exactly how horny I am. Oh god.

My eyes fall shut, and I feel the room spinning.

"I'm going to stay with him," Cash says, almost insisting it, but I want them both to stay, to crowd me on this small bed and hold me. What a way to fall asleep.

"Yeah, that works, man. I have an early day tomorrow," Ford says, his hand lifting from my arm. I hear footsteps and then the door closing.

Then it's just Cash and me. One eyelid pops open, and I see him staring down at me. I pat the side of my bed sloppily.

"Come," I slur, and Cash shakes his head, his eyes trailing down my body. "Come sleep with me."

It's a whisper as my eye shuts once more, enveloping me in darkness.

I feel the bed dip as Cash lowers himself next to me.

"You need to drink some water."

I snort and sigh. "I need to drink your cum."

"Jesus," Cash says, and I whine, turning to glance at him. His face swims in my vision.

"I'm so fucking thirsty." I reach out and drag my hand along his chest, and I feel his breathing pick up.

"Not when you're drunk," he says, and I whimper at that.

My poor, unfortunate soul.

"Fine," I pout, turning onto my side, my back facing his chest. I feel him shift a bit closer and then his hand lands on my stomach, pulling me into him. The warmth of him, the scent of him has all of my senses firing. I lean back, my head hitting his chest and sigh.

He feels so right, holding me like this. A small part of me knows that he shouldn't, that this is crossing lines, but my drunk brain doesn't care. I'm gonna just bask in his warmth, in how strong he is. Just for tonight.

"Missed you," I say almost incoherently as I drift off to sleep. The only thing that would make this even better is if Ford had stayed.

I want them both to stay.

———

When I wake up the next morning, I feel like death. *I'm now the Grim Reaper*, I think as I groan and smack my lips together. My mouth is the lake of fire.

Oh god, why did I drink so much?

I peel my eyelids open and see Cash sitting in my desk chair, his eyes hooded as he watches me.

"Oh shit," I moan as I try and sit up. My head throbs, and I feel like my skin is going to fall off.

"Here," he says as he moves toward me with a bottle of Advil and a cup of water. He hands them both to me, and I take them with shaky hands, sipping at the water and popping a few pills.

"You didn't need to stay," I say, not able to meet his eyes. Fuck, what did I say to him last night? I didn't divulge any secrets, did I?

Although I'm not sure he would have stayed if I had.

"I had to make sure you didn't die. Dean was busy with Avery, so someone had to make sure you were okay all night."

My eyes flick to him, and I feel my cheeks flush.

"You didn't have to," I whisper, feeling my heart sink at how he's looking at me. It's not with lust, but more like veiled disgust? Or maybe I'm projecting.

I'm disgusted with myself at the moment. And I smell. Like old toilet.

"I need a shower."

I push myself up and wobble slightly. Cash appears at my side and grabs on to my arm.

"Come on."

"I've got it," I say, but he still walks me to the small bathroom.

He only lets me go so he can turn the shower on as I lean against the counter and begin scrubbing at my teeth. I do an extra good job too, trying to wash away the taste of bile. When I'm done, my mouth rinsed, I see Cash reach for the hem of my shirt, pulling it up over my head. And I let him.

Just want him to be with me, just want him close to me.

Fuck.

The shirt plops onto the ground, and I feel my chest constrict as he steps away from me. I want him to undress me, to place his hands on me. But he doesn't. He's probably disgusted with me, with the fact that we aren't exclusive. That I've been with someone else.

I pull off my pants and kick them to the side, not even bothering to look at Cash as I stumble under the hot water. I don't want to see him look at me with revulsion, with derision. I can't stand it.

Scrubbing at my head and body quickly, I wash and rinse before turning to see if Cash is still in the bathroom with me. Our eyes catch through the slightly foggy glass. His chest is rising and falling quickly, and I realize, as my eyes drop to his crotch, that his cock is hard and jutting out from his jeans.

Oh fuck.

My own dick lengthens between my legs, and I grab on to it, trying to keep it under control.

Shutting off the water, I turn toward him, feeling a shiver of lust slide through my body as I face him fully. His eyes have darkened, his jaw muscles working back and forth as he grinds his teeth. I see his hands fisted at his sides, and I know he's trying not to reach out for me.

"I'm not drunk anymore," I say, despite the ache in my head still making itself known. But right now, it's a dull throb. What hurts more is my dick. It needs attention.

"No, you're not," Cash says as I grab a towel and start to dry myself off. I can't look sexy while doing this, but the way Cash's nostrils flare as he watches me, I know it's doing something for him.

"Did you think any more about what you want from me?" I ask softly, peeking up at him.

Cash lets out a shaky breath. "Oh, I want a whole lot from you. Want your lips on my dick again, want to suck your cock into my mouth, want to try fucking you. But I don't want to share."

I wrap the towel around my waist and hold it tightly around my hips.

Cash's eyes swivel down to where my cock is straining against the fabric, and he wets his lips.

"I don't fucking share."

"I know," I say and then reach out and press my hand against his chest, feeling the steady beat of his heart under my palm. "I get it."

We stare at each other for a long-drawn-out moment, and then Cash lifts a hand and presses it against mine. I feel that touch all the way to my toes. It consumes me.

"Thank you for last night."

"Always," he says and then he lets me go and steps back. "I'm going to go."

"Okay." I watch him go and feel my stomach drop, both in nausea and despair.

Well, if that isn't clear, I don't know what is. It's over between Cash and me. I flew too close to the sun and got burned. And I have no one to blame but myself.

I dress and meander to school, having missed my first class already. I've lost motivation for today anyways. Tatum can see it and despite trying to cheer me up, he can't quite manage it. And neither can the ladies at the senior home. It doesn't help that Ford doesn't message me either.

It makes me wonder what's going on with him when just two days ago he was insatiable. Maybe he's over me too.

I need to know, but I can't bring myself to show up at his place uninvited. Doesn't mean I don't sit outside his house that evening like the creep I am.

I've hit a low point, for sure.

I wasn't invited over, my phone screen sits blank. Not that I should have been. But it hurts nonetheless. I let out a shaky breath. I can't go marching up there and knock. That would be absolutely insane. That would make me seem needy and insecure, like a baby who needs coddling. I got myself into this mess, I can see my way out.

I lean my head back against the headrest and pull out my phone. It's time to go on another date and get over these men. It was good while it lasted.

I'm going to move on.

No more pining. I am not a tree.

I'm a man.

....

CHAPTER SIX

....

FORD

"What's up, man?" I ask, loving that Cash is here in my house, that he feels comfortable enough to be here with me. Part of me wishes that I could spend a few hours inside of Ben first. But my best friend is going through a crisis. And bros before...hoes?

Not sure how that saying would go when Ben is a dude, but whatever.

No Ben tonight. I don't want Cash walking in while Ben's getting his ass railed. I don't need Cash knowing what I've been up to in my free time. He'd probably judge me for going after Dean's son.

But it's not like I ever had any inappropriate thoughts about him in the past. It wasn't until the last few months that things began to change for me. It was the way he'd look at me, the way he'd adjust himself while watching me work. How he'd wet his lips and how his pupils would dilate.

And then those words he uttered one evening when we were alone at the shop.

I'm not fragile, Ford. I can take anything you give me.

That innuendo made ideas pop into my mind, ones that I've acted on.

Many times.

"Not much, you sure you don't have plans?" Cash asks as he pulls his jacket off and moves past me to the fridge, grabbing a beer.

I snort. "No plans when you're here."

Cash pops the top and then eyes me. "What do you have on your skin?"

"Paint," I say and then shrug. "Was painting a room earlier."

"Jesus, you can't sit still, can you?"

"Nope. Wanna see what I'm doing? You can actually help me with some stuff."

Cash narrows his gaze at me and sighs. "Is that why you told me I could come over? You wanted to put me to work?"

I smile widely at him and then reach out and slap his ass. "More like put that ass to work, bi-boy."

"Shut up," Cash grumbles, and I pull him into me, smearing some still-wet paint onto his shirt. He stares down at it and then side-eyes me. I just smile wider and nuzzle into his neck. He smells really fucking good, like gasoline and wind.

I nip at his chin and then poke the tip of his nose. "You love me just the way I am."

"Fuck me. I do," Cash sighs and then steps away from me. "Alright, show me what you've gotten yourself into, and I'll see how I can help since you've already gotten my shirt all fucked up."

I laugh as I grab on to his hand and pull him into the back bedroom.

———

"Shit, you weren't kidding. That was more than painting, you asshole," Cash grumbles from his spot in the hot tub. I peer over at him, all those tattoos peeking out over the top of the water. He looks real fucking grumpy and yet at the same time, relaxed. We've been friends for decades and he's always been like this. A real push and pull and a pain in my ass.

Well, he's never been in my ass, but then again, he was in a long-term relationship with a woman, and I didn't want to fuck up a decades-long friendship. But I digress.

"Your back hurting, old man?" I ask as I place my arms on the back of the jacuzzi, my fingertips brushing against Cash's shoulder.

"I'm just fine. Didn't think you meant that I was going to be installing cabinets all fucking evening."

"Yeah, but it kept your mind off shit, right?"

I eye my best friend and watch as he arches an eyebrow at me. Damn, he looks good right now. Not that I let myself go there. Never in a million years would I go there.

Although he is bi.

And he is hot.

Hm.

"It did."

"See," I say and then lean back a little more, sliding over slightly and letting my hand settle on the back of Cash's neck, massaging it. He groans and my dick twitches in my swim trunks.

Down boy, I think as I close my eyes. I have Ben. Just Ben. I really need to talk to him, to get inside of him again. That's the only reason my libido is so out of control. Cash hasn't ever been an option. Our friendship is more important. At least, that's what I tell myself.

"God, your fucking hands," Cash groans, and my half-hard dick chubs up the rest of the way. Meh, it's fine. It's under the water. He'll never know. It's not like I can control this thing anyways. It has a mind of its own.

"God made them just right, huh?"

"Fuck yeah."

He smiles softly, and I feel something flutter in my stomach as I continue to massage him. My arm starts to fall asleep at the angle I'm at, so I slowly adjust myself, moving closer to him to get a better grip on him.

"Could you have smaller shoulders?" I ask as Cash peeks an eye open at me.

"Maybe you need to be more flexible."

"I'm plenty flexible."

Cash huffs a laugh, his hand snaking around my waist and pulling me onto his lap without another word. I straddle his thick thighs and let out a grunt. This isn't the first time I've sat on his lap.

I sit on his lap a lot actually.

Hm.

"If you wanted to fuck me, you could just ask," I tease as my hands land on his shoulders, massaging his tight trapezius muscles.

"Not gonna fuck you. This just works better."

I smile at him as I happily continue to slide my hands across his body. He's built like a linebacker, thick and coiled. For a second, I have a vision of him over me, that big body dwarfing mine, but I quickly discard it. Don't need Cash feeling my boner.

I'm gonna save that for Ben. Maybe I can head to his place, park down the road, sneak into his apartment, and slide into that tight hole.

My breath comes out faster at the thought.

"Why you breathing like that? I can hear it over the jets," Cash says, and I glower at him.

"It's been a few days since I've fucked and being on your lap is giving me ideas."

Cash snorts at that. "Fuck you."

"I'm serious," I say and then squeeze his muscles really tightly, making him hiss.

"Feel my dick, if you don't believe me."

"I'm not touching your dick."

"I have a nice dick, man. Don't hate."

"Sure you do. I've seen it."

I puff up as his eyes open and our gazes meet. I see his flushed cheeks, and I move my thumbs up the sides of his neck, brushing along his scruffy jaw.

"I know you're a secret fan. You probably watch me when I'm not looking," I tease, and Cash's eyes crinkle in the corners.

"You're so full of yourself."

"I can't help it. When you're made like me, you just have to push through. Big dick and all."

Cash's hand drops from my waist, and then I feel the squeeze of his fingers on my dick.

My mouth drops open and my eyes widen.

"You're touching my cock, man," I say, and Cash shrugs like it's no big deal. When it is. It's a big fucking deal. I mean, I've never let myself go there with him, but here I am, his hand on my motherfucking ding-dong.

"Just wanted to see if you were telling the truth."

"Pfft, I never lie."

His fingers squeeze my dick, and I fall forward, my forehead hitting his as I breathe deeply.

"Your dick is so damn small."

"You're a fucking liar," I say with a smile, leaning back and arching my hips up slightly. Cash's eyes are hooded now, and I can see the way his chest heaves.

"This is fucking weird," I say, and Cash nods, but his hand stays right where it is, massaging a slow orgasm out of me.

"Yeah, it is."

Suddenly his hand is gone, and he rests it on the seat next to him.

My breath is still coming out heavily and so is his, but I don't push him. I'd never push him to do something he didn't want to do.

I slide off his lap and sit next to him, our hands brushing.

"Did that make it weird?" I ask, and Cash turns his head toward me.

"Nah, no weirder than when you pooped on my bed in college."

"Jesus, you're never going to let me live that down are you?" I say with a laugh, pushing at his shoulder. He shoves me back and before I know it, we're wrestling in the jacuzzi, our wet bodies rubbing all over each other. It's not doing my dick any favors. And when I move my thigh slightly to the left I can feel his is standing at attention too.

"This turning you on, Cash?" I say with a laugh as he pins me beneath him, his body pressing mine against the edge of the jacuzzi. His hands bracket my sides and his thighs are between my legs. I wrap them around his lower back and he grunts at the extra weight on him.

"You're a fuck," he says with a smile and then he leans down so his elbows are resting on the edge and his hands cup my head, those thick fingers sliding into my hair.

"You gonna kiss me," I tease and Cash's eyes flick down to my lips. He's so damn close, inches away. I could lean up and press my mouth to his before he could even blink. I think I'd like that. I think I'd like kissing Cash.

Instead, he presses a kiss to my cheek and then pushes off of me, standing up and adjusting himself.

"I'm gonna go get changed and head out," he says, and I sigh, running a hand through my hair.

"Probably a good idea," I say as I grab a towel and throw it at him. He catches it and starts to run it across his body. I try not to look. But my eyes can't help but admire the view.

"You could just stay here tonight. My bed is big enough."

"And risk you trying to get me to kiss you again," Cash says with a smile. "Not a chance in hell."

"I don't want to kiss you, asshole."

"Sure you don't."

I flick the towel out and get him in the ass. He glowers at me and then winds up his own, trying to get me, but I'm too fucking nimble. I manage to evade him and scuttle into the house, Cash right behind me.

"You're too slow, old man."

He winds up the towel once more and nails me right in the balls. My vision goes white as I bend over, a wheeze escaping me.

"Shiiiiit," I moan and suddenly Cash is before me, on his knees, his hands on mine as I try to breathe. If this were any other time, I'd joke about him being on his knees for me, but my balls are on *fire*.

"Got me in the nuts, man," I gasp. "I think one is bruised."

Cash's eyebrows furrow. "Is that a thing?"

"God," I groan as I suck in a breath. "I think one is gonna fall off. I think it's falling off right now."

Cash scoffs and then before I can even blink, my swim shorts are wrenched down and his hand is between my legs, knocking my half-hard cock out of the way and scooping my balls into his hands.

I lose the ability to breathe for another reason altogether. I mean, we've seen each other's dicks, but he's never touched mine. Let alone my balls. We've never done anything like this before.

"Your balls are just fine," he says, rolling them this way and that, trying to get a closer look at them. "A little small and shriveled, but just fucking fine."

I stand up a little farther, my legs shuffling wider as Cash examines me methodically.

One of my hands threads through his hair and his eyes shift up to meet mine.

"Suck my dick to make it feel better."

It's mostly a joke, but the way Cash's eyes darken and the way his tongue pokes out has my cock standing at full attention. The pain in my balls dissipates as blood continues to flow south. I'm almost lightheaded from the rush of it.

"I'm not sucking your dick," he says, but the way he's still touching my balls has me losing the ability to breathe. And he's not moving away either. He wants to do this as much as I want him to.

"You so should," I say, my fingers tightening in his hair and gently pulling him forward. He doesn't resist, just lets the tip of my cock brush his lips. "Just give it a nice little lick. An apology for being so fucking rough and careless."

"Fuck no," he says, but he doesn't move.

"You're so curious. I know you are," I say as I arch my hips, letting the tip of me slide across his lips.

Cash is frozen in place, but his eyelids flutter as his lips part slightly. Just the barest hint of acceptance.

Oh my god, I think. This can't be happening.

There is no way Cash is gonna blow me in my living room.

Not in my wildest fucking dreams would that ever happen.

CHAPTER SEVEN

CASH

Seems my mind has been having inappropriate thoughts about my best friend. Seems Benjamin unlocked things in my brain, and now I'm on my knees, Ford's cockhead at my parted lips.

I'm not sucking his dick. No way in fucking hell will I. That's a line we shouldn't cross.

"Just a taste," he teases. "I bet you like sucking dick. Bet you become a whore for it."

"Never gonna happen," I murmur.

My heart is hammering in my chest, my pulse point throbbing in my neck. His fingers flex in my hair, and I feel the scrape of his nails against my scalp as I press my lips to his dick. I shouldn't do this, should abso lutely stop, but my head keeps moving forward, my lips keep opening further.

Seems my body doesn't want me to stop.

Seems I want to try this with Ford.

He lets out a shaky breath as I widen my mouth and take more of him inside. I've never sucked a cock before, and the taste of him explodes on my tongue. It's so foreign and yet so familiar. It's Ford. My best friend of decades.

"Fuck yes," he gasps and then bends his knees slightly, pushing his dick deeper into my mouth. I open wide, my tongue sliding underneath him, my hand still holding his balls, the other coming to rest on his bare thigh.

This should be weirder than it is, but my body is only thrumming with need, my cock half-hard at the fact that Ford's dick is my mouth.

"Damn, Cash," Ford says as he rocks his hips. "Do you not gag?"

My eyes pop open, and I meet his stare, my mouth stretched wide across his hard length. His eyes meet mine, a small smile spreading across his face.

"Shit. You look so hot on your knees. Now suck me like you mean it. Show me how gay you are."

I let go of his balls and reach around with both hands, cupping his ass and dragging him as far back as I can manage. Ford lets out a choked groan. *Asshole asking me to prove myself,* I think as I pull off him and then take him all the way back into my throat. My cock is throbbing now. I want nothing more than to reach down and give my dick a long squeeze, but my hands are preoccupied with Ford's muscular butt. A butt I might have stared at a time or two.

"Fuck yes. Like that," Ford says, his hand tightening in my hair, showing me the pace he wants me to move. And I let him direct me, trying like hell to fight the feelings rising up in me. I should feel weirder about this, should feel so fucking strange, but it's Ford.

The only other dick I'd suck would be Ben's.

Just the thought of him has my cock hardening all the way, and I shift on my knees, feeling my mouth start to leak as Ford bobs my head up and down his length. My jaw is starting to ache, my tongue growing sore from rolling down the underside of him, but I'm not going to stop. Not when Ford is moaning above me, his cheeks flushed, his legs shaking as I take him over and over.

"Jesus, yes, do that tongue thing again," Ford grunts and then rams into me, his movements becoming sloppy and rough.

I grunt and grab him a bit tighter, wanting to pull off him, but also not wanting this to stop. I want to watch him come. Want to taste this part of him.

Ford's head is thrown back, his hips arching forward quickly, nearing his release, when suddenly the front door creaks open. The sound is deafening in the open space, and the two of us freeze. I peek over.

Ben. Here in this motherfucking house.

Ford's cock drops from my mouth, the two of us just staring at him. Ford's hand is still in my hair and one of my hands is still on his ass. I don't know what the fuck to do. I just told him that I wanted to be exclusive, and here I am sucking Ford's cock.

I swear to god, only Ford could get me into this kind of shit.

"I'm—" Ben stutters, and I can see his cheeks reddening. "I'm—I—"

Neither of us moves, the air thickening between us as Ben just stumbles over his words, his mouth opening and closing like a fish out of water. He looks damn good, tired, but still hot as fuck. His eyes are a little wild and so is his hair, and his shirt is a little too tight on his lithe body.

He looks like a piece of candy.

"Ben," Ford says, his words a little raspy.

He wets his lips, and my eyes drop to his groin where his cock is pressed out from his pants.

"I—" He shakes his head, taking a step back and then pausing. He looks as if he's warring with himself and then comes to a decision in seconds.

He takes a step forward.

My heart rate picks up as his eyes swivel from me on my knees to Ford standing before me.

"Again," he says lowly and my entire body flames. I feel like I'm going to combust. What is it about this guy that gets me going like this? I have no fucking clue.

"Again?" Ford asks dumbly, and Ben swallows.

"Again."

I know what he wants. I know what he wants to see.

And deep down, I want it too. I want it with the two of them.

I turn my head and engulf Ford. He lets out a gasp, his chin falling to his chest as I hollow out my cheeks. My hands grab on to his ass, pulling him into me over and over again, gagging when he moves too far down my throat, but I don't let up. I'm doing this for Ben now. Doing this for him. So he can see me on my knees.

Ford is moaning loudly now, his hand grasping my hair roughly. We're a cacophony of sounds of need and lust.

"Shit. Shit. *Stop*," Ben says suddenly.

The urgency in his voice has me pulling off of Ford, my chin wet, my eyes glazed over. Glancing up, I see Ford's chest heaving, his cheeks pink, and then I turn to see Ben standing right beside us. His hand is cupping his cock through his jeans.

He looks so fucking hot that I want to grab him and draw him down with me, want to press my lips to his, but I don't.

He wouldn't want that. He's made that clear. But then again, here he is. I don't fucking understand. My mind is too muddled.

Suddenly, he drops to his knees.

"What—" I begin but he just grabs on to Ford's cock and brings it to his mouth. He spreads those pouty lips, and I watch as he engulfs that big dick expertly, like he does with me. Oh shit. Watching him do this makes my cock leak. Ford gasps, his free hand moving into Ben's hair, now touching both of us as he thrusts his hips forward.

"Fuck, Ben," he moans as I watch Ben's mouth stretch over his hard length over and over. He takes him so good. So damn good. Fuck, I like watching this more than I thought I would. I love the way Ben grips his own cock, squeezing it, as if he needs to come. Reaching out, I move his hand away and run my palm over his hard length through his jeans. Ben whines and arches his hips forward, trying to fuck my hand.

I want him naked, want him sprawled out. I want to stick his cock in my mouth, want to watch as Ford fucks him.

Oh god.

Ben suddenly pops off Ford's cock, leaving my best friend reeling.

"Take it out," Ben says.

I stare at him, not understanding what he wants. I can't understand English right now. I just see his lips moving and want my dick in his mouth.

"Take it out, Cash."

The way he's bossing me around does something to my nuts—they draw up to my body and I feel like I'm gonna come.

When I don't move fast enough, he leans forward, his trembling hands tugging at my swim trunks. I sit up a little taller, helping him pull out my dick, and then it's just Ford and me, our hard cocks out. Ben wets his lips, his already red cheeks darkening, his pupils dilating. I can almost see the throb of desire move through him.

"Let me just do this. Just this once," he moans and then he falls on my cock, sucking me down. I arch up, my hands shifting through his hair like I've done so many times.

I know I should stop him, should pull him off, but I just push him farther down on my cock, making him choke and sputter, moan and writhe. I can see Ford jacking himself slowly as he watches us, his breathing still labored, his cock leaking.

"Fuck, this is hot," he groans and then Ben wrenches his mouth off of me and takes Ford back into his mouth. My hand grips my cock, my brain in such a state of lust that I can't see straight as I watch him suck and *suck*. The sloppy, squelching noise of his wet mouth is making the tip of me leak. Ford is groaning loudly, filthy words pouring from his mouth. Then Ben's back on me, making my eyes cross, making me moan. I grab on to Ford's cock, jerking it in my hand as I thrust my hips forward, right down Ben's throat.

What the fuck am I doing? Why the fuck am I doing this? Just as those thoughts form, Ford turns my face and presses his dick into my mouth, forcing a gasp from me as Ben groans.

The sounds we're making, they're obscene. I've lost my mother-fucking mind doing this.

And yet, my dick doesn't seem to mind. The way Ben is sucking me, the pleased humming he's making—like this is his dream come true, like this is what he was made for—has me shooting down his throat with a grunt. Ford follows me over a moment later, his cock twitching, his fingers grasping my hair as he cries out, his load exploding into my mouth without warning.

Fuck.

I swallow and sputter, choking on the obscene amount of cum that's unloaded into my throat. But Ford doesn't let up on my hair as he rides his orgasm to completion.

And then we just sit there, Ben's cheek on my thigh, my forehead on Ford's hip. It's silent except for our breathing.

"Well, shit," Ford manages to mutter and just like that, the spell is broken.

CHAPTER EIGHT

BEN

I don't know what I just did, but I did it. And I didn't even have the decency to come. My cock is still hard, pressing painfully against my zipper. My entire body is shaking as I sit up and take in a wide-eyed Ford and a frowning Cash.

"I—" I begin, the lust-driven spell broken. I don't know why I thought it was a good idea to join in on Cash and Ford's fun, but I saw them there—Cash on his knees, Ford with his hand in Cash's hair—and my first instinct was to crumble. They didn't want me. They'd chosen each other over me. Of course they did. They're best friends.

But then the sight of it—the way their cocks strained out from their bodies, the look of them *together*—had me moving toward them. I was powerless to stop myself.

Oh god. I joined in, and it was the hottest moment of my life. I will never forget this. All of my fantasies came true in those few minutes.

But now it's over, and they're in shock.

Ford's dick is wet and hanging down on his leg, and Cash's sits spent on his swim trunks that are haphazardly pulled down his thighs. My eyes swivel to his face, and I see that he still has cum on his lips. I want to lean forward, stick out my tongue and lick them clean. But I don't. I can't. Oh my god. What have I done?

I curl my hands on my thighs and breathe deeply.

The two of them continue to stare, confusion filling the space between us. I need to leave. I need to get out of here. I can't stay or I'm going to have to start answering questions I don't want to answer.

"Where the fuck are you going?" Cash asks gruffly when I stand to leave.

His eyes pivot to my crotch where my cock pulses in desperation, and I let out a shaky breath.

"I'm leaving."

"Like hell you are," Cash says.

"Hey, be nice," Ford reprimands, but Cash ignores him, standing up and stuffing his cock away. He glances over at Ford who is still standing there, his swim trunks around his thighs.

"Put that shit away, Ford."

Ford just blinks at him dumbly, so Cash reaches over and pulls Ford's shorts up his thighs, tucking his cock away in the process. The way they touch holds so much familiarity. As if they've been doing this for ages. For a second, I wonder if they've sucked each other's dicks before, but then shake it away.

No, Cash hadn't been with another guy before me. He told me that.

I was his sexual awakening. Motherfucking me.

When Cash looks over at me and finds me still not sitting, he moves toward me and gently settles me into a kitchen chair. His palms scrape against my arms, and I bite back a moan. My cock likes his hands on me far too much.

"He didn't come, Cash," Ford says, blinking back to reality.

Cash's gaze settles on my straining cock, and I press my hands over the bulge. They don't need to see this.

No, they really don't.

I gave all of my secrets away minutes ago and now I don't know what to say. I should make a run for it, but the way that Ford and Cash are watching me, I doubt that I'd make it very far. I'm not the most athletic. They could tackle me quickly.

The thought of both of them lying on top of me only makes my dick harder. There's a wet spot forming on the front of my jeans from how much it's leaking.

"I can see that," Cash says. "I think the real question is why he joined us in the first place."

Ford scoffs. "I mean, we're hot."

Cash eyes him and then slugs him in the shoulder.

"Why the hell was Ben here, Ford?"

"I was just—" I begin, but Cash cuts me off with a look.

"Let Ford answer this."

Ford shuffles on his feet. "Man, come on. My dick was in your mouth."

"Yeah, it was."

"Ben was just here for... we were gonna hang out."

Cash's eyebrows go up and he looks suspicious, as he should be. I walked right in Ford's front door. And here I am, hard dick and a cum-filled stomach—wanting to do whatever that was over and over again. If only they'd just fucking let me.

"Hang out?" Cash asks, his eyes narrowing. "Since when do you hang out with Ben alone?"

Ford shuffles on his feet and then scrubs a hand down his face.

"Don't," I plead, but Ford shakes his head.

"We're fucking."

Cash's mouth drops open and his arms fold across his chest.

"So are we."

Ford looks a bit surprised and then he shakes his head. "Wait, is this the guy you're into?"

My heart throbs in my chest. *Cash is into me?*

"Yeah, I didn't know he didn't want to be exclusive because he was fucking you."

They stare at each other and then their gazes swivel to me. I swallow so loudly that it clicks. Oh my god. I'm going to faint, my vision goes a little blurry, and I grab on to the edge of the table to steady myself. I should have eaten dinner. *Or maybe not*, I think as my stomach clenches deviously.

"You're fucking both of us?" Ford asks, and I shake my head.

"No."

It's a lie, but I have to do it. I can't admit it. It's the one thing in my life I've ever done that was completely reckless, and I can't fucking tell the truth. I'm too ashamed.

Cash scoffs, and Ford takes a step toward me, bending down and taking my hands in his. They're so big that they engulf mine. They're so fucking warm, so fucking strong.

I peer into his eyes and then my gaze flicks to Cash. He looks so fucking upset with me. Not that I blame him.

I would be too.

The amount of jealousy that surged through me when I saw them together was unreasonable. I can't imagine what they're feeling right now. I can't stand it. I can't fucking breathe.

I pull my hands away and stand up, the chair scooting back loudly. Ford and Cash watch me intently, and I shake my head.

"I—I'm going. I'm not doing this. I can't do this."

Ford pushes himself up, and I glance at the two of them standing there—two devastatingly handsome men who star in all of my fantasies —and swallow back my tears.

"I'm so fucking sorry."

And then I dash from the house, stumbling out the front door and jogging to my car. My dick is still hard, not at all ashamed for being the slut it is as I fumble with my car keys. *I need to get a newer car so I can make a hastier escape,* I think as my keys fall to the ground. I grab them with a curse and jam them into the lock. My vision swimming, I slide inside and turn the car on, swiping at my eyes as I peel away from the curb. I don't even look to see if they're watching me. I don't need to look.

Without thinking about it, I drive to Tatum's place. He lives with several roommates and they all know me, so I don't even knock, just walk right in, waving at a few people gathered on the couch. They don't even blink at my intrusion as I make my way up the stairs to his room. I knock once and then push the bedroom door open, finding Tatum on his bed, bright green headphones covering his ears. He has a purple pencil in his mouth and when I appear before him, his bright eyes meet mine.

"Hey," he says, pulling the headphones off so they hang around his neck. "What's wrong?"

I shake my head, kicking off my shoes and crawling into bed with him. His arms pull me into his chest, and he sighs.

"Oh god, what happened?" he asks, his hand rubbing up and down my back, trying to soothe me.

"I sucked their dicks at the same time," I manage to say with a hiccup.

"And that's a problem?" Tatum asks, his fingers threading through my hair gently.

"It is because now they know what I've done. What I've been doing."

Tatum sighs. "You've done nothing wrong. They both knew this wasn't exclusive. They went into this with eyes wide open."

"Yeah, but they're mad."

"Obviously not that mad if they let you suck their dicks."

I peer up at him and his eyes twinkle. "It's not funny."

"I'm not laughing. I swear. I'm just amused that you're here with me and not getting your greedy butthole split open over and over."

"They wouldn't do that. They—it was just a moment of insanity."

Tatum snorts, and I glower at him.

"Sorry, I'm sure it was a moment of insanity, but I guarantee you that it'll happen again. And again. Those men are so horny for you, and you're just as bad. I'm sure they'll come to that realization very soon."

I snuggle up against him and let him just hold me. I'm not sure he's right. I think I've fucked it all up.

———

"Hey! Benjamin. How are you doing?" a friendly voice says. I turn my gaze up and see Colin standing there beside his boyfriend, Ethan, the man who glowers at me nonstop whenever they come to the senior home to visit Colin's grandma, Beth. *Well, I got the point, buddy*, I think as I scrub at my tired eyes. I peer up and see Colin looking so damn good in his tight athletic pants and shirt. But on top of that, what makes him shine, is how happy he looks. Content. I'm sure I don't look like that at the moment.

After leaving Tatum's room at midnight last night, I went back to my place and tossed and turned for hours before deciding I should get back to the gym. I've missed a lot of yoga classes the past few weeks, mainly because I was getting my exercise elsewhere.

Now I need to find an alternative to cardio fucking.

"I'm okay," I say, taking in the scowling British man next to him. He's wearing loose athletic shorts that show off his muscular legs and a tight-fitting long-sleeved shirt. He's absolutely gorgeous. No wonder Colin is so damn happy—the way Ethan looks at him with nothing but adoration. It's so opposite to the way in which Ford and Cash looked at me last night.

Just the thought of it has my stomach rolling.

"So good to hear," Colin says, spreading his mat out and sitting down cross-legged. He turns to Ethan and begins talking quietly, so I just face forward, catching my reflection in the mirror. I look horrendous. Like I haven't slept in a week. There are dark purple smudges under my bloodshot eyes. My hair is in disarray and I just look sallow, sunken, anemic.

I should eat more, but fuck, the stress of everything is making my appetite nonexistent. Perhaps working out with some yoga will give me some of that back, will help me relax. But by the end of class, I only feel like I'm going to throw up. I shouldn't have gone this long without working out. I feel the burn of stretching and several under-worked muscles scream at me as I roll up my mat and gulp down water.

"Alright, well, it was good to see you again. Catch you again soon?" Colin asks, and I nod before watching him lean into Ethan as they make their way out of class. I can't believe I ever went on a date with him—that *that* man was even interested in me. Perhaps if I could have stayed awake during our date, I'd be happily dating Colin right now. But no, that couldn't have happened. By that time, my trysts with Ford and Cash had already started, and I was only on that date because I'd already made plans with Colin and didn't want to cancel.

To say that Cash was upset when he found out I was on a date with another man was an understatement. He punished my mouth with that tattooed dick when he got me alone. Made me see stars and then caressed my face after, looking down at me in awe. That's a look I'll never see from him again.

Oh god. I walk on shaky legs to my car and sink into the driver's seat. I feel like I'm going to pass out. My vision swims, and I grab a discarded, unopened granola bar from my console and force it down, nearly gagging on it. But I know this is what my body needs. Sustenance. Food. Fuck, I hate it. Such a goddamn chore.

I wash down the scratchy bits with some water and then start up my car, pulling out of the parking lot and driving home. It's still so early, and I feel like I could sleep for a week with how exhausted I am, but I know it's useless. I won't be able to, not with the anxiety bubbling inside of me.

So I just shower and head to the senior home, knowing that as soon as these oldies get a look at me, the comments will flow endlessly.

"You look pooped!" Vikki exclaims, her eyes bugging out from behind her glasses. When my eyes water slightly, my poor, tired brain telling me not to cry, she sighs. "Oh dear. This is more serious than I thought. I'm going to get you some coffee and something to eat. You look far too thin."

She turns around and shouts, "Norma! How do you use InstaGrub! Or is it DoorCart? Damn names," she mutters. "Norma!"

I crack a smile at that, my eyes burning. Fuck, I just want to sob. I want to bawl until I can't breathe, but I have too much to do. So I can't. I need to hold it together for a little while longer.

Thirty minutes later, Vikki emerges with Martha and Norma in tow, setting a large cup of coffee and a breakfast burrito in front of me. It reminds me of Cash cooking me breakfast, and I inhale sharply.

"You guys," I say as they pull up chairs, crowding around me. "You didn't need to do this."

"Yes, we did. Took us no time at all," Martha says, and Norma snorts.

"Took us longer to find our phones than actually ordering it."

"Had to find my magnifying glass," Vikki says, and I snort a laugh.

Sipping the coffee, I nearly groan at how good it tastes, vanilla and hazelnut notes exploding on my tongue. How they know what I like only makes my eyes leak profusely.

"Oh bother. Why are you crying?" Martha pats me on the back as Vikki rubs at my leg. Norma is unwrapping the burrito and shoving it in my hand.

"He needs to eat. He's crying because he's hungry."

It's true. I am hungry, but fuck, I don't feel like eating. I take a bite anyways, hiccupping after I swallow and then taking another sip of my drink. Someone walks up to the check-in desk, and Norma scowls at them when they try and ask me a question.

"Can't you see we're in the middle of something?" she hisses, and I manage a wobbly smile, swiping at my eyes.

"Norma, I have to check them in."

"If I can figure out how to use a fancy phone, you can use that screen yourself, young man."

The older man—who is not that young—blushes, looking thoroughly chastised and signs in quickly, walking away with his hands in his pockets.

"Jesus, people these days. They can't read a room," Norma grumbles.

"*Norma*," I say, but she just stuffs the burrito in my hand again and watches eagle-eyed as I take another bite. "I can't get fired."

"If they fire you, I will burn this place to the ground," Martha says with a huff, and I stare at her in shock.

"That's illegal."

"Not if we don't get caught," Vikki pipes up, and I let out a horrified laugh.

"Do not burn the building down. You cannot do that."

"At least we got him to laugh," Martha chimes in with a wink, and I feel my chest tighten.

"I needed it," I say softly and then sip at my drink. I really did. I haven't laughed in ages. And now I feel like my whole world is crumbling. All I want to do is cry.

"So are you going to tell us what's going on?" Vikki asks, adjusting her glasses and watching me intently. "We may know a thing or two. We have been alive since Jesus."

"We know it all," Norma says assuredly. "So spill."

I eye the three of them, the little old ladies who have befriended me this past year, and give in with a sigh.

"I was doing two guys. I already told you all that..."

"Doing? You mean fucking?" Norma asks as Martha says, "At the same time or separately?"

"Well, yes and yes. God. Yes, fucking," I say lowly and then add, "And at first it was separately, but last night..." Norma waggles her eyebrows as they all lean forward. "I was with them both."

"Oh yes! Thank the Lord, hallelujah," Vikki shouts, choking slightly and coughing until her face turns red. I worry she's about to keel over dead, but she manages to recover after a few minutes, her eyes leaking and her face still a splotchy red. I let out a sigh of relief. I don't want her to die.

She waves her hand around her face and then sniffles, "Go on. Why were you crying?"

"Well..." I pause and take a deep breath. "They now know that I've been doing them both behind each other's backs and they're mad. I ran out of there as soon as it was over. Just the looks on their faces... This thing between us is definitely over."

Martha purses her lips, deep in thought, and Vikki is picking something out of her ear.

"How do you know? If anything, they're probably mad you left. They probably want another round. Several more, in fact," Norma says loudly, and I shake my head, swallowing roughly.

"I think it's over. I messed up. Bad."

Vikki wipes her finger on her shirt and then leans forward. "Had some wax in my ear and couldn't hear. You mean to tell me that it's over?"

"Yeah."

I squirt some hand sanitizer in Vikki's hands and she rubs them together, the smell of alcohol and disinfectant piercing my stuffy nose.

"I ruined it."

They all lean closer to me, patting my legs and shoulders as I swipe at my eyes. "I'll be fine. I'm just upset and tired, and I have to go to my dad's shop and see them after this."

"Oh, they work at the shop?" Vikki asks. "That's right. Lex said something about the dad's best friends."

I flush red and feel the admission well up inside of me. I can't keep it inside anymore. "Yeah, well, he was right."

"Woooheeee," Norma chortles, and I press a hand against my cheek.

"It's so bad. I'm a terrible son and an even worse person."

"No, you're not," Martha says as Norma chimes in that only the best people are secretly bad. It makes another laugh slip out of me, and I shake my head, sniffling loudly.

"Maybe you just shouldn't go. Take a couple days for your mental health," Vikki says, a voice of reason among us. It's surprising really, but then again, they do tend to impart helpful nuggets at the most random times.

The idea isn't terrible, and honestly, I could do without seeing them. I've never called out of work at the shop, and I'm sure they won't miss me. All I do is file paperwork and help Avery when he's overwhelmed. I'm not even paid that well. I won't be hurting anyone if I skip out just this once.

So that's what I do. When I'm finished at the senior home, I call Avery to say I'm not feeling well, then go straight back to my apartment and throw myself onto the bed, letting out the tears I've been holding in all day. It feels good, lying here in my own fluids, just being the saddest sack to ever sack.

When I'm finally done, my entire body exhausted and strung out, I close my eyes and fall into a fitful sleep.

Later. I can deal with all of this later, but I'm no good to anyone exhausted. Especially myself. That's who I need to focus on now.

Me.

And no one else.

CHAPTER NINE

I wake up the next morning with Ford lying half on top of me, a pool of drool on my shoulder. I don't know why he does this, but he's the cuddliest fucker on the planet. I shift beneath him, and he grunts, moving even closer to me.

"Get the fuck off," I grumble and shove at him lightly.

He rolls off of me, his eyelids blinking open, and I smile at him.

"You drooled on me."

"Don't know why you aren't used to it by now. Why the hell did you sleep over? Thought you were gonna leave."

I run a hand over my face and sigh. "Yeah, well, you pinned me down and I couldn't move."

Ford sighs and then sits up, running a hand through his dark hair and making it stand up even more sideways than it was.

"Well, I'm glad you stayed. I'm worried we fucked it all up," he says candidly.

I am too. I think we did.

"I mean you and I, we're solid. And honestly, I'm not even mad that Ben is fucking you, but Ben—well, shit, he's so fucking skittish."

"Yeah."

I know what he means. After the initial awkwardness of learning that we were both doing the same guy, nothing much changed. The blow job, while not forgotten, isn't an obstacle at all. We just moved past it. It almost seems like it was meant to be. I mean, I'm barely even bothered that Ford is the other guy in this equation. Anyone else and I'd have lost my mind...but because it's him, I mentally shrugged.

If it's Ford, it's fine.

"But the blow job was hot, Cash. Just sayin'," Ford says, and I sigh. Apparently, I've moved past it, but he hasn't. The thought of it, the three of us together, does things to my libido I don't understand.

"Yeah, how about we don't talk about that anymore."

"Why not? It was sexy—you're good with your tongue. I want to do that again."

"With Ben," I say, and Ford nods.

"Of course with Ben."

"So, how do we get him to do it again?" Ford asks, standing up, his cock half-hard in his boxer briefs, his arms thrown behind his head as he stretches. My eyes swivel down to his cock, and I feel my own morning wood start to throb.

"Don't know," I say and then run a hand down my face. "I don't fucking know."

"Hm, well, let's shower and we can brainstorm. I always do better after a morning blow job."

I glower at him, and he winks at me, pulling his shirt off and heading to the bathroom.

"Come on, Cash. You had my dick in your mouth last night with Ben. Come wash my body!"

"Fuck you!" I shout and then sit up, looking around the room I've spent more than one night in. Usually in his bed. Usually waking up with Ford sprawled across me.

Maybe that blowjob last night was inevitable. I don't fucking know. All I know is I'm not getting in that shower with Ford, and I'm not washing his goddamn body.

———

"Knew you'd cave," Ford says with a broad smile, one arm up as he washes his pits. I roll my eyes as I kick off my boxers.

"I'll shower with you, but I'm not washing your body."

Ford snorts as I step inside and shut the glass door behind me. He hands me some soap and then turns, grabbing the shampoo. His bare ass is facing me, and I sigh. This isn't the first time we've showered together either. In college, there were more times than I could count where I'd ended up with him bare-ass naked in the bathroom. Usually it was to clean him up after he spilled on himself, or even worse, vomited everywhere.

But now, things are different. Now his cock has been in my mouth, and I liked it.

"Here," he says, turning around, his erection poking me in the stomach as he reaches up and starts to slide his fingers through my hair.

"Your dick is poking me," I say, and Ford just scoffs, moving a little closer so our dicks bump.

"Yours is poking me too. Who cares? Let's talk about Ben and how we can get him to join us in the shower next time."

I glance away from him, willing my eyes not to close as he massages my scalp so deliciously but failing. Ford is such a fucker.

"I'm thinking we text him and tell him to come over after work. You know, play it cool at the shop and then have a repeat of last night when we get home."

His hands have moved from my head and are sliding down my chest now as he keeps blathering his nonsensical plan.

"...or we could go a crazy route and unplug his battery so his car doesn't start, keep him stranded at our place and then fuck him silly. Make him see sense."

"How are you not mad at him for keeping me a secret?"

He shrugs. "He never said we were exclusive, and his ass kept me coming back for more. And we shouldn't be too hard on him," he says as he grabs on to my hard dick and strokes. A small gasp leaves me at the sensation. "I mean, he is a lot younger than us. And don't forget, we're fucking our best friend's son."

"I haven't fucked him," I say as I arch my hips forward, letting his soapy hand slide all the way down my cock.

"You're missing out."

I huff a laugh and then groan when his grip tightens.

"Shit."

"You're gonna have a very clean dick after this," he says with a smile and then shifts a little closer, moving one hand around to my ass and scrubbing at my cheeks. Our cocks slide together and he gathers them both tightly in his fist and strokes, making me grunt and moan.

"So, we have a plan then? You wanna do creepy or more reserved?"

"Oh fuck," I say as my head hits the tile behind me.

"Yeah, I was thinking that too," Ford says as he picks up the pace. "I think kidnapping is a good idea."

I let out a huff and then clutch on to his shoulders.

"Shut the fuck up and get me off, you ass."

"Working on it," Ford says and then tweaks my nipple with one hand, making me hiss.

"That's not helping."

"It helps me. Love my nips played with."

"Jesus."

"What do you like played with, Cash? When Ben sucks you, does he do anything else to you? Play with your balls? Lick your hole?"

My eyes narrow.

"He just sucked my dick."

"Hm," Ford says, cocking his head, his cheeks looking a little flushed, his breathing growing labored. "Well, we'll have to fix that, Cash. You need more than just head from him. God, the things that ass can do."

The thought of it, Ben bent over, my cock sliding into his hole makes me explode. And then Ford gasps, his head thrown back as he follows me over.

Our breathing is stunted and Ford slowly removes his hand from my cock, finger by finger until we're finally separated.

"Come on, rinse. You look like a bubble bath."

I shuffle around him and close my eyes, rinsing myself clean and then watch as Ford does the same.

"We aren't kidnapping him," I say, and Ford smiles at me.

"Yeah, I was mostly kidding about that. But for real, at work—we behave normally, then get him to my place. Somehow, someway. You want a repeat of last night, right?"

"Yeah, but maybe you could be sucking my dick instead."

"Yeah, or we could take turns fucking Ben."

I scrub a wet hand down my face. "I don't know—"

"Trust me," Ford says with a wink, moving past me and patting my chest. "Once you get in his ass you'll be loath to leave."

"So, just to clarify," I begin, trying to make sure this is clear between us. "You want to keep fucking him—together?"

He shrugs. "Together, separately. So long as we're all consenting and having fun, who cares?"

I eye my best friend as he winks at me.

And for the first time in a long time, Ford actually makes sense.

———

He's not here. He called out sick. The way that Ford is eyeing me makes my heart rate pick up. We both know why he's not here, and it makes me sick to my stomach. Instead of talking it out with us, he ran, and we let him. But we had stuff of our own to discuss. Not that we did much of that. Ford fell asleep halfway through, and then so did I.

Maybe I should be more upset with Ben, but I can't be. Especially not when he walked in and saw Ford's cock down my throat.

Besides, it's not really sharing when it's Ford. We've never really been good with boundaries anyways.

So we pulled together a half-assed plan, but Ben's not here to enact it. Well fuck.

"I just messaged him," Ford whispers, and I nod. "No response. Don't worry, man. We'll get him."

Our shift ends later than we thought and we move out of the building together as the sun is setting. Dean took off with Avery earlier, not that I blame him. Seems that Dean has eyes for his assistant in those skirts and crop tops.

And I might have taken a peek at him out of curiosity, but it did nothing for me.

Ben does it for me.

He really fucking does.

There's just something about him—his pouty pink lips and piercing eyes and just the way he looks at me with intense desire. And maybe it makes me a bad person that Ben is Dean's son, but it hasn't stopped me yet. And it seems Ford is on the same page. But then again, we have always been similar. Apparently we have the same taste in men too.

"We can't just show up at his place, so what the fuck do we do?" Ford asks, and I scratch at my jaw.

"I don't know. Maybe we should just go back to your place to figure shit out."

Ford doesn't seem to like that plan because he comes up with a thousand others on our way back to his place. And then once there, he starts to get antsy. He's pacing the living room, his energy almost out of control.

"I mean, we could sneak over. I could park down the street and we could go through his window."

"Are you going to wear a ski mask too?" I ask, and Ford eyes me.

"I could. All black might not be a bad idea."

I shake my head, a smile forming on my lips. "How about instead of scaring him to death, we just call that guy, Colin?"

Ford's brows furrow. "Who the fuck is that?"

"Ben asked me to do him a favor that one time. I took Colin out on my bike and got him ice cream."

Ford cocks his head, and I add, "He owes me."

"Hell yes. Do it."

I pull out my phone and search my contacts for the number and then hit call.

Colin better come through like I did for him. I showed up on my motorcycle and took him out to make some British guy jealous. And I did it for Ben, because he asked me to. Colin owes me a happily ever after. And my goddamn leather jacket.

CHAPTER TEN

FORD

"When the hell is Colin going to get here?" I ask, my feet pacing the room. Cash just leans back in his chair and eyes me. He's the perfect picture of nonchalance. It's ridiculous. How can he be so calm when Ben is out there? When he's not here with us?

"He'll be here soon. He has a kid to take care of."

"Shit," I say, running my hand through my hair. I'm anxious to see Ben, to make sure he's okay. I hate that he called out of work today and disappeared, that he stopped answering messages from both of us.

Makes my mind spiral.

"Come here," Cash says, pointing to his lap.

I roll my eyes. "Not gonna happen."

"Get your ass over here," he says more gruffly this time, and I stride over to him, helpless to do anything but what he asks when he uses that tone on me. Leaning forward, his hands land on my hips and he brings me down onto him, my ass connecting with his thighs.

"Now chill the fuck out," he says as he adjusts me on his lap.

I squirm and wiggle before settling in, my nervous energy abating somewhat from being so close to Cash. But this is how it's always been.

He's been my rock for so many years. Which might seem strange considering his tumultuous upbringing, but it is what it is. He's always been so goddamn strong.

Suddenly car lights shine through the front window, and I scramble up, moving quickly to the front door and wrenching it open. Cash is right behind me, his chest pressed up against my back as we watch Colin get out of the driver's seat.

"God, why is Colin so hot?" I mutter, hating him just a little bit.

"I know, but he's taken."

That makes me feel somewhat better. I don't like that Cash took this guy for a ride and for ice cream. He usually only does that shit with me.

And he gave him his leather jacket and never got it back.

I never get to wear his leather jacket.

"He refuses to get out," Colin says and then sighs. "He's also pissed at me that I tricked him into coming here. Told me we aren't friends anymore and then denounced me."

I let out a snort as we move off the porch to the passenger side door, and I open it, glancing in at a worn-down Ben.

"You tricked me," he says softly, and I bob my head before reaching in and unbuckling him. He doesn't even fight it, just lets me gently tug him out of his seat and into my arms.

He smells clean, fresh like he just showered, and I inhale the scent greedily before walking him toward the front door.

"You have my jacket?" I hear Cash ask Colin, but Colin just loudly says goodbye and hops in the driver's seat, locking the doors. Cash shakes his head and follows us inside.

"That fucker still has my jacket and won't return it," Cash grumbles as he locks the front door. His comment goes ignored as I feel Ben pull away from me, moving to the far corner of the room, his arms folded across his chest, his cheeks pale.

He looks so fucking pretty in the worst way.

He looks tired. Like he needs a long nap.

"Why the fuck do you look like that?" Cash says, and Ben scoffs, rolling his eyes.

"You kidnapped me."

"We didn't. We just had you delivered," I say.

"I'm not an Amazon package."

"No, you're definitely not," I say, my eyes raking over him. Fuck, even tired and worn out he looks hot. "Amazon doesn't have anything as hot as you."

I never looked at him this way when he was younger, he was always just Dean's kid—too young and not even an option. But then a few months ago, something changed, and I suddenly couldn't wrench my eyes away. And now that I've had him, been inside him, he's the only one I want. Well, and of course Cash. But that's a given.

Cash and Ben and me.

"So now that you dragged me all the way here, what do you want?" he asks, sounding less angry and more wary.

"You didn't show up for work," I say, and Cash moves to stand near me, the two of us an impenetrable force as Ben seems to curl up into himself.

"I wasn't feeling well."

"You were avoiding us," Cash grumbles, and I nudge him.

"Shut up, man."

"Well, it's the truth," he murmurs, and Ben shakes his head and then sways slightly. It's then that I notice how pronounced the dark purple smudges under his eyes are and the fact that he looks almost sick.

I don't waste another second. I move toward him, scooping him into my arms and bringing him to the bedroom.

"Get him some water and something to eat," I call behind me as I move toward my bed.

"I'm not hungry."

"Yeah, well you're gonna eat something and drink some fucking water," I say as I sit him down. He wobbles slightly and his eyelashes flutter.

"I don't feel well."

"Of course you don't. You don't take care of yourself."

Ben swallows roughly as I move to take his shoes off.

Cash appears beside me, handing Ben some water and a granola bar.

He sips at the liquid as I discard his shoes and socks, and then the two of us stand and watch him intently as he slowly bites into the bar.

"All of it," Cash says, concern lacing his tone.

Ben rolls his eyes but does as he's told, and when he's done, we move at the same time. Cash grabs the cup and granola bar wrapper, and I move to grab the hem of his shirt.

"What the hell?" Ben grumbles as I start to pull it up. "What are you doing?"

"I'm helping you get undressed. We're going to bed."

Ben's cheeks flush, that bit of color in his skin making him look so much healthier.

"I'm not staying here. I'm going home."

Cash grunts and then brushes me aside and yanks Ben's shirt off, tossing it across the room.

A gasp leaves him and he covers up his chest as if he's suddenly indecent. It makes me chuckle.

"Been inside of you, Ben. Had my tongue up your ass. You don't need to act like you're some virgin."

Ben's mouth opens and closes, his skin flushing even darker.

"Pants off," Cash says and then moves when Ben continues to sit unmoving.

He wrestles them off until Ben's clad only in his boxers, and I run a hand down my face to keep my dick in check. My horniness levels are at an all-time high with Ben here, on my bed. My mind is conjuring up all the filthy things I've done to him on those sheets. And at the same time, my dick is throbbing because I like watching Cash touch Ben.

I would totally watch them fuck.

Would be so fucking hot.

"You sleep in boxers or naked?" Cash asks, and Ben sighs.

"Naked."

"Good," Cash says as he pushes him to lie back and nearly rips his underwear off. Ben's dick is straining up from being manhandled and he gasps when he notices, covering it with his hands. Not that it does any good. We can see it. We've seen it all.

"Don't worry," Cash says. "We aren't gonna fuck you. We're gonna sleep."

Cash reaches up and pulls his own shirt off and begins unbuckling his pants.

"We aren't?" I ask, feeling a little disappointed. I mean, I could totally fuck right now.

"He's exhausted. Can barely sit up straight. His dick can wait. And so can ours."

I sigh and follow Cash's lead, discarding my clothes until I'm only in my boxers. My dick is hard and Cash's is too. I can see it bulging out from the fabric of his briefs. But it goes ignored. Sadly.

He reaches out and pulls the sheets back, and Ben eyes us.

"Get in," Cash murmurs.

"I can't stay."

And yet he still scoots back until he's under them, his head hitting a pillow with a sigh. We watch him for a second before moving at the same time, the two of us sliding in beside him, me on his left and Cash on his right.

"You sleep and when you wake up, we'll talk."

Ben's gaze shifts between us and then he rolls onto his side and closes his eyes, his lips parted as he drifts off. I look over at Cash as he moves in closer to Ben from behind, and I follow suit, blanketing him against us. Ben sighs and curls up tighter against us and something shifts inside of my chest.

Cash meets my eyes and smiles softly at me.

"We're gonna take care of him," Cash whispers, and I nod once.

Hell yes, we are.

CHAPTER ELEVEN

BEN

I wake up feeling a heady throb beating through my body. It's a persistent drum of inexplicable need. I need them.

Need them.

I stretch my naked body out and feel the hairy legs of someone beneath me and another behind me.

Cash.

Ford.

The two men I never thought I'd have again are in bed... with me.

My eyelids slowly open and despite the dark room, I notice I'm half sprawled out on Cash, my arm thrown over his chest, my head tucked into his shoulder. And Ford is behind me, his hand resting on my stomach, his leg thrown over mine.

I'm in a man sandwich, I think and then shove the silly thought away.

Oh god, it's not silly. It's real. I'm between these two men and my cock is throbbing painfully. The need to be filled is so intense I almost lose my ability to breathe. I shift my hips backward and feel Ford's hard cock slide up against my ass. Even through his boxers, I can feel the hard heat of him.

Oh god, oh my fucking god.

My fingers curl up on Cash's chest, and I hear him groan as I rock my hips forward and drag my bare cock against his side.

"Mm," Cash hums after a moment, and I feel Ford shift behind me, the two of them starting to wake up.

I don't even know what time it is. Don't even fucking care. All I know is it's time to be fucked. It's fuck o'clock. It's been so long since I've had them, and here they are, crowding me with their body heat, their scent. Individually, they smell delicious but combined, their fragrance is almost orgasmic.

I continue to rock my hips back and forth, and I feel the two of them wake up, their hands and bodies starting to move.

So many hands on me. Rough hands, manly hands. I can feel the slip of their metal rings dragging across my skin.

Ford's fingers drift down my stomach and brush my cockhead, making me exhale sharply as Cash's hand slides up my arm and curls around my neck.

"You awake?" Ford asks, his hand wrapping around my dick, and my hips jerk forward.

"Yeah," I breathe as Cash's thumb slides across my lower lip. My tongue slips out and traces his skin, and I hear him let out a long shaky exhale.

"You need us, Benjamin?" Ford asks as he slowly works his hand up and down my cock.

"Yes," I groan, moving one hand back to pull Ford's face into my neck while the other cups the side of Cash's face. I can't fucking move, too turned on to try and pivot my body so they can have better access to me. But neither of them seems in a hurry. They're taking their time, teasing me with their small touches until I'm panting and groaning. Practically begging.

"Think he needs to be fucked," Ford says softly, his hips rocking against my ass, foreshadowing what's to come, what he's gonna do to me.

"I need it," I nearly wheeze, my entire body writhing between the two of them.

"What do you need?" Ford whispers.

"Everything," I hiss and then groan when he moves his hand off my cock and drags his fingers up my side.

"Cash told me he hasn't fucked you," Ford says, biting at my ear and then lifting his head slightly to look at Cash. "Did you know Ben can come multiple times? That's how much of a slut he is for it."

Cash lets out a groan as he turns toward me, both bodies now bracketing me.

I'm grinding my hips back and forth, my cock sliding against Cash's while my ass presses into Ford's. It's too much, too fucking much for my mind to comprehend. I've always dreamed of this but never thought it would actually happen. Just hours ago, I thought it was all over, and now here I am, squished between them.

"Get me the lube and condoms," Ford says. "They're in the drawer."

Cash arches back and then a second later, a large bottle plops down on the pillow.

"Really?" Cash asks, and Ford laughs softly.

"Ben really is insatiable, and you'll be thanking me once you take his ass. We'll go through this really fast."

The thought of it, the two of them taking turns with me has me nearly coming on the spot, but I hold back, not wanting this to be over anytime soon.

Ford and Cash move at the same time, almost in sync, as if they can read each other's minds. Ford grabs the lube and flips me onto my back, positioning himself between my legs as Cash moves up to kneel by the side of my head, his thick thighs bracketing my shoulder.

I feel his hand drop to my chest, caressing me gently as Ford flips the cap of the lube open and squirts some on his fingers.

"Knees up," he says softly, and I do as I'm told, opening myself up for whatever Ford and Cash want to do to me. I'm just a vessel to be used.

A second later, I feel the press of Ford's finger at my hole, and I bear down as he slides his entire finger inside of me. Oh hell yes. *About time*, I think on a sigh.

"Fuck, tight as ever," Ford says as he twists his wrist and brushes against my prostate. I arch my hips up on a gasp and Ford chuckles, adding a second finger.

"Think he needs something in that mouth of his," Ford says, and I nod, parting my lips and reaching up. Cash's hard cock is already out and I grab on to it, bringing it down to my mouth. I lick and suck on the underneath of him and Cash leans forward a little further for better access.

I need more. I need it in my mouth. Need it choking me, down my throat. I don't want to be able to breathe.

I turn my head and take the tip of him into me as Ford adds a third finger into my ass, stretching me wide.

Cash's hand is cupping my head now, helping me take more of him as Ford adds a fourth finger. I cry out at the sensation of being so full, of being so deliciously used.

"He's ready," Ford says, and then I hear the ripping of a condom wrapper.

No. No. I want more.

I want it differently this time.

Cash's dick slides out of my mouth, and I shake my head, almost delusional with lust.

"No condom. I've only been with you two. Please."

Ford pauses, the wrapper still between his teeth as his eyes flick to Cash. He must see something there because he tosses it aside before scooting closer to me, taking some lube and coating his bare cock as I arch my neck once more and take Cash's dick deep into my mouth. He's leaning over me, sliding down my throat as Ford presses into me. I groan loudly at the intrusion, my mouth stretched wide, my jaw aching from the pressure of it.

Fuck, it's only been a few days, but it feels like it's been years.

I needed this. I needed this more than I needed air.

My legs wrap around the back of Ford as he enters me slowly, tunneling his hard length into my slick, wet hole.

"Fuck, he feels even better bare. Oh fuck, I can't explain it—"

I groan just as they do, our sounds filtering through the darkened room. Fuck, this is too good, it's euphoric. Cash pulls his cock out of my mouth and thrusts back in, the two of them pushing inside of me like a well-oiled machine. As if they've done this a thousand times before. Perhaps in another life, the three of us were together. Perhaps, this is just old souls finding each other once again.

Ford's hips punch into me as Cash pulls out of my throat, and all thought disappears. My eyes shut in bliss, my entire body thrumming with the need to come. I can feel it in the base of my cock, in my heavy, tight balls. They're full and needing to be emptied.

"Fuck, look at him," Ford grunts, leaning forward slightly and fucking into me faster. "Make him choke, Cash. Stick it down his throat."

Cash shifts slightly, cupping the back of my head and pulling me closer, his dick sliding down my esophagus, cutting off my air and making my entire body tingle with the need to breathe.

Who needs air when you have cock?

"Yes, like that. Look at it. The whole thing," Ford groans as he starts to fuck into me harder. Cash pulls out and does it again, their thrusts going out of sync, my body just being used. Just holes. But it's glorious. I wouldn't want it any other way.

"Look at his cock. Look how hard it is for us," Ford gasps as he reaches down and tugs at it.

I cry out, my mouth still full of Cash, but loving that their hands are on me. Put them all over me.

They both groan at the sight of my dick as it leaks in response.

"You sure you don't want a turn in this ass?" Ford asks. "He feels so damn good."

Cash just chokes me on his cock again and grunts out, "So does his mouth."

Ford chuckles and then moans as he continues to fuck into me. Cash replaces Ford's hand on my dick and he starts to work me toward the edge, but it's when he pivots and leans down to suck my cock into his mouth that I lose all ability to exist. I come with a muffled shout.

I don't even give him any warning. The minute his mouth surrounds me, I jerk up and explode. Cash moans around my pulsing length, and I'm left to moan and grunt as he continues to fuck my mouth. We're nothing more than groans and bodily fluids at this point. Reason and thought have fled.

"Fuck, that's so fucking hot," Ford says as his hips go wild, pounding into me as Cash sits up once more, the back of his hand swiping across his mouth. I arch up, letting him fuck my mouth in earnest.

It's too much, too much of a sensory overload. I never want this to stop. I want them to do this to me all night. I'd cock warm them with my mouth and my ass—just fall asleep with them inside of me.

But my dreams are dashed.

All too soon, it's over. Cash unloads in my waiting mouth with a groan, his cum spilling over my lips and onto my chin and neck. And then Ford follows him over a minute later, his cum pumping into my ass.

Our breathing is ragged, our sheets and bodies a mess of cum and sweat.

"Well fuck, I wanted to keep going—" Ford sucks in a deep breath and pulls out of me, his eyes swiveling down to my exposed hole that's assuredly leaking now. "But that was too hot. I— Fuck. Me."

Cash lets out a low chuckle and then groans as he moves off the bed. I'd follow him, but I can't move, my body sprawled out on the sheets, my chest covered in cum, my face and neck too. But I don't even care. I could fall asleep like this and wake up a happy man.

"We need to clean him up," Ford says, but I shake my head.

"No. Leave me," I croak.

I will die like this.

"He does look good like that," Ford says, and Cash scoffs.

"He needs a shower and we need to go back to bed. It's three a.m."

"Let me die here," I say dramatically, and Cash chuckles as he reaches beneath me and pulls me into his arms.

"You can die after we've fucked you a few more times."

"Oh god. It's a deal," I whimper, my head rolling onto his shoulder. "As long as that dick ends up in my ass."

He smiles down at me, the three of us shuffling into the shower. I let them wash me, those hands moving across every part of my body, getting me all worked up by the end of it. But neither of them puts me out of my misery, they just bring me back to bed, make sure I drink some water, and then climb in beside me.

I don't want to sleep. I want to stay awake because this could all just be a dream.

But as soon as my eyelids flutter closed, I'm gone.

Lights out.

I can only hope that when I wake up, they're still here.

———

The sunlight pierces my eyelids, and I slowly blink them open. Last night filters through my mind, and I groan, my jaw and ass sore in the most delicious way.

"Morning, sunshine," Ford says, and I turn my head to look at him. He's rumpled, and just the sight of him gets my libido going. I'm turned on and ready to go. Drive me, Ford. Stick your cock in me and pump me full of rocket fuel. I am ready to go to the moon again.

I'm an astronaut now.

"What's that look for?" Ford asks, and I feel my cheeks heat.

"Nothing. Where's Cash?"

"In the kitchen making us breakfast."

The smell of bacon hits me, and my stomach grumbles.

"You're hungry, come on."

"I have to pee first," I say, and Ford sits up and gestures toward the bathroom. I quickly go about my business, pulling on my sweats and one of their discarded shirts, and then make my way into the kitchen where I see Ford and Cash at the stove, their wide shoulders brushing as they dish up plates of food. Fuck, they're so damn hot together. Flashes of last night filter through my mind, and I feel my cock stiffen between my legs.

It was too fucking good, my dream come true.

I want to do it again and again.

"Here he is," Ford says with a smile, and Cash turns around with a full plate in his hand. He sets it before me and then hands me a fork.

"Eat and then we talk."

I gulp nervously as Ford sets a cup of water down next to my plate and then they join me. Their legs bump mine under the table, and I bite back a groan as I force myself to eat. I want to rut against the table leg, but that's a bit too animalistic. I've gone full feral now.

But, I'm actually ravenous so the pancakes, bacon and eggs go down easily, and when I've scraped my plate clean, Ford and Cash are leaning back in their chairs looking a bit smug.

I swipe at my mouth and take a large gulp of water.

"What? I was hungry."

"You should be," Cash says, and I flush. "Last night was quite the workout."

I nod and shift in my chair, wishing I was in their laps instead, their dicks inside of me, stretching me open. *That's how I want to eat breakfast every morning,* I think, but of course, I don't say it. That would be insane.

I've lost my mind.

"I know what you're thinking, Ben, but we aren't fucking you right now," Cash says, and Ford's head snaps to his friend, his brow furrowed.

"What? Why the fuck not?"

"He's exhausted and he needs to focus on himself. I'm sure he has things he needs to do today, and we have to get to work."

Ford purses his lips and then nods in agreement. "Yeah, okay. But later. When we get home. Will you be here?"

I roll my lips between my teeth.

"Yeah, I can be. I just need to go home and grab my school stuff." Today is my day off, and I usually spend my time catching up on home-work and studying.

A key slides across the table, and I grab it, the metal cold in my warm palm.

"Thank you."

Ford nods and then Cash unfolds his arms from his chest.

"Now, before we go, can we talk about what this is?" he asks, and Ford nods, his eyes flashing.

"It's—" I clear my throat and then take another sip of water. "I don't know, but I'm only fucking you both. I swear it."

"Alright. And will you be exclusive with us and only us?" Cash asks, and I flush.

"Yeah. I only want you two. If that's okay."

Ford nudges Cash and then nods his head. "Hell yes, it is. Right?"

Cash looks a little more unsure. Oh god, what if this isn't what he wants? What if this is too much?

"I could give it a try," Cash says, and Ford beams.

"Fuck yes, you can because it was hot, right?" Ford says, shifting in his seat with a groan. "It was *so fucking hot.*"

Just that throaty sound has my entire body flaring with need, and I press down on my hard cock with the heel of my hand.

"What do we tell your dad?" Cash asks and then runs a hand down his face. "Fuck."

"We don't tell him, we can't," I say almost desperately. "He can't ever know."

Ford rolls his eyes. "He won't care. He was wild in college before your mom—"

"He will. He so will," I say and then stand up. "If you tell him, it's over. I wouldn't be able to live with myself. It would ruin everything. So it needs to stay a secret."

"Ugh, secrets are the worst, and I'm the worst at keeping them," Ford says, and Cash nods.

"He really is."

"You've made it the past several weeks. You can do it for a while longer," I say, my voice firm, and Ford's shoulders sag.

"Yeah, fine. Okay, but don't blame me if this shit gets out. I warned you."

Cash eyes his friend and then reiterates once more. "So, just so we're clear. We're exclusive. You don't fuck anyone else and neither do we."

I nod my head. "Yeah, that works."

He nods. "Alright, good talk. We gotta get to work."

Ford grumbles under his breath, but stands up, and the two of them head out. I just sit there at that kitchen table and press my hands to my cheeks. I cannot believe this is my life. I can't believe this is happening.

CHAPTER TWELVE

FORD

Work is dragging. I feel like I'm going to combust. I just want to go home and sink into Ben, to feel his ass contract around my cock and milk my cum from it. But at the same time, I also want to hold him, to kiss my way across his neck and feel his heartbeat under my palm. I want more than just sex with Ben, but right now, that's all he's willing to give us.

I can tell Cash is feeling antsy too because he's a little more spacey than normal. Several times throughout the day he's dropped tools, and more than once I've caught him staring at the wall.

I bet he's reliving those moments with Ben last night.

I know I am. They're on a loop, just going round and round in my brain. The sight of him stretched out beneath me, how wrecked Cash looked as Ben sucked his cock. God. That was a sight. Better than the Seven Wonders of the World. Ben and Cash fucking is glorious. The three of us together—spectacular.

I adjust myself in my work coveralls and grab a wrench. I need to focus so we can get this shit done and go home. To Ben. Who I'm sure is waiting for us with a hard dick. If there's anything I know about him, it's that he's a total slut for it.

"What's up with you two?" Dean asks as he approaches, wiping his greasy hands on a stained rag. Cash jolts at his voice and nearly bangs his head on the propped up hood of the car we're working on. "Yeah, like this weird shit. You've both been distracted and clumsy. What is it? It's not your parents again?" Dean asks Cash who just runs a hand through his hair.

"No, fuck. It's not them."

Dean bobs his head and then cocks it to the side in worry. "Yeah, okay, sorry. Shouldn't have mentioned them, but I was worried maybe they were up to their old shit again."

"No, not at the moment. And it's fine, man. Just a lot on my mind at the moment."

"Not Claire?"

"Fuck no."

Dean nods, and I feel something like guilt move through me before it disappears entirely. I can reason this thing with Ben away in my mind. I can come up with a hundred different excuses of why we're not telling Dean. Initially, this wasn't exclusive, just a bit of harmless fun. Plus, he's an adult and he can do whatever he wants.

And what he wants is me and Cash.

This has never been about taking advantage of him. Before, it was just a mutual exchange. Just lust and passion. But now that we're exclusive... the three of us. Well, that's even better, isn't it? Our intentions are noble.

We are basically gentlemen.

Sir Ford.

I smile at that, and Dean's eyes swivel to me. "And why the hell are you so happy? You getting laid finally?"

My smile drops and I swallow, suddenly feeling nervous. I did manage to keep this thing with his son under wraps for weeks, but Dean never asked me about my sex life at the time. But now he is, and I can feel the truth start to bubble out of me. Luckily, Cash steps in, obviously seeing what's about to happen.

"With Ford, it's never serious. Probably has a few guys he's fucking at the moment."

I scoff. "Or girls. I am bi."

Dean eyes me and then runs a hand down his face. "Yeah. Yeah, I know."

At that moment, Avery appears wearing a black skirt and form-fitting shirt, and Dean's cheeks flush red. Yeah, maybe Cash isn't the only one in this garage having a sexual awakening.

"You need to eat your lunch," Avery tells Dean in a bossy voice. "You've been putting it off."

Perhaps that's where Ben gets it from. Between Dean and Ben, it's a wonder anything ever gets eaten.

Except ass. I bet Ben would love to eat ass.

Dean looks a little guilty as he nods and tosses his dirty rag in the bin. Avery arches an eyebrow at him. "Yeah no, that's not good enough. Wash your hands first. With soap."

Dean grumbles, but I watch as our boss moves to the bathroom, doing as he's told. Avery narrows his eyes at us too. "You too. No dirty oil smudges on bread. My stomach can't handle it so it can't be good for your stomachs."

"But it gives it more flavor," I tease, and Avery rolls his eyes before disappearing up into his office. Dean appears a moment later, wiping his wet hands with a paper towel.

"You're whipped, boss," I joke but Dean ignores me, trudging up the stairs without a backward glance. The door closes with a bang, and Cash turns toward me.

"Jesus, Ford. You almost spilled the beans, didn't you?"

"Pfft. No. I had that *totally under control*."

Cash cyes me and then a small smile pulls his lips up. "Yeah, you didn't. I saw the words starting to roll off your tongue."

"Why you looking at it anyways? You like my tongue, huh?" I poke it out, and he rolls his eyes.

"Yeah, put that shit away."

I nudge him and we get back to work, the two of us working in tandem until it's time to leave. I can feel the excited energy as we get into my truck, the two of us eager to see what awaits us at home. We didn't even bother to pull our coveralls off. Cash pulled his halfway down, but I didn't even want to waste a minute more. So I left completely clothed and filthy.

But I don't fucking care. I can shower and change later.

After I get inside of Ben.

"Think he's there?" I ask as I nearly bounce in my seat, my body unable to sit still.

"Eyes on the road," Cash says gruffly, and I scoff.

"Well, I think he's there, waiting for us. Think he'll be naked?"

"Jesus," Cash says as I grab on to my dick through my coveralls. "Hands on the wheel."

"Ugh, I can't. I'm so horny."

"I know. I could see your hard dick all through work."

I chuckle at that. "Yeah, well who's fault is that? You were looking and some of the fault lies with you too. Last night, you were just as hot as he was."

Cash's cheeks flush in the setting sun, and he stares out the window.

"So were you," he admits softly.

I beam at that small admission as we pull into my driveway and get out. We're quiet as we unlock the door and step inside.

And there he is. Ben's on the couch, books piled on the coffee table, his laptop on his legs. He's dressed in loose jeans and a black t-shirt. His gaze is intently focused on the screen in front of him, but as soon as the door shuts behind us and I lock it, his focus turns to us.

Immediately, I see his pupils dilate and his cheeks flush red.

Oh, I knew it. He's just as horny as us.

"You get your work done?" Cash asks, not moving forward. I glance at my best friend and then turn my eyes to Ben.

"Yeah, I'm almost caught up."

"Did you eat?" he asks, and Ben wets his lips.

"I forgot."

"Jesus," Cash murmurs, and Ben shakes his head.

"I'm fine, I'm still full from breakfast."

He closes his laptop, setting it on the table, and I can see the bulge of his hard cock straining against his jeans.

"I can eat after."

"After what?" Cash asks, and Ben presses his hand against his cock with a whimper.

"After we fuck."

"Hell yes," I say softly, and Cash elbows me.

"Is this a negotiation?" Cash asks like this is a hostage situation. I swear, if he didn't end up a mechanic, he could have worked as a policeman.

"No, I'm telling you what's going to happen." Ben's voice is wobbly but firm, and it turns me on more than I already am. Love a bossy bottom.

"Is that so?" Cash asks and Ben nods.

"Yeah." He wets his lips again and then swallows nervously. "Now... kiss."

That last word is said on a wheeze, and Cash and I both freeze.

"Excuse me?" Cash asks lowly. "What did you say?"

Ben's hand presses against his dick again and his cheeks flame. "I want to see you two kiss."

Cash's lips part, and he narrows his eyes. "We don't kiss."

"Well, you should. Because I want to see it."

"I'm down," I chime in, and Cash turns those dark eyes on me.

"You are?"

I shrug. "It's just a kiss and it'll make him happy."

Cash doesn't look so sure, and I swear the seconds tick by as he considers Ben's proposal. But then Cash opens his mouth and says something that makes my heart skip a beat.

"Fine, but if we do this, then we get to kiss you too."

Ben's mouth drops open, and I wonder if he's gonna accept this. He's never kissed me, and I'm assuming he hasn't with Cash either. It was a hard rule for him and one I don't think he's gonna break easily.

"He doesn't kiss," I hiss, and Cash just reaches out and squeezes the nape of my neck, putting pressure on it and making my mouth snap shut. Oh fuck, my dick likes this a whole lot. Seems I have a bossy bottom and a bossy top.

Am I in heaven?

Ben mulls the proposal over for a few seconds and then almost in slow motion, he nods. His chin touches his chest and Cash lets out a long breath, his hand tightening on the back of my neck and pulling me into him.

Without hesitation, his lips crash onto mine. I'm shocked momentarily but that dissipates in seconds as his tongue slips out and presses into my mouth. I groan into it, at the feel of him entering me. I can immediately taste the familiarity of him. This. *This is what we've been missing*, I think as my hands reach out and clutch his shoulders before moving into his hair.

Our tongues glide against each other's, and I feel my cock hardening. I'm kissing Cash, my best friend in the whole entire world. And shit, he's a good kisser, good with his mouth, with his teeth, with his tongue. The commanding way that he controls the kiss has me sinking into him, my fingers tightening on his scalp, holding him in place.

He grunts and then his hand slides to my jaw, tilting my head a little more, exactly as he wants it as he continues to eat my mouth. And when he finally pulls away from me a minute later, my lips are swollen and so is my dick.

So fucking hard. Almost ready to burst and just from a kiss.

Cash wets his lips and then turns to Ben who is panting, wide-eyed on the couch.

"Get your ass over here," he rasps, and I watch as Ben pushes himself up and strides on wobbly legs to us. His cock is hard and he's unbuttoned his jeans, his zipper half undone.

He liked what he saw. Seems we'll have to do that more often.

Cash reaches out and pulls Ben into his chest, his hand landing on the back of his head as he leans down to press his lips to Ben's mouth. He's gentler with him than he was with me, but I love it. Love watching as Ben whimpers as Cash's tongue sneaks into his mouth and he subtly grinds his hips against Ben's dick. And while he sucks on his lips and tongue, Ben's hands are fisted in the front of Cash's shirt as if hanging on for dear life. And I don't blame him.

Cash kisses like he's taking over your world, like he's plundering your free will.

When he's kissing you, you don't care that you're now a slave to him. He can have me.

When he finally pulls away, Ben's eyes are hooded, his breath coming out staggered. He looks like he's just been fucked, and it was only a kiss. Yeah, buddy, I know exactly how you feel. I could probably come untouched after a long make-out session with Cash. That's how good it is.

Cash reaches out and presses his thumb against Ben's swollen bottom lip, the exact place that he sucked a second ago.

"Show him how much you want him," Cash commands softly, and Ben nearly falls into me, his lips crashing onto mine. I pull him into me, cupping his ass in my hands and grinding our hips together. I lick into him without asking permission, and of course, he opens like the good boy he is. As soon as my tongue slides across his, I taste the cherry bubblegum.

Addicting.

I tilt my mouth over his a little more and suck on his tongue, pulling a low groan from him. Fuck, I could do this all day, could press him against the wall and make him whimper, but he pulls away too soon and whispers, "Kiss again. Please."

Cash eyes me and then we fall into each other, licking and sucking until a low moan from Ben pulls us apart. His hand is down his pants, his hand working his cock frantically.

"Fuck me. Fuck me," he begs. "I need it. I've been waiting all day. I can't take it anymore."

Cash doesn't even hesitate, just pulls Ben's shirt off and tosses it onto the floor. He starts yanking on his pants, but when I start to remove my coveralls Ben shakes his head.

"Leave them on."

I freeze and my lips turn up. "Turns you on, huh?"

He nods and then steps out of his pants and underwear, pressing up against me once more and kissing me deeply. Fuck, I won't get tired of this, of his taste, of his lips.

Cash moves up behind him, our hands sliding against each other's as we glide our palms across Ben's warm skin.

Ben is lost. He's moaning loudly, grinding against us both, like a dog in heat, like a wild animal. And I'm here for it.

Suddenly, he pulls his lips away from me and turns to Cash, kissing him with just as much fervor. I touch my lips to his exposed neck, nipping and biting at his skin while my hand slides to his front and cups his cock in my palm.

He groans and then rips his lips away from Cash and leans his head back on my shoulder as I start to slowly jack him off.

"Oh my god," he groans as the two of us work our lips across his shoulders and neck, licking and kissing him on every available inch of skin. And when Cash and I finally meet in the same spot against his neck just under his ear, Cash takes my lips in a searing kiss that leaves me breathless.

Fuck, I'm addicted to both of them.

I should be afraid, but I'm not. I'm elated.

"Oh fuck. Fuck me. Please," Ben begs. Before he can even finish uttering the last word, Cash moves, tossing him onto the couch and striding to the bedroom to grab the lube.

Ben is heaving, lying on his back, clutching the end of his cock as I pull my coveralls down.

"This is a dream," he breathes, and I shake my head.

"Nah, Benjamin. This is your life now."

He grips his cock so hard that I can see the white on his knuckles as I pull my dick out and stroke it slowly. Ben's eyes track the movement and he lets out a shaky breath.

Cash emerges with the bottle of lube and sets it down next to me.

"You wanna fuck him this time?" I ask, and Cash stares down at Ben, a look of severe concentration on his face.

"No. Not yet."

I nod my head, not quite sure what's holding him back, but the thought dissipates as I lean down and flip Ben onto his hands and knees, exposing his lush ass to me. I could get lost in this ass. Could die in it.

Cash pulls his cock out and then positions himself in front of Ben, one knee on the couch as he grabs on to his jaw and slides two fingers inside his mouth. Ben moans as he sucks on the digits while I start to stuff him full of lube. And just like he always does, he takes me so easily. Two fingers, three, and then four until he's loosened up and gaping for me.

I glance up and see Cash's cock in Ben's mouth, his cheeks flushed, his eyes hooded as his cock disappears entirely down Ben's throat. Fuck, that's so damn hot. And what makes it even hotter is that Ben loves this. I reach around him and grab on to his stiff dick and jerk it a few times, making him cry out in need.

"I know what you need," I say into his ear, hearing the slurp of Cash's dick moving in and out of his wet mouth.

I lean back, take my dick, and slide it into his ass in one harsh thrust.

Ben cries out once more, his lips stretched open around Cash's hard length, but then the muffled cry turns to moans as I start to pump into him, my hips hitting his ass with a loud slap.

"Shit," Cash says, his hand fisting Ben's hair as he thrusts forward, making Ben gag and choke, but Ben doesn't let up, just takes it like the slut he is.

"Such a whore for it, isn't he?" I moan. "Look at his ass. Taking my cock. Look, Cash."

Cash thrusts deep into his throat, grabs on to Ben's waist, and leans forward, assuredly choking him in the process. But none of us seem to care because Cash's dark eyes are glued to where my dick slides in and out of Ben's hole.

"Hot, right?" I say.

Cash reaches out and slides a finger around his rim, touching my dick in the process. The sight of him against us both has me gasping, my balls drawing up against my groin.

"Fuck that's—god." I groan as Cash leans back up and pulls himself from Ben's mouth, giving him a slight reprieve. Ben gasps, trying to catch his breath but before he fully can, Cash is back inside of him, thrusting in and out of his mouth almost ruthlessly.

"Fuck him harder," Cash says, and I groan as my skin slaps against Ben.

"He'd take us both. His ass was made for two," I grunt, and Ben moans at that, almost as if in agreement. "His ass likes that idea, Cash. God, the way he grips my cock."

"His mouth is just as tight."

"So is his throat."

Cash's eyes slam into mine as he pulls Ben down his length and fucks into his esophagus. Ben swallows and groans as we take him over and over, using him just the way he wants until my balls can't take it anymore.

The heat of him, the way his ass keeps contracting around my dick, not to mention the sight of Cash, makes me explode into his hole with a long shout. It's euphoric as I unload into him, wave after wave making me nearly see stars.

Cash watches my jerky movements and then when I slump forward, he pulls out of Ben's mouth and explodes across his face, covering him in cum.

Ben falls to the couch and turns over, his face dripping with Cash's release. But that's not all I see. His cock is still hard, a dark angry purple.

"Look at how much he needs us," I say as I fall to my knees, sucking him into my mouth, tasting him. He tastes like sex, like cherries, like fucking pie.

"Taste him," I tell Cash as I pull off of him and lick at his slit. Cash moves toward me, kneeling down next to me and taking Ben into his mouth. Ben is wild beneath us, his hips bucking up as he fucks into Cash's mouth. But Ben needs more. And Cash needs a little motivation. I grab his hand off of Ben's thigh and guide his finger to Ben's hole, showing him how magnificent it is.

Cash pulls off of Ben and meets my stare as I push him knuckle deep inside.

"Feel it," I say and then fall onto Ben's dick as Cash fucks his finger into Ben's wet, dripping hole. Ben is writhing underneath us and it doesn't take long for Cash to find his prostate and for my cheeks to hollow at the same time.

Ben explodes into my mouth with a shocked cry, his orgasm drawn out by our combined efforts. He shakes, curses, and screams until he shudders and goes entirely limp.

I pull off his dick at the same time Cash pulls out of his ass, and we stare at Ben who is breathing shallowly with his eyes closed.

"Think we killed him?" I ask, and Cash leans over and presses his lips to mine, shutting me up with that kiss. His tongue sweeps into my mouth, tasting Ben's release on my tongue.

"Shut up," he says softly as he sucks on my lower lip for a minute before leaning down and kissing Ben gently.

Ben sighs under Cash's mouth and then after he pulls away, Ben reaches up for me. I lean down, kissing him softly, swiping my tongue into his mouth before sitting up. Shit. This is too fucking good to be true.

We stare down at Ben for a minute before a small snore escapes his parted lips.

"We fucked him to sleep," I whisper, and Cash smiles at me.

"You fucker."

"You loved it."

Cash is quiet for a moment and then nods.

"I did."

His eyes drop to my lips and he leans forward once more, pressing his mouth to mine. It's so easy, so familiar, like we've done this a thousand times before. But all too soon, it's over.

"Carry him to bed. When he wakes up, we'll make him eat."

I nod and then stand, shucking off the rest of my clothes and pulling Ben into my arms. His face nuzzles into my neck and he sighs contentedly.

Yeah, Ben, I feel the same damn way.

This was pretty damn special.

CHAPTER THIRTEEN

CASH

"Why's he still sleeping?" Ford asks, his voice laced with worry.

"He's exhausted," I reply. I know for a fact he hasn't been taking care of himself. Between work and school, not to mention being a fuck boy for the both of us, he's been run ragged. If I came as many times as he did, I'd be in a coma.

"It's been two hours," Ford says, and I nudge him.

"Just let him sleep."

Ford eyes me from our place in the doorframe and then walks toward Ben, who is still passed out in the middle of the bed. Ford pulls his clothes off and climbs in next to him. I watch as Ben sighs, cuddling into his side. I should join them—should place myself at Ben's back and wrap myself around him, but I have an unread message on my phone. One I've been putting off opening.

I haven't been in the mood.

But it can't wait any longer.

Leaving the two of them, I make my way to where my coveralls were discarded earlier and fish my phone out of my pocket.

My mom.

Shit.

I pop open a beer before tapping the message open, my heart rate accelerating as I read it. I'm forty-two years old, and I still get nervous whenever my parents call or message. It's some kind of minor PTSD.

"Shit," I murmur when I see what it says.

I click the phone off and set it on the counter, gulping down my beer quickly. God, I don't even want to answer, but I know I need to.

Fuck familial responsibility. I just want to be left alone, but at the same time, I know that I can't ignore it forever. Despite their disappointment in me, I still have to show up to shit.

"Fuck."

I sigh and then run a hand down my face. I'll deal with this shit tomorrow. I have Ben and Ford waiting in bed. The two of them are more important.

I replay those kisses in my head, that unanswered message on my phone dissipating as I make my way toward the bedroom. For now, I'm going to put all that aside and focus on them. Ben needs us both right now.

When I appear in the bedroom and see Ben pressed up against Ford, his eyes still shut, his chest rising and falling and the content look on Ford's face, I just melt.

I strip and slide in next to them, pressing my hand to Ben's stomach, feeling his warm skin beneath my palm.

"I am obsessed with him," Ford whispers, and I nod.

"I know."

I watch as Ford leans up a little and presses his lips to the crown of Ben's head, and then I do the same. Ford smiles at me, and I nestle into Ben, hearing him sigh and relax as we surround him.

He needs us. We might not make sense, but he needs us.

And we need him.

———

"I'm so hungry," Ben grumbles as he stretches between us, his naked body warm and needy.

"I bet you are," I say as I run my hand along his side. "I'll get up and make you something."

Ben groans as I move away from him, almost whimpering in sadness as I walk to the bedroom door but Ford is there, soothing him.

"I've got you," he whispers softly, his hands running up and down his chest.

I want to stay, want to see where this goes, but I need to make them breakfast. It's an easy task and one that I like to do for people who appreciate it. And Ford and Ben appreciate it. I love seeing my men satisfied.

"It's ready!" I call out twenty minutes later, but when they don't appear, I cover the breakfast sandwiches and make my way back to the room.

"Oh god," I hear Ben moan lowly, and my dick instantly perks up.

I know what Ford's doing, what *they're* doing, and for some reason it doesn't bother me at all. No, it turns me on. I want to watch them fuck, want to see their bodies moving in tandem.

I want to stroke myself and come across their bodies.

I step into the room, the blinds still pulled shut, but I can see the shape of them moving. Ben's on his side, his back to Ford, his leg pulled up and back as Ford slides his cock in and out of Ben's hole.

"Fuck yes, you take it," Ford groans and then thrusts harder, making Ben cry out. It's a desperate cry, one filled with need and longing. He needs this fucking, he needs Ford inside of him.

Me inside of him.

Perhaps I should fuck him too.

But not yet. Instead, I watch them writhe from the doorway, reaching into my pants and squeezing my aching dick.

"He's watching, you like him watching?" Ford says, and Ben groans, almost delirious from being fucked awake.

"Yes. Yes. Yes," he chants as Ford pushes into him over and over.

"Want him to join?"

"Yes!" Ben cries out, and I feel my heartbeat throb in my neck. It's pounding so hard that I'm almost lightheaded from it.

"Please. Please," Ben is begging now, and it's an impossible request to resist. I push my pajama pants off and walk over to them, holding the base of my dick while I watch them. Ford is propped up on his elbow, his hips snapping back and forth as he works himself in and out of Ben's ass. I watch his muscles move, watch as his ass clenches with each forward thrust.

And for some reason, some inexplicable reason, I want to try something new.

Something I've never thought about until now.

I grab the lube that's sitting on the side of the bed and snap the cap, watching as Ben's eyelids flutter open.

"You gonna fuck him?" Ford asks, slamming into Ben and holding him there, his cock stuffed inside of him.

Ben whimpers and I roll my neck, wetting my two fingers with the gel and approaching Ford.

"God, I wanna watch you fuck him for the first ti—," Ford groans, but then his words are cut off when I reach down and slide my fingers up his crack.

Ford's lips part and he leans back, meeting my stare.

And then without another word, he arches his hips forward, pressing into Ben a little more to give me better access.

So I do it again, squirt some lube onto my fingers and swipe it up his ass, making Ford's breathing come out harder, making his already pink cheeks darken.

"Oh fuck. Yes."

I swirl around his hole, feeling it clench around me, and then slide a finger inside.

Ford lets out a long groan, a pent-up one that seems as if it stems from his abdomen, and Ben gasps, his lips parted, his hand on his cock.

"Is he in you?" Ben asks, his voice throaty and worn. "Is he finger fucking you?"

Ford only nods as I slowly work my finger into him, feeling the warm heat of his body against my skin, feeling the way his muscles loosen and open for me.

I'm in Ford. Inside my best friend.

Ben's eyes roll back into his head at the mere thought of it. "Oh god. Yes. Yes. I want to watch you two fuck."

But I'm not ready for that, I'm not even sure I'm ready for this, but my dick is. It's throbbing, leaking, straining out toward the two of them as I crawl onto the bed and sit on my haunches, twisting my wrist slightly to find that small raised bump inside of him.

And when I do, Ford lets out a slew of cuss words, his hips bucking. Ben gasps and I bite my bottom lip as I feel his wet hole suck me in and out of that tight entrance.

"More. I need more," Ford grunts, and I add a second finger, spearing him as he continues to fuck Ben speechless. And that's it, the way the next several minutes pass, Ford fucking into Ben before falling back on my fingers, the two of them groaning and panting while I try to keep my wits about me.

They look so good together, the two of them.

But the three of us are... perfection.

I add a third finger and the stretch makes Ford lose his mind. And so does Ben, the two of them going wild with lust as they start to orgasm, first Ben who pumps his dick almost frantically before unloading onto his chest and then Ford who slams forward and unleashes himself into Ben's tight ass. I can feel Ford's hole clench around me, can feel the way he shudders and shakes, and I help draw it out by massaging his prostate the entire time, until he shouts at me to stop.

So I still my fingers, very reluctantly, Ford's cock still in Ben.

"Oh my god," Ben groans, his body going limp. "I can't... I can't handle this hotness."

I slowly pull my fingers out of Ford and he whimpers at the loss of me before I pull Ford back, his dick slipping from Ben with a squelch. Ben watches as I straddle Ford's waist and then walk on my knees to his mouth.

"Open," I say, grabbing on to my best friend's jaw and pressing my hard cock to his waiting mouth.

And Ford does it, just opens and takes me in whole. Ben is panting beside us as I fuck Ford's mouth, those eyes looking up at me, leaking slightly as he fights to take my entire tattooed cock.

I let him try and prove himself, but I'm bigger than him and he knows it.

He sputters and shakes beneath me, his tongue doing sinful things to me, but it's when he reaches up to my ass and presses his finger against my hole that I detonate, pulsing into his mouth with a loud groan.

And then it's done, the three of us replete and exhausted.

I'm ready for another nap.

Fucking Ben is a full-time job. Add Ford into the mix and I'm well into overtime.

Slowly, I pull my cock free of his lips and sit back on his thighs, watching as Ben leans up and kisses Ford slowly, licking across his lips and tasting me on him.

It's the most depraved and sensual thing I've ever seen, and I want to do it all again.

"Well, I'm not hungry for breakfast anymore," Ford says, and I roll my eyes as I push off of him onto my wobbly legs.

"You both need to eat and you better get up before the food gets cold."

They grumble and groan, but both manage to pull on boxers and follow me out to the kitchen where the food awaits.

I watch as Ford sits daintily on the chair, and I smirk at him.

"You have thick fingers," he says, and Ben lets out a small laugh as I hand them their food and pour them coffee.

"It's good practice," Ben says, taking a bite of his English muffin sandwich and then a sip of coffee. "For when Cash fucks you."

We eye each other, and for a moment I wonder what Ford will say, but he just shrugs, like it's a possibility. I haven't even fucked Ben. I'm not thinking of fucking Ford.

But then again, his ass did feel all kinds of right. I can only imagine what Ben's will be like.

I adjust my hardening cock as I take a seat at the table with them.

"God this is so good, I'm famished," Ben says softly as he takes another bite.

"Yeah, you should be," Ford says and then engulfs half of his sandwich in one bite. "Cash is the best cook. He just looks at shit and it's delicious."

Ben nods as he takes a big gulp of his coffee.

"Even the coffee is good."

I feel my cheeks flush, and I shift in my seat. "Enough about this. What's the plan for today? You're off right?"

Ben sighs and then shakes his head. "No, I have to work for a bit this afternoon, but I can come by after."

Ford eyes him. "You better."

Ben flushes and then nods. "Yeah, okay, I can do that. And um," he hesitates and glances down at his plate. "If you guys fuck around without me... it's okay. I mean, I want you to."

I stop chewing and glance at Ford who is eyeing Ben intently.

"We don't want anyone feeling left out."

"I won't. It will turn me on knowing you two have been messing around. And you know, you could send me some dirty pics."

I swallow loudly and Ford's eyes turn to me.

"We'll see," he says, and I nod, not sure if he and I will mess around without Ben in the picture. I mean, we did that one time, but Ben showed up halfway through, so it almost doesn't count.

"I just don't want to hold you two back."

Ford reaches out and settles his hand on the back of Ben's neck.

"We want you, Benjamin."

He blinks rapidly and then nods, finishing off his sandwich and coffee quickly before standing up.

"I need to shower and then go home before work."

Without thinking, I wrap my hand around his waist and pull him onto my lap. He falls onto me without resisting.

"What time do you work?" I ask, not wanting him to leave yet, knowing Ford is going to go feral once Ben takes off.

"I have to be there from twelve to six."

I glance at the clock on the oven and then press my lips to his neck. He shivers slightly and leans back against me.

"You have two hours. Let's shower here and take our time and then you can go."

He lets out a shaky breath and then nods.

"Okay. If you want me to."

"Hell yes, we do," Ford says and then stands up, his cock nearly hitting the table as he goes.

We both eye it, and I see Ben wet his lips from the corner of my eye.

Yes, a shower is what we need. One where we get filthy first and then wash ourselves clean.

And then, when Ben is gone at work, Ford and I can discuss what we plan on doing from here on out. Because it's clear that we're in this together now, that this isn't just a fling.

I'm serious about making this work between the three of us. I want Ben just as much as I want Ford.

I want all of us together.

And like hell I'm gonna fail.

CHAPTER FOURTEEN

BEN

The shower with the two of them scrambled my brain, and I wonder how I'll manage to make it through work as a functioning adult. Because the minute we were inside those glass doors, they were on me—almost delirious with need, their cocks jutting out from their bodies, their thick fingers raking down my skin, and I just melted into a lust-filled coma. They used me, Cash rutting his dick through the crease of my ass, Ford, grabbing my dick, bringing us together, and frotting until we each came, our bodies wet and shaking as we tried like hell to wash it all away.

I was barely able to stand, my entire body wrung out. And they weren't much better, their movements sloppy and uncoordinated.

"We still have an hour," Ford says as he watches me dress.

I meet his stare, and he wets his lips. "Can we just hold you for a bit?"

I swallow, feeling like I shouldn't let this happen but wanting it all the same.

"Yeah, we can do that," I say, moving toward the couch and lowering myself onto it. Ford joins me, pulling me into his side and then Cash sits beside me, his hand running down my thigh.

"I have a crazy idea, but hear me out."

"Love when Cash gets crazy ideas," Ford says with a laugh.

"I think we should go on a date."

"A date?" I ask, and Cash nods.

"Yeah, the three of us."

I turn to peer at Ford, but he's just nodding along.

"But what will people think?" I ask as Ford starts to slowly massage my tight shoulders. He does have a way with his hands. Love them on me, soothing me.

"That we're the hottest throuple on Earth," Ford says smugly, and I scoff.

"Guys, that's—it's too risky. What if someone sees us?"

"Who's gonna care?" Cash asks, and I bite my bottom lip.

"Can I think about it?" I ask, and Cash nods.

"Yeah, you can. Think all you want, Benjamin, but listen," Ford says, grabbing on to my chin softly and forcing me to look at him.

"We're gonna date the fuck out of you. Cash and I. There's no running away this time."

My mind spins, my heart rate thundering. If I do this, if I agree to this, it's serious. It's more.

"Okay," I say, and Ford beams.

"Fuck yeah," he says, and Cash pulls me in for a long kiss before tilting my head and letting Ford lick into my mouth. But that's where it stops, the two of them closing in on me and making me feel warm and drowsy instead. Nothing about this moment is sexual. It's just them soothing me, making me feel safe and surrounded.

I want to call out of work and spend my day with them, want to just let them take care of me. But I can't. I have to work, have to play it cool.

I might have agreed to let this be more serious, but I can't let myself dream too big.

When it's time to leave for work, they both walk me to the door clad in only their boxers and take turns kissing me, long and slow until I'm panting with need once more.

I have to wrench myself away and refuse to look back at them as I leave or else I might never make it to work.

But when I get to work, I am useless, just sitting at my desk with my head in the clouds. I'm just counting down the minutes until I can get back to them, until I can fall into their arms and let them hold me, fuck me, make me lose my mind with pleasure.

I can't believe this is my life.

But I know I can't hold on to this, can't cherish it because this is gonna end in the worst way.

It's the only possible outcome.

Because if my dad finds out, it will have to end. There isn't any other option. I went into this knowing it and did it anyways.

And yet, I still run out of work at the end of my shift, driving like hell to make my way back to them.

They want to date me.

They're serious about this, I think. Serious about me.

My god, why am I so lucky?

When I'm only five minutes away, my dad calls, the ringtone I assigned for him blaring through the car. I fumble with my phone and answer, worried that something's happened. My dad never calls me.

I didn't even know he owned one anymore, he rarely has it on him.

The last time I saw it, it was on his workbench covered with tools.

Perhaps Avery found it and made him put it to use. What's the point of having a phone plan if you don't use the damn thing?

"Hey, you okay?" I ask, pulling over to the side of the road and trying to catch my breath. I'm bracing for bad news.

Maybe he found out about Cash and Ford.

About me and what I've done.

Oh god, I'm not ready for this to be over.

"Hey, yeah," he chuckles awkwardly and then says, "Nothing's wrong. Just thought I'd invite you over to dinner with Avery and me."

I let out a strangled breath. "Jesus, Dad. I thought you were dying."

He scoffs, and I can almost see him running a hand down his face. "No. Not dead, just wanted to know if you wanted to come over for some food and conversation. It's been a while since... well, you know, since we talked."

Well, shit. I want to go back to Ford's and get my ass railed, but I don't want to turn my dad down either. Not when it's been so long since we've had a chance to connect. I do love spending time with him, no matter how different we are. It's one of the reasons I took that job at the garage.

Well... that and so I could watch Cash and Ford work. I've had a crush on them for ages. All that masculine energy, those dirty hands, those coveralls.

My dick perks up, and I flick it. Now is not the time.

"Okay, yeah. I can do that."

He almost beams through the phone. How could I say no to him when he's sacrificed so much to raise me? He's loved me unconditionally. I remember coming out to him, how nervous I was that he might not accept me.

I don't know why I was ever worried. He'd just looked at me and said, "Thanks for telling me, Ben, but I already knew."

And then he took me on a motorcycle ride and bought me a burger at a small, run-down bar.

Nothing changed after that, except his occasional dad comments about finding myself a man.

"Great. I'll tell Avery. I can't wait to see you, Ben."

"Yeah, Dad. Same." And then we hang up, and I press my forehead to the steering wheel. I am looking forward to my time with my dad, but I'm also regretting the fact that tonight will have to wait.

Shooting off a few texts to both Cash and Ford, I turn my car around and head to my dad's place.

———

"You want something to drink?" my dad asks me, and Avery eyes him. He's wearing a bright purple dress and his hair is pulled into an intricate French braid. He's a pop of color in this house, and I can see why my dad looks at him the way he does.

I think he has a little crush. Not that I blame him.

Avery is something else.

"Yeah, sure. I'll have some water."

"Not a beer or anything?" my dad asks, and Avery holds out the spoon he's using to stir something in the pot on the stove. A noodle plops to the floor, but it goes ignored as my dad almost seems to lean into him.

"He told you what he wants, Dean. Get your son a water. The last time Ben had something to drink he had to be carried home. He's a lightweight."

"You did a heavy pour," I say, and Avery winks at me.

"I did. And boy, was it worth it."

My dad clears his throat and then moves to the fridge, brushing against Avery in the process, his hand dragging across his lower back, and I see Avery arch into his touch.

Quickly, I look away and focus on a new piece of art hanging up on the wall adjacent to me. It's a bright abstract floral arrangement, and I get lost in the colors.

"You like that?" my dad asks, setting a bottle of water before me. "Avery painted it."

I study it and then uncap my water, taking a small sip.

"It's really good."

"It is. He's really talented."

"Dean, god, stop," Avery says, his cheeks flushed pink.

"What? It's really damn good."

Avery's eyes flick to my dad and then back to the stove. "Thank you, and as much as I love to talk about how talented I am, we should get the meat on the grill. The mac and cheese is almost done."

My dad nods and grabs some trays from the fridge, meandering into the backyard and starting the Blackstone.

"That a new grill?" I ask Avery, who turns to face me.

"Yeah, I convinced him to get it. He made a fuss about the cost, but he loves it."

"I can tell. He's been talking about getting one for years, but he always said he didn't have anyone to cook for."

Avery's cheeks flush and he peeks up at me. A small smile forms on my lips, and I utter the words before I can stop myself. "I'm glad it's you."

His mouth opens and then closes, shaking his head. "It's nothing... we're just friends."

"I can see the way he looks at you. He hasn't looked at anyone like that in a long time."

Avery's cheeks darken and then we both turn to look at my dad, who is throwing the meat on the grill.

"He's really happy you're here. He's been wanting to reconnect. Says that since you started college he's seen you less."

"Yeah, I've just gotten a bit overwhelmed with my life."

"Totally makes sense. He's just glad you're here for a last-minute invite. On a Saturday. I told him you'd probably have plans…"

I shake my head, lying through my teeth. "No plans."

Avery looks at me like he doesn't quite believe it, but he thankfully keeps those thoughts to himself.

"How about we bring everything outside and then we can just chill and watch the sunset? Catch up on life."

"Yeah, that sounds good," I say and help Avery carry everything outside.

All through dinner, I can see how happy my presence makes my dad. He smiles and chats happily, looking at me with a twinkle in his eyes. We see each other at the shop but rarely have a chance to really talk. I should make more of an effort to spend more time with him, but it's hard when our hobbies are so different. I'm not one for rebuilding cars or motorcycle rides. I prefer reading and school. I like going to art museums and spending time people-watching.

Although, with the way my dad is watching Avery, perhaps we could bond over that.

"You have any plans tonight? We could watch a movie…" my dad's voice trails off, so damn hopeful. I clutch on to my thighs tightly.

I can't fucking say no. "I could stay for a movie."

My dad beams and my hands relax.

Yeah, I can totally stay for a little while longer. Maybe one day, Cash and Ford can sit on this couch with me snuggled between them.

I shake that thought away.

No, that can't ever happen. It won't ever happen. I might go on a date with them both, but my dad can't ever find out.

It would crush him, and I don't want to see that smile fade because of me.

———

I finally arrive at Ford's house and stand at the front door for a minute before realizing that they gave me a key. I can use that to let myself in since it's pretty late.

The key feels serious to me, almost symbolic. I clutch it in my hand as I walk inside, only two lamps lighting the entire space.

Immediately, my eyes scan the open living area, and I don't see either of them. My heart drops slightly, wondering if they went out without me or went to bed and fell asleep in each other's arms.

I shake that thought away. We talked about this, very briefly, this morning. If they choose to be together while I'm away, I'm okay with that. I can't always be present and they have needs too. I can't expect them to wait around for me to come home every day. My schedule is busier than theirs at the moment and my free time is hard to come by.

Plus, I have a feeling that Cash and Ford are only now discovering long-dormant feelings for one another.

This is new for all of us.

I check in the bedroom, and when I don't see them there, I make my way out back. The moon is out, the stars mostly hidden behind gray clouds, and I see them sitting in the dark, both of them in the hot tub, their arms spread across the back of the tub, their eyes swiveling to me as soon as I make an appearance on the back porch.

I stand there awkwardly, feeling guilty for changing my plans this afternoon, but at the same time, I know they understand. They know my dad, they know me.

I had to go. And if they saw how happy my dad was that I was there, they'd probably tell me to do it more often. They care about both of us deeply.

I know that.

I fiddle with the end of my shirt, not sure what to do now that I'm here. What do they want from me? What are they expecting?

We stare at each other until Ford's hand moves and he grabs on to Cash's chin, pulling him in for a searing kiss. My heart rate picks up, and I feel my cock harden as I watch them bite and lick at each other's mouths.

God, they're so hot together. They could set an entire room on fire.

Cash's ringed hand moves into Ford's hair as he tilts his head and sucks his bottom lip into his mouth.

Ford groans loudly and then shifts closer, almost trying to crawl onto his lap, but Cash pulls away, Ford chasing his mouth.

They meet each other's stare for a long, heady moment before the two of them turn to face me.

Well. Fuck. Me.

I know where I'm headed.

I move toward them, pulling my shirt off and dropping it on the ground as I go. Cash and Ford wet their swollen lips as I approach. I still don't know what they see in me, how I ever caught their eyes, but the way that their breathing changes, the way that they look at me tells me that they like what they see.

"Took your time," Ford says, his hands clenching tightly on the lip of the spa, and I know that he's trying his best to behave. Cash reaches back and presses his fingers against the back of Ford's nape, holding him in place. He wants to lunge at me, wants to maul my mouth.

I wouldn't mind it. I wouldn't mind being consumed like that.

"He came when he could," Cash says steadily.

Ford lets out a shaky breath and my gaze swivels between them.

"Did you fuck while I was gone?" I ask, and Ford lets out a wheeze.

"Fuck no. We were waiting for you."

I nod and slowly unzip my pants. Both of their eyes flick down to my open jeans and Cash wets his lips.

"All of it *off*," Cash says.

I hesitate a moment, knowing I hold all the power in my hands. I could make them do anything I want in this moment. Shit, that makes me feel ten feet tall. "Only if you take yours off too."

Ford moves so quickly that he nearly slips, throwing his wet swimsuit onto the ground with a plop. Cash eyes him and then arches his hips up under the water, producing his trunks and tossing them aside.

"In," he says, and I kick off my pants and boxers and do as I'm told.

Their hands are on me almost immediately, pulling me against them, my ass straddling both thick thighs which are pressed together under the water. My back is against their chests, and I love how they dwarf me completely, how small I feel between them.

Ford nuzzles into my neck with a sigh and Cash presses his lips to my shoulder, his fingers flexing against my stomach.

I let out a long exhale, feeling like I can finally relax.

It shouldn't be this way with my dad's two best friends, but god, it is. It so is.

"How was it?" Cash asks, his lips brushing against my skin as he holds me against him.

"Good. I'm glad I went. He misses me."

"Yeah, I know he does."

"I think he and Avery have a thing going on," I say, and Ford snorts.

"Yeah, well, that's not news. Your dad's been eye fucking him for ages."

I lean back and eye him. "I had no idea he was into men."

"Me neither," Ford says just as Cash pipes up.

"Sometimes just the right person makes an impression and things change."

I turn my gaze to Cash, our eyes clash and I can't help it. I turn into him, reaching out and pulling him in for a long-drawn-out kiss. Our tongues sloppily slide together and the sensation of him being inside of me, in any way, has me hardening almost painfully. What I would give to have him press his dick up into me right now.

I feel Ford's hand drag down my stomach to my dick. He wraps his hand around me, and I gasp into Cash's mouth. I love how often they touch me. How they seem so ravenous for it.

For me.

I pull away from Cash and turn to Ford, kissing him with just as much desperation. Ford groans into my mouth, his hand snaking into my hair and grabbing on tightly.

"I want to eat your ass," Ford says when our lips part, and I let out a moan at the thought.

"But the neighbors," I say, and Ford glances around.

"They can't see in, so you better be quiet. Don't want the cops to show up for murdering your hole with my tongue."

My ass clenches in anticipation as Ford moves me off his lap. My gaze slashes to Cash who is watching me with hooded eyes. I'm not sure what he's going to do to me tonight but even if he just watches, that's enough to push me over the edge.

I lean over the side of the hot tub, my ass in the air as I push my hips out. Ford's finger slips down my crack, and I bite my lip to keep the sounds I want to make inside. God, I don't want the police to be called.

I don't need anyone to see what these men are doing to me.

I don't want to set the whole entire neighborhood on fire.

Ford's finger swirls around my hole, and I press my forehead onto the lip of the tub and turn to see Cash watching me.

"You like a tongue up your ass?" Cash asks lowly as Ford spreads my cheeks and starts to kiss and suck at my hole. Oh fuck, that feels so damn good, so damn wrong and right at the same time.

"I do."

Our eyes connect, and I can see his arm starting to jerk below the water. He's turned on just from looking at my face.

My mouth parts as Ford's tongue starts to slide in and out of my ass. He wastes no time entering me and slashing at my opening.

"You gonna come like this?" he asks, and I whimper.

I can. I so can.

Ford holds nothing back, spearing me over and over, making small whines slip from my throat. Ford is grunting like an animal in heat as he eats me, and I can tell Cash isn't unaffected.

"Sounds like he's enjoying himself. Maybe I should have a taste."

Those words from Cash make my cock jerk and my balls draw up toward my body.

"Yes, please," I whisper. "I want that."

Cash blinks slowly and then he moves, his hard cock jutting up from his body.

I glance back, watching as he moves Ford out of the way and presses both palms to my ass cheeks. I can't breathe, can't fucking inhale.

I just hold my breath as he lowers his face and licks a long stripe up my crack. My hips buck forward, and I bite my lip so hard that I draw blood.

I can't believe Cash is eating my ass. Can't believe he's even trying this.

"Mm," he says as he does it again. He wastes no time in flicking his tongue across my hole, and I grind my ass back to feel more of him. This isn't enough. I need him inside of me.

"Fuck yes," Ford moans lowly as Cash swirls the tip of his tongue around my hole before impaling me with it. He's more methodical about rimming than Ford, and I love the difference between the two of them. Ford is more wild and unexpected whereas Cash is more precise.

The way he thrusts his tongue in and out of me rhythmically, the way he's groaning softly as he does it has me nearly coming on the spot.

"He tastes good, huh?" Ford says, standing up and jacking his cock. "Could eat his ass every day."

Cash grunts his response, and Ford runs his free hand down my back as Cash continues to thrust his tongue inside of me.

"Make him come, Cash, and then we can fuck him."

Cash seems to double down on his efforts, his one hand reaching around me and grabbing onto my dick, angling it down and jerking it in time with each thrust of his tongue.

And that's all I need. I explode at the sensation, my cum hitting the water and swirling away.

Ford curses as Cash continues to eat me through the orgasm and when I'm slumped over and trying to catch my breath, Ford swoops me into his arms and manages to maneuver me out of the hot tub and toward the house.

They don't even dry off, just enter the house, leaving puddles on the floor.

"Get the lube, Cash. I can't fucking wait. That was too fucking hot. My dick is gonna explode."

I'm pushed over the kitchen table, and I shiver when my naked torso hits the cool wood. But I immediately start to heat up as Ford enters me a minute later, not even bothering to prep me. He just sticks his lubed cock right into my already loose hole.

"Hell yes. Look how he just takes me. Jesus. Fucking. Christ."

I groan as he slams his hips into me, his wet skin slapping against mine as he fucks into my stretched hole. My fingers tighten on the edge of the table as our thrusts scoot me forward inch by inch.

Cash is standing off to the side, watching us, his hand slowly jerking his dick, and I meet his stare as Ford takes me.

I want him to fuck me. Want him inside of me.

Take me, Cash. Take me.

I beg him with my eyes as Ford's rhythm starts to get choppy and then a second later, I feel his cock jerk inside of me as he unloads into my ass. He lets out a long moan as he fills me up, and I rest my cheek on the table as he presses kisses to my back.

"Fuck. Always so damn good."

My fingers loosen their grip on the table as Ford pulls out of my ass. I can feel the release dripping out of me, but I don't move.

No, I wait. I'm fucking *waiting*.

"You gonna try this ass?" Ford says behind me, and Cash's eyes flick from mine to his best friend.

He seems to think on it for a second and then he steps behind me.

"Oh god, yes. Please. Please."

I lose the ability to breathe once again.

"He's already open. Look at it gaping," Ford says as the snap of the lube resounds around the kitchen.

"Yeah," Cash replies, spreading my cheeks and looking at me.

My hole clenches around nothing once more, almost as if telling him that I can take it—can take him.

And it seems to convince him because he slots his cock at my entrance and then pushes forward slowly.

I let out a wheeze as Ford groans.

"Fuck, yes."

Cash's fingers tighten on my waist as he pushes balls deep into me.

"Shit, how does it feel?" Ford asks, shifting on his feet.

"Tight," Cash says lowly as he holds himself inside of me. My cock is already hard again, straining against the table. I can't believe he's fucking me. Can't believe this is my life.

This is my literal dream come true.

I have to be dreaming.

"I know, his ass, right?"

"That ass," Cash replies as he pulls all the way out of me and slams back inside.

I groan loudly, letting all of the noises I held in while having my ass eaten explode out of me.

"Fuck yeah, harder. He can take it. Loves it rough," Ford says and those words spur Cash on, his hips slamming into me.

"Shit. Shit," Cash grunts as he pummels my ass with his dick. He's bigger, thicker than Ford, but hell, it's the most delicious stretch. The most wonderful sting.

"More!" I cry out when he arches my hips up and penetrates me impossibly deep.

Cash continues to work me closer and closer to the edge. I won't even have to touch myself to come. No, I can come completely untouched like this.

"I want to see you. Want to see your face when I come," Cash says, pulling out of me and flipping me over. My back is on the table now, my ass being dragged to the edge as Cash slots his cock at my hole once more and pushes forward. His balls slap against my ass as he sinks into me entirely.

Oh god, this is so much better. I can see it all, all the emotions on his face. His hooded eyes, his clenched jaw, the way his gaze settles on my cock and then my face and then my cock again. As if he can't decide what to look at.

I lean up and see his dick sliding in and out of me, and Ford moves closer to watch too. It's like a fucking porno.

This is my porn.

"So damn pretty," he says as he thrusts in and out of me. "So fucking hot."

I groan and arch my back as he continues to use me.

"You gonna come?" Cash grunts, and I nod my head, trying to speak but being unable to.

"I want you to come."

I cry out when he lifts my hips an inch and slams into me.

"There!" I nearly scream as he continues to peg my prostate. "There! Yes! Yes! Yes!"

My cock jerks and I come untouched, my cum spilling across my stomach, and Cash watches it all, his fingers tightening on me almost painfully as he grunts and unloads into my ass with a few uncoordinated thrusts.

"Hell yes," Ford says as he moves toward me and leans down to kiss me tenderly. "You did so good."

I kiss him back lazily and then watch as Ford stands up and presses his mouth to Cash's. They kiss furiously, their tongues warring with each other's until they finally pull away.

It's only then that Cash pulls out and all of the cum inside of me spills out.

I should be embarrassed, but the way they watch it only makes me proud.

I took them both, those big dicks right up my ass.

"He's gonna fall asleep again," Ford says, and I shake my head.

"Hell no," I manage to rasp lazily. "I'm totally awake. Completely energized."

My eyelids flutter closed, and I hear the two of them let out a small chuckle as I pass out.

CHAPTER FIFTEEN

CASH

Well, if I wasn't gay before, I am now.

I stare at Ben who is curled up on the couch between Ford and me, his head on my lap, his feet on Ford, and I run my hand through his hair. He woke up after we cleaned him up, his eyes droopy, his body limp.

Wish I could have slept after that, but Ford and I were both wired.

Ford even pressed his finger against my pulse and said, "It's racing, huh?"

Yeah, because that was *so fucking hot*.

I want to do it over and over again. But then again, I don't want to wear him out or hurt him. How much can one ass take?

That's the question, huh?

"Think his ass is okay?" I ask Ford, and Ben peers up at me with a soft smile. He's almost purring right now, arching into my touch.

"It's perfectly fine. I could be fucked all day long."

My brows meet in concern, and Ben reaches up and touches my face gently.

"I swear I'm fine. I'd never let you really hurt me."

I press my lips to his fingertips, and he closes his eyes again. I glance over at Ford, and he cocks his head at me while threading his fingers through mine.

I squeeze them lightly as Ford tucks himself further into the couch.

"Can it get any better than this?"

No, I don't think it can. Although, it would be nice if his dad knew about us and approved. I'm not doing this for shits and giggles. I don't just go around fucking guys.

Ben is the exception.

Well, Ford too, I think as I glance over at my best friend who is still holding my hand. He looks real fucking hot, and for the first time in... well, ever, I wonder if I'm gonna end up fucking him too.

The thought doesn't make me nervous. Actually, it only makes my cock jump between my legs.

Don't know if I've ever had this much sex. Intimacy with Claire was nonexistent toward the end, so to go from nothing to sex multiple times a day is something my cock and mind can get on board with.

Who knew a forty-two-year-old guy could get it up so often?

I turn my gaze to the TV and watch for a few minutes before my phone lights up. Glancing down, I see my mom's name flash across the screen.

Fuck. My face feels hot and my heart rate increases slightly. And not in the good way, either.

I forgot to message her back. And I know how she gets when she thinks I'm ignoring her.

I remove my hand from Ford's and grab my phone, staring down at it in silence.

"What's wrong?" Ford whispers.

I glance over at him and sigh. "My mom."

His eyes roll. "Oh, fuck her. What does that bitch want now?"

His outburst makes Ben stir and he sits up with a yawn.

"What's going on?" he asks, rubbing at his tired eyes.

I purse my lips and throw Ford a glare, but he ignores me.

"Cash's parents are the biggest knobs."

"Why?" Ben asks, looking worried, and I reach out and massage the back of his neck, making him lean into me a little more. I don't want him stressed out, especially if it's because of me.

"It's just how it is. It's fine."

Ford rolls his eyes and snorts. "No, it's not. They keep bugging him, trying to make him into something he's not. It's been this way since we met. They keep trying to parade him around in suits and ties when he'd rather be in his garage in jeans and a t-shirt."

I sigh and run a hand down my face. "Ford, enough."

"Nah, nope. I hate them."

"Jesus Christ."

Ben eyes me and then asks softly, "What do they want now?"

"Probably for him to attend some fancy, pretentious party…"

Ford isn't reading the room. Ben doesn't need to stress about this. It's a nonissue, it's not a big deal. But now Ben's eyes are fraught with worry and he's chewing on his bottom lip.

"Is it a party?"

"Yeah, my parents' anniversary party. They go all out."

"Oh."

"And I bet Claire will be there," Ford scoffs and then narrows his gaze at me. "You know what? Fuck that. If you go, I go. Keep that bitch away from you."

My chest tightens. "I can manage just fine."

"No, I'm going," Ford says, sitting up a little straighter. "You're mine now, Cash. Ours."

Ben blinks up at me. "Yeah, yeah you are."

I sigh and quickly respond to my mom that I'll be attending, and then a minute later she asks if I am bringing anyone.

I glance at Ford and then Ben, not sure what the fuck to do.

"I can go too, if you want," Ben says softly, his cheeks flushing as he says it. He probably thinks I'm going to reject him. Like I'd ever.

I roll my lips between my teeth. I don't want to go alone.

"Fuck it."

I type back that I have two guests I'm bringing and then turn my phone off. My mom can sit with that all she wants. She always makes judgments about me no matter what I do. Showing up with Ford and Ben won't change anything on her end.

"We're gonna give her something to gawk at that isn't you," Ford says loudly, and then pulls Ben into him and kisses him deeply.

I watch their mouths move and feel my heart rate slow.

Yeah, I've never been good enough for my parents, and even at forty-two, it still stings, but knowing that I have these two makes me feel a little better.

I can probably withstand the scathing comments and looks with them there.

"Come to bed with me," Ben says as Ford kisses his way down his neck. I stand and help him up before following them to the bedroom, peeling my clothes off as I go.

Ben and Ford fall to the mattress, and I crawl in after them.

Yeah, this.

This feels right.

Nothing else matters.

"When do we go to get fitted for our suits?" Ford asks me the next day as we're working on a 1962 Roadster for some shady dude. I'm pretty sure he's a mobster. Anthony Costello. I'm totally extrapolating and making inferences, but the way he looks, the way he speaks, and that bodyguard he brings around with him only confirm my suspicions.

He just looks dangerous, but Dean took the job anyways. I told him if we ended up in the river with no fingers I'd be pissed.

I happen to like my life right now. I have shit to live for.

I have two people to live for.

"After work. I got us all an appointment," I say.

"Awesome," Ford says and then bites his lip, his eyes flicking to my mouth. I can see his pupils dilating and my cock chubs up in my coveralls.

"Stop it," I grumble. "Not here."

"Yeah, well you're both here, and I'm getting all kinds of ideas." He leans in a little closer to me. "Can you imagine what he'll look like in a suit and tie? I'm gonna wanna strip him naked and suck his dick."

"Suck whose dick?" Dean asks, and I drop my wrench onto the ground with a curse. Damn Ford and his big mouth. He can't keep it shut.

"Don't mind me, Dean. Just running my mouth," Ford stammers.

I glance over at Ben and see his cheeks flushed red. He obviously heard that and is starting to squirm. If Ford spills the beans, I'm going to spank his ass.

Just the thought of it makes my cock jump.

"Yeah, okay, probably don't wanna know anyways. Where are you off to after work? Want to come over for some beers?"

"We have an appointment," I say and then sigh. "My parents' wedding anniversary. We are getting fitted for suits today."

"Shit," Dean says and then shoves his hands in his pockets. "What a shitty thing to have to do."

"I know."

"Yeah, well, I'll suck Cash's dick to make him feel better," Ford blurts.

Dean's head swings around to Ford and his eyebrows meet.

"Wait, you two—are you two together? Or is that a joke?"

I sigh and then shake my head as Ford says, "Hell yes, we are."

Dean looks confused, and I swear to god, I don't know what to say. I feel slightly nervous that Ben is watching this too, that he can't be included in this revelation.

But it has to stay a secret for now.

"Which is it? Yes or no?"

"Yeah, I guess we are."

Dean ponders that a moment and then nods his head. "Yeah, well, I guess whatever works. You were always really close. I'm not really surprised."

It's true, we always have been close, more so than most men our age. But then again, it's Ford. How could you not be close to him? He attaches himself like a koala and doesn't let go.

"Yeah, it works. It so works."

Ford waggles his eyebrows, and I roll my eyes as Dean pats me on the shoulder.

"Well, I hope everything goes well with your dad. If you want to take one of the loud cars, really make an appearance, let me know."

"Fuck yeah, we do," Ford nearly shouts, and I eye him. His dark eyes are nearly dancing with mischief. My parents hate Ford with a passion.

They'll hate him even more if I show up with his hand in mine and kiss him for all to see.

That would really get the party started.

"You know where the keys are. Just make sure you give them hell," Dean adds and then slaps me on the back once more, turning around and making his way to the other side of the garage. Ford eyes me and then we both look at Ben who is peeking over at us.

"Think I distracted him enough?" Ford asks, and I smack him upside the head gently.

He smiles widely at me, and I sigh once more.

"Yeah, you did good, man."

He beams and then leans forward, pressing his lips to my cheek. My entire body heats from just his lips on my skin, and I wish Ben could come over here too and do the same. But his gaze is focused intently on the paperwork before him, his fingers shuffling through the piles before he files them.

I've told Dean multiple times to go digital, but he's not budging. Perhaps Avery can work a little of his magic on that guy because it's ridiculous we even have a file cabinet in the first place.

But then again, if he got rid of it, Ben wouldn't need to come in anymore.

I stare at him for far too long and then pull my gaze away. I need to focus. I can kiss his soft lips later, when it's just the three of us.

I can't fucking wait.

CHAPTER SIXTEEN

FORD

God damn. My men look hot in suits. Fuck, this fitting is killing me, putting me in an early sexually frustrated grave.

I tug at the tie around my neck and then adjust my hard dick. It's poking out from my slacks and waving around at customers, but it's not my fault.

Cash and Ben look exquisite.

I mean, they always do, and it makes me damn proud to think that they're mine.

"Jesus, Ford. Put that shit away," Cash hisses, and I sigh.

"I tried, man, but you bent over and I got all sorts of ideas."

Ben laughs at that and then turns around, facing the mirror and arching his ass out a little, teasing me.

"That's not helping," I murmur and Ben meets my gaze in the mirror. He looks so goddamn happy that my dick is forgotten as I smile back at him.

"You think these work?" Cash asks, moving to stand near Ben, and I move up behind them, grabbing both their asses as I do, squeezing hard.

Cash rolls his eyes as Ben pushes back into my hand.

Fuck, he's needy for it.

"I think you guys look hot. I think your parents are going to lose their shit."

"Good," Ben says and then turns around and takes my mouth in a scorching kiss which leaves my head spinning.

It's fucking awkward too. The man at the counter taking our payment is studiously trying to ignore my hard dick. Well, it's not my fault. I'm horny for both of them. This man obviously has no clue the torture I've had to endure all day. If he could only fathom the amount of times my dick has complained, he'd end up having to go to HR.

"Is this going to get back to my dad?" Ben asks when we make our way back home. "Like, will your parents tell him that I went with you guys?"

"No," Cash scoffs. "They don't talk to Dean, know nothing about him. They probably don't even know he has a son."

Ben relaxes a little in his seat, and I reach forward from the backseat and massage his shoulders.

His head falls back against the headrest and he moans. It sets off my hair-trigger dick, and I bite my lip to keep myself in check.

I can see Cash isn't unaffected either by the way his hands tighten on the steering wheel.

"I wish I didn't have to go to this study group. I already feel like I haven't seen you all day," Ben says when we finally arrive back at my place. Cash turns his car off and faces him.

"When will you be home?"

Home. Hell yes, it is.

"Late, probably. I should probably just go back to my apartment—"

"No, come back here," I interrupt. "Come back to us."

Ben looks at the two of us and then nods. "Okay, if that's what you want."

"It's what we want," Cash says and then leans forward and pulls him in for a kiss. Ben goes willingly, almost crawling into his lap as he slants his mouth over his. I watch it all, feeling horny as fuck, but knowing I'm gonna have to wait for some relief.

Unless Cash wants to get me off alone.

I could go with that too.

Ben kisses me goodbye before hopping out of the car and we watch him walk to his car and drive away.

Cash glances down at my crotch and rolls his eyes.

"Come on, let's keep you occupied. It's going to be a long evening if we don't."

I follow him inside, curious what he has in mind. He walks to my room and kneels down beside the bed, reaching underneath and pulling out a box. My cock jumps, and I meet Cash's stare.

"How do you know about my box of shame?"

Cash smirks. "You got drunk one night and showed me."

I smile widely and then my cheeks darken when he puts it on my mattress and pulls the top off, gazing into it.

"You have a lot of things in here, Ford."

I roll my eyes. "I'm adventurous."

"You are," he says and then turns to me. "Drop your pants and bend over the bed."

I don't think twice, my cock already leaking as I do as I'm told. My face is turned toward Cash as he rifles through the box and then produces a plug.

"Think this will help you keep your ass occupied until he comes home?"

"I think I'm going to be edged into oblivion with that," I murmur.

Cash chuckles as he moves up behind me, grabbing on to the lube bottle. I hear the cap pop open and then feel the drizzle down my crack, his thick fingers pushing it into me. One finger, two, until I'm panting.

"Good enough?" Cash asks, and I nod, swallowing hard.

Then I feel it, the press of the plug at my hole. I let out a long exhale, relaxing my muscles as he pushes it in. It's bigger than my other ones, and I struggle to take it, but it finally settles in me with a small pop and Cash moves away from me, eyeing his handiwork.

"Hot," he says, and I turn over, wincing at the sensation of being stuffed full. It's been a while since I've been the bottom.

Not that I don't enjoy it.

I'm just out practice.

"You gonna suck my dick now?" I ask, feeling a little like I might riot if my dick doesn't get some attention.

Cash eyes it and then nods, sinking between my legs.

"Just so you can make it until he gets home."

———

The blow job helped, but thirty minutes after emptying myself into Cash's mouth I'm ready to go again. Probably doesn't help that I'm still wearing the plug and it's giving me all sorts of ideas.

"Suck my dick again," I tell Cash, but he shakes his head, reaching behind me and pushing on the plug through my pants. I gasp and then glower at him, my dick already starting to leak.

"You are evil."

Cash smirks at me just as the doorbell rings. I adjust my dick and then point to the door.

"You need to answer that. It's your fault I'm like this."

Cash chuckles as he presses on my plug once more before walking to the front door and pulling it open. I scoot behind the kitchen counter and then am glad I did when I see my mom standing on the front porch. Her gray hair is a bit windblown, her mascara a bit smudged, and I spot a stain on her cat t-shirt, but she looks like home.

I really do have the best parents. I wish Cash had half the love I get from them. Even half could change a person.

Too bad I forgot she had messaged me earlier to say she was stopping by on her way to visit her sister.

"Cash!" she cries as she steps inside and pulls him into a tight hug. "I was hoping you'd be here!"

My best friend wraps his arms around her and squeezes. I can see him eyeing me, and I shrug. Yeah, buddy, I forgot too, and I'm the one with the plug up my ass. Thankfully she isn't planning on staying.

"You've been avoiding us. Where have you been?" she asks him, and Cash shuffles on his feet, looking a little bashful.

"Mom, he was at your place last month," I say.

"Yeah, well, that's a little too long for me. I miss my boys."

She presses a kiss to his cheek and then points to some bags lining the front porch. "Can you bring those in for me, hun? I have something in there for you too."

Cash does as he's told, and I move out from behind the kitchen counter, thankful that my dick has gone down as I pull my mom into a hug. I don't need her seeing that and wondering what the fuck is going on. I mean, she knows I'm bi, but I don't know if Cash is ready to explain why my dick was hard.

"Did you forget I was coming by?" she asks me as she takes a seat at the kitchen table, the same one we fucked Ben on top of, and I hope like hell Cash sanitized it.

Jesus, we are filthy, I think as I shake my head.

"Never. I always remember when you're coming over."

She smiles at me and then starts to rummage through the bags, pulling out a stack of towels and setting them on the counter.

"I made you more," she says, and I resist an eye roll. I have hundreds of these homemade kitchen towels. They're ones you can hang on drawers and wipe your hands on. The ones I'm looking at are floral and don't match anything in my house, but knowing me, I'll hang them up all over. Just like I already have.

"They're awesome, Mom," I say and she beams at me.

"You can have some too, Cash," she says and then pulls out a folded quilt, handing it to him. "But this is for you."

He takes it and opens it up, looking at the intricate needlework. I know my mom spent a lot of time planning this out. It's just how she is. She does everything with care.

"It's gorgeous," he says roughly.

"Made it just with you in mind. I know you said you liked the one on my couch, so I thought I'd make you one too."

He swallows roughly and then hugs it to his chest. "I'll use the hell out of it."

My mom waves her hand in front of her face, looking bashful at Cash's show of emotion before handing me two shirts.

"I made these for you too. Just so you didn't feel left out."

I hold them up and see that she's embroidered little farm animals on the bottom of these button-ups. I'm going to be mocked relentlessly for wearing these, but like hell I won't.

"They're awesome. Thanks, Mom. I love them."

"You're welcome. I just wanted to stop by and see my boys and give you this stuff. Are you coming by next weekend? Dad wants to talk shop with you. He bought another old car, can you believe it?"

My eyebrows fly up. "Shit no, really?"

"Yes, really. It's becoming a bit of a problem." She sighs and then pats her legs. "Well, I won't keep you any longer. I'm sure you guys are busy, but both of you are expected at our place. And bring Dean, will you? I haven't seen him in ages."

I eye Cash and he rolls his lips between his teeth.

"Sounds good. I'll see if he and Ben can come."

"Oh yes, bring Ben. Such a cute kid."

Well shit, I think as I follow my mom to the front door and give her a hug goodbye. As soon as it shuts behind her, I turn to Cash, who is watching me silently.

"A cute kid?"

I snort a laugh. "I mean, he is cute."

I walk up to him and take the quilt from his hands, setting it on the back of the couch.

"Now come on. Let's stay busy or else I'm gonna have to jack off like a hundred times," I say, and Cash snorts a laugh as he follows me out back. We'll find a project to do until Ben comes home.

CHAPTER SEVENTEEN

BEN

"You sure are in a hurry to get home," Tatum teases, and I roll my eyes as I close my book and shove it in my backpack.

"Yeah, well I have shit to do."

He waggles his eyebrows at me, and I lean forward and punch at his arm.

"Stop it."

"Hey, come on. I have to tease you about this. At least you're getting some."

I freeze and stare at my best friend, his pink hair sideways, his lip ring glinting in the light. "What do you mean? I thought you were hooking up with that Brandon guy."

"Brayden. And I was, but then he quit me. Didn't think it was possible, but apparently I'm quittable."

I stare at him and then scoot a little closer. "Are you okay?" I ask softly and he shrugs, looking a little sad. His bright blue eyes a bit dimmer than normal.

"I liked him, but I'll be fine. He wasn't that great anyways. Too far in the closet and you know me, I hate those things."

"Yeah, I know."

"But enough about me. I think we're good for the midterm and you need to go back and get your ass ripped up."

I let out a bemused laugh and then stand up, feeling my knees pop. Shit, I sat cross-legged far too long. I ache.

"Yeah, I really need that."

"I know you do, you slut."

He walks me to the front door of his house and gives me a small hug before I jog down the walkway to my car. And to be honest, I break a lot of laws to get back to Ford's place as quickly as possible.

It's been a long-ass day and once again, my ass feels empty.

I just want to sandwich myself between the two of them and let them have their way with me.

But I also just want to be with them, to listen to them talk, to have them cuddle me and make me eat dinner.

Shit, I forgot to eat dinner.

That's my thought as I unlock the front door and walk inside. I see Cash and Ford on the couch, Ford with his head in Cash's lap.

"How was it?" Cash asks as Ford sits up with a small whine. He shifts on the couch looking a little flustered as I set my book bag down on the ground and toe off my shoes.

"Good. I'm glad I went. I think I'll nail the midterm."

Cash and Ford nod and my stomach rumbles.

Both of their brows furrow, and I smile at them sheepishly.

"Forgot to eat."

"Damn you," Cash says as he stands up and moves to the kitchen, pulling things out to start reheating. God, I love being taken care of. My dad did a great job while I was growing up, but he was gone a lot, always working. He was trying to provide.

I never had someone at home to watch me and care for me.

Maybe that's why I love this so much.

For the first time in a long time, someone cares enough to actually do something about it. This is a dangerous game I'm playing, but for the first time in a long time, I don't want to run away.

I want to embrace it.

Ford steps up to me and pulls me into a hug. "We missed you."

"Yeah," I say and then tilt my chin up and press my lips to his. He moans into my mouth, his tongue sliding into me and tangling with mine.

Forget dinner, I think, I would rather just fuck.

But that's shut down when Cash announces that my food is ready. Reluctantly, I pull away from Ford and move to the table where I see some tacos laid out on a plate. I realize now how hungry I am and demolish them quickly before sitting back and patting my full stomach.

"Better," Cash says, grabbing my plate and rinsing it off. "You really need to make sure you eat, Ben."

"I know, but I just forget with everything going on."

"That's what we're here for," Ford says as I rub at my eyes, feeling far too full and very satiated. I could go to sleep right now—could just close my eyes and snooze. But my dick is hard just from being near the two of them and it's ready to go.

"Okay, I've been good for so long. Now can we fuck?" Ford nearly whines as he moves up to Cash and leans into him. Cash eyes him and then reaches out and presses against Ford's ass, making Ford groan.

My eyebrows rise. What have they been up to while I was gone?

"We didn't do anything. Well, I mean, he sucked my dick after he put a plug up my ass..." Ford says, and I realize now that I spoke my question out loud. "But really, we have been waiting for you to come home. Thank fuck you're home."

He sounds almost desperate.

"Shit, Ford, calm down. Maybe Ben doesn't want to do anything. Maybe he just wants to sleep."

I stare at Cash. "Do you not know me at all?"

He narrows his eyes at me, and I smile. "Show me this plug, Ford. I wanna see."

Ford obliges, ripping his pajama pants off and bending over a chair. I can see the flex of his strong ass and my mouth goes dry. There between his cheeks is a bright blue silicone knob. I can envision it—Cash sliding it inside while Ford whines and squirms.

I wish I could have been there to watch.

I wanna watch.

I reach out and press against it, making Ford gasp.

"Shit, you guys keep doing that, and I'm gonna come. I swear to god."

"How long have you been wearing this?" I ask, feeling my entire body heat in response. This is how it always is with them. Just being near them makes me combust.

Ford stands up and clutches the base of his dick.

"Since you left."

I wet my lips and then meet Cash's stare.

"I want to watch you two fuck."

Cash's mouth falls open, and I stand up moving toward the bedroom.

"I want to watch you both fuck while I get off," I amend as they move in behind me.

When we make it into the bedroom, I start to undress and they both watch me, their eyes heating as I strip bare. My hands run up my stomach, and I play with my nipples, my mouth opening in a moan as I watch them wet their lips.

"You guys make me so hot. You're gonna be so hot fucking each other."

My hands move to my cock and I tug on it, my mind conjuring up all sorts of filthy things that they could do. With each other. With me.

"Undress," I tell Cash, and when he doesn't move fast enough, I help him pull his shirt off and tug his pants down his thighs. When I'm on my knees in front of his engorged cock, I pull it into my mouth, just for a taste. It's too tempting not to, and I am not one to resist that.

He groans above me and fucks into me a few times before pulling away.

"You have to stop. I could come just like this," he says lowly, and I nod, standing up and moving onto the bed. I spread out on my side and watch as Ford and Cash stare at one another. This is a monumental moment for them, and I'm so fucking glad I'm here to watch it unfold. I've been jacking off to the thought of them fucking for months... years even.

And now I get to see it.

In real life.

"Gotta remove the plug first," Ford teases, and Cash swallows nervously.

"Ass out then," Cash says, and Ford obeys, sticking his butt up in the air, his elbows and torso resting on the bed.

Cash stares down at Ford's ass for a few seconds before slowly working the plug free, tossing it onto the ground. Ford's eyes are on me, his cheeks flushed, his fingers grasping on to the sheets beneath him.

Cash slides his hand along Ford's crack and then slides a finger inside of him.

"Still wet," Cash says, and Ford moans at the intrusion.

"Jesus, just do me already. I've been waiting all fucking day."

"So impatient," Cash says with a chuckle, slotting his dick right at his hole. I sit up, wanting to see him enter, wanting to see Ford take his best friend's dick.

Ford moans as Cash starts to push forward, his back arching up slightly as he takes Cash balls deep. I'm panting now, wanting to join in but also wanting to watch, wanting to see this.

"God, you're big," Ford gasps, and Cash chuckles.

"Your hole is just tiny."

"Oh, fuck you, it's perfectly fine," Ford says and then grunts when Cash snaps his hips forward.

"Jesus, take it easy."

"You don't take it easy on Ben," Cash replies, and I smile at them when they turn their gazes to me.

"You really don't, but my ass is magical."

They smile at me in tandem, Ford's slipping first into an open-mouthed gasp when Cash slams his hips forward again and again.

I watch with hooded eyes as Ford takes Cash's cock over and over, the smell of sex and sweat filling the room, the sound of skin slapping together making my cock leak.

"He likes this, watching you get fucked," Cash says, and Ford scoffs.

"He fucking better."

I lean forward and kiss Ford, shutting up his grumbling. I want them to do this again and again. I'll use anything as an incentive. Ford licks into my mouth hungrily, and I moan just being near him. I want to join in, want to sit on Cash's dick, want Ford to impale me on his cock while he's being impaled by Cash.

I want it all. The possibilities are endless.

"Oh shit," Ford cries out and then leans down on his elbows, fucking back on Cash's cock.

"Found it," Cash says smugly as he continues to smash into Ford's ass. And he's not complaining.

No, Ford is whining, his eyes shut, his lips parted in lust.

Fuck he looks good like this, getting railed and enjoying it.

I pump my dick faster, watching as Cash leans forward and jerks Ford's dick, making him explode a minute later. The sight, the smell of it has me falling over the edge too, my cum splattering across my stomach. Cash is the last to go, his rhythm faltering slightly as he empties himself into Ford's hole.

He falls down on top of Ford's back and gasps, still inside of him.

"Jesus." Ford is breathing heavily, his entire body trembling.

"Yeah," I say and then sit up, leaning toward them and kissing across their sweaty skin. They taste like salt, like man as I let my tongue slide against them.

"My ass needs a break after that," Ford says when Cash finally sits up and pulls out.

I scramble to the edge of the bed and take a long look at his release dripping down Ford's thigh.

"Next time, I want you both to fuck me," I say, reaching out and trailing my finger through the mess. "Then I want you to plug me up. I want to keep you both inside of me for as long as I can."

They both groan as I smile wickedly.

"Come on. I just came," Ford grumbles looking down at his dick which is already starting to harden. "You did that on purpose."

I giggle at that as Ford moves, trying to tackle me, but I manage to escape, running for the hallway, my bare feet slapping on the floor. And they give chase.

I'm squealing as I try and outmaneuver them, but they catch me quickly, their hands slipping on my sweaty, filthy skin as they haul me into their arms.

"Trying to run?" Cash asks lowly as I link my ankles behind his lower back.

"I know you'll always catch me," I say sappily, but he loves it. He just walks me back to the bedroom, Ford following behind.

Cash sets me on the bed, and I scoot back, pulling the sheets back and silently asking them to join me.

And they do, sandwiching me in against them. I sigh, burrowing closer to the two of them, making sure my skin touches theirs and finding that my eyes close easily.

"Yeah, you sleep, Ben," Ford says from behind me. His deep voice rumbles through me. "Tomorrow when you wake, we're gonna stuff you full."

"For fuck's sake, Ford," Cash chastises, but I shush him up.

"That sounds good to me. I want to wake up to you both fucking me."

And they let out a synchronous groan.

———

As promised, Ford and Cash delivered, fucking me awake, each taking their turn filling me up and then sliding a plug up my ass to keep it all inside.

I didn't want to move, but they made me get up for breakfast.

If I keep this up with them, I'm going to gain a hundred pounds. They're always feeding me.

For fuck's sake.

"God, I'm so full," I groan. "I can't eat any more."

They eye me and then Ford rolls his eyes. "Yeah, good. You were too skinny before."

"So much like his mom, huh?" Cash says, and Ford chuckles.

My heart clenches, and I stare at them. "That's what my dad says."

"Yeah, she was a stress case, but in the best way. We'd always laugh at how ridiculous she could be."

I find myself smiling at that, my heart fluttering in my chest.

"God, we miss her," Ford says, and Cash nods.

"I'm sad I never knew her," I say softly and they both move at the same time, their hands on me, pulling me into them.

"We know, but... shit, we have those pictures still, right?" Cash says, and Ford nods.

"Yes, we do. God, where did I put those?" He moves away from me quickly, and I watch him go before my eyes turn back to Cash.

"Think she'd be pissed at me for fucking you both?" I ask softly, and Cash's brows meet.

"Honestly, I don't know."

That doesn't sit well with me, and I shift in my chair, my ass still stuffed full from the plug.

"But I know she loved you very much. And so does your dad. I think it might come as a shock to him, but he'll come around to the idea of the three of us. Because this is more than just fucking, Benjamin."

I swallow and avert my eyes. I don't know what this is, just that I feel things when I'm with them both. And it's not just lust.

No, I feel safe, protected, cherished.

"You'll see. You'll see that it's more."

I nod just as Ford makes an appearance, a shoebox in his hand.

"Found it. Was in my closet under some quilts my mom made and a mountain of those little towels."

I smile at that and then hold my breath when he sets the box down in front of me.

"I should scan these into the computer, but for now, here you go."

I pull the lid off and peer inside. There are hand-written notes and a stack of pictures—a young Ford, Cash, my dad, and my mom—Elaine—smiling at the camera.

"This from when you were in college?" I ask as I look at each picture, my mom posing and laughing.

"You guys had so much fun," I say, and they each nod.

"Yeah, we did. A blast, and Elaine was so good for your dad. He was far too serious, stoic."

"A bit like you," I tell Cash, and he rolls his eyes.

"I'm nothing like your dad."

"You so are," I tease, and then look at Ford.

"Why didn't you two... you know? Did you ever mess around in college?"

"Hell no," Ford says and then waggles his eyebrows. "You were his sexual awakening."

I look at Cash and see his cheeks flushed slightly.

"Shut the fuck up, Ford."

Ford just chuckles and then pulls Cash's seat out, straddling his lap and kissing him on the mouth sloppily.

Cash's hands go around his waist, and I watch them with hooded eyes until they finally pull away.

"And now look at us," Ford says, his eyes flicking to me. "The three of us."

I swallow and turn my gaze back to the photos before me.

"I wish I could have known her. I feel like she would be able to tell me what to do about you two."

Cash reaches out and cups the nape of my neck.

"No one needs to tell you what to do. You do what you feel is right."

"And what's right is us," Ford chimes in.

A smile cracks my lips, and I sigh, putting the pictures back and closing the lid.

"Yeah, it feels right," I say, and Cash and Ford both grin.

"Want me to show you something?" Ford asks, and I nod, letting him lead me outside. The air is cool and crisp, stinging my cheeks.

They each take one of my hands and pull me forward to the far end of the yard.

"What is it?" I ask, and Ford gestures toward a large tree.

I stare at it, confusion in my gaze.

"Your mom would make the best apple pie. I planted this for her. It's an apple tree," Ford says, and I feel my eyes sting.

"Yeah?"

"Yeah, I have the recipe in the house somewhere. One day, I'll make it for you."

Cash squeezes my hand, and I gulp back tears. "My dad has a lavender bush at his place for her. Says that it was her favorite flower."

"It was," Cash says.

"I feel like I don't know her. I feel like I was robbed."

"I know, Benjamin. But we can tell you whatever you want to know. We knew her."

Ford nods and then leans down, kissing me gently. "She would have been so happy that we found you."

They pull me into them, and I sag against their strong chests, inhaling them. Would she be upset that I'm with them right now? I don't know, but they seem to think she wouldn't. They clearly loved her. They knew her.

Maybe Cash is right, maybe my dad won't be so upset if he finds out. He knows how much they loved my mom and how much they love…

I gulp that thought back and shake my head. No, that's not what this is.

Right?

"Yeah, okay, I think I'm gonna take a shower and take this plug out…"

"We're coming with you," Ford says, tugging me toward the house and then down the hall to the bathroom, Cash on our heels. I let out a laugh as he pulls me into him, kissing me wildly, his hand snaking down to press against the plug.

Oh god, I'm so full, so fucking stuffed.

"Alright, let him breathe, Ford," Cash says, and I whimper when his lips finally peel off of mine.

"I don't need to breathe," I say grumpily and Cash just pulls me closer, helping me undress.

"You need a break."

Ford huffs but lets me go, turning on the shower instead. I let Cash strip me down, his hands caring, his movements gentle as he tosses my clothes aside. His fingers graze the plug, but he doesn't do more than that. Just helps me into the shower.

When I'm done, my ass empty and my body washed, I step out to a waiting towel that Ford wraps around me and a cup of coffee that Cash brings me.

I've never in my life been so well taken care of.

"When do you get off of work tonight?" I ask as I sip on my coffee and then lazily start to get dressed.

Cash and Ford lean against the wall, watching me closely.

"Dinner."

I peer up at them as I button up my pants.

"Want to go out? The three of us?"

Ford's lips turn up in a smile, and Cash nods. "Fuck yeah, we do."

I grin widely as I pull on my shirt.

"It's a date then."

CHAPTER EIGHTEEN

CASH

Well, fuck. I'm nervous. Ben is due home any minute, and I have tried on far too many shirts.

None of them look good.

"You look hot, dude," Ford says when he appears from the shower, a towel around his waist. "Stop stressing about it."

"But it's a date."

"Yeah, but it will be chill. It's Ben."

I sigh when I feel him come up behind me, his hands spreading across my chest and bringing me back against him. His face tucks into my neck, and he kisses my skin softly.

"He's gonna be thrilled with what we have planned. I just know it," he says, and I relax against him. "And then we can bring him home after and fuck his brains out."

I let out a laugh and then shove away from him, adjusting my hardening cock in my pants.

"Don't give me any more ideas. I'm already fucking horny for it."

Ford waggles his eyebrows and drops his towel, bending over and pulling on some boxers. My eyes linger on his ass for a little too long. I was in him, in that tight hole. And honestly, I'd do it again.

And again.

I want Ben and Ford to take turns sitting on my dick.

My mind is awash with those filthy thoughts as he gets dressed, and then we wait for Ben to arrive. And arrive he does, looking so fucking hot in tight black jeans and a light blue button-up shirt. He's wearing Converse and his hair is styled, and I want nothing more than to peel him out of those clothes and sit him on my cock.

"Enough growling," Ford says as he moves up to Ben and kisses him softly. "Let's go before he mauls you."

I shake my head and move toward Ben, kissing him slowly, savoring him, until he's panting and pressing his hardening dick against me.

But enough is enough. We could easily end up in bed and forgo the date, but I want this. We need it.

We have to show Ben that we mean this, that this is more than just sex.

"Where are we going?" Ben asks, and Ford waggles his eyebrows.

"Well, Cash and I had a talk at work and then we decided to split it up. Cash planned the first half, and I planned the second half."

"And god help us on the second half," I say.

Ford rolls his eyes. "No, it's going to be romantic, just you wait."

"So basically neither of you know what we're doing?" Ben asks, and I place my hand on his lower back and lead him out to my car.

"Yeah, it's gonna be a surprise for all of us."

"I can't fucking wait."

———

Ben shifts in his seat, the three of us crowded into the front of my car. Thank fuck for old-school bench seats. My hand rests on Ben's thigh, and I squeeze. Ford links his hand with Ben's, and I feel so fucking complete for the first time in forever.

Who would have thought that I'd feel this way with two men?

Not fucking me.

"So, gonna give us a hint where we're headed?" Ford asks, always so fucking impatient.

"Can you wait and see?" I ask, and Ford huffs.

"Yeah, I can wait, but I don't wanna."

Ben leans his head against Ford's shoulder, then squeezes the hand I have settled on his leg.

"Let's just wait and see. I love being surprised."

Ford glances down at him with a smile. "Like being awoken by a surprise dick in your ass."

"Jesus," I murmur, remembering how the two of us took turns waking him up the other morning. Fuck, remembering it has my dick stirring. I don't know why I waited so long to fuck him. Because while his mouth is glorious, his ass is heaven.

Ford's is fucking nice too.

I could fuck both of those for the rest of my days.

"I did like it. I wouldn't mind waking up like that all the time. Free use and all that."

"What the fuck is that?" I ask, and Ford chuckles.

"Means we can use him anytime we want."

Fuck. Me.

I stare at Ben and his cheeks are flushed a pretty pink. He wets his lips and then nods. "Yeah, I am totally down for that. I just want to be used."

My hand wrings the steering wheel, and I let out an exhale.

"Yeah, okay. We can do that. After our date."

He squeezes my fingers in his and then sighs as I pull the car into a parking lot.

Ford whistles. "Well, fancy shmancy, Cash."

"Only the best for you two."

Ben's eyes are wide as we get out of the car, his gaze veering down to what he is wearing.

"Shit. I don't think I'm dressed nice enough for this," he says, and I pull him into me, kissing the top of his head.

"You're beautiful."

Ford nods. "You are."

Ford reaches out and grabs Ben's hand, pulling us all to the entrance of the Haven, an upscale restaurant in the Hills. It caters to the rich fucks up here—a place my parents would love if they lived closer—and I know we don't really fit in, but I wanted to impress Ben and Ford.

And I can see that I have. Ben's eyes are starry, and Ford is looking around the dimly lit interior with a smile.

"This is really fucking nice," Ford says a little too loudly.

The hostess turns to look at us, and I wave it away, hoping that maybe she can let this one go.

Perhaps coming here was a bad idea, I think as she leads us to our table, tucking us into the corner of the restaurant.

"This is way too fancy, Cash," Ben says softly as he sits down, Ford and I sliding in next to him in the booth. The hostess gives us the menus and doesn't say anything about how close we're sitting. This is obviously a date and Ben is far younger than us.

Fuck, does this look bad?

Ford doesn't seem bothered by it and neither does Ben, not with the way he leans into Ford and pulls the menu open to glance down at the items inside. Ford places his arm around his shoulder and presses a kiss to the top of his head, uncaring that people might be staring.

I wish I could be more like him at times. I've always admired that about him.

"There aren't prices," Ben says, and I reach out and brush my hand against his cheek.

"That's the point. You order what you want."

"But I can't read these things."

I smile at him, so fucking young and innocent. Well, maybe not so innocent. Not with what that tongue can do. And that ass. And those hands.

Fuck. Me.

I shift in my seat and look down at the menu, my eyes crossing at the fancy words.

Well, fuck. Maybe I overthought this.

"I'm gonna go wild," Ford says, licking his lips. "I'm gonna get a few of these weird things."

My worries dissipate as I take him in, and my chest swells. Ford and

Ben. My world couldn't exist without them. I can't have one without the other.

"Yeah, me too. Maybe we can all share?" Ben asks, and I feel lighter than I have in years.

"Yeah, we can do that. It's what we're good at. Sharing."

Ford winks at me. "You know it."

CHAPTER NINETEEN

FORD

"That was fucking amazing," I say as we all walk out of the restaurant, not really full because let's be honest, the portions were tiny, but they were delicious. Like little appetizers bursting with flavor. Could have done with an American-sized portion of it. Would have gobbled it up.

"It was good, huh?" Cash says, looking proud. Well, he should be. That restaurant was amazing. I wasn't so sure when we entered because everyone seemed a little snooty, but they had a right to be. The food and service was another level. I don't know if we'll be going back anytime soon because the bill made me nauseous, but I'd sure as fuck go back there if given the option.

Maybe for our anniversary. We could come back here every year and stuff our faces. And yeah, I'm thinking of the future. Who wouldn't?

"Yeah, it was amazing. And you know it," Ben says, rubbing at his stomach. "I'm stuffed. Can barely move."

The way his hands are rubbing across his stomach turns me on, and I lean into him and kiss him. He had two glasses of wine with dinner and looks a little flushed. Like maybe he's a little buzzed, which is fine by me.

I want to stuff him full of my cock and then suck his dick into my mouth—a nice sixty-nine after dessert—but first we have places to go.

Now it's time for my part of the date, and it's something I'm really fucking excited for.

"Cash, let me drive, since this is part of the surprise."

Cash shakes his head "Yeah, you driving my car... don't think so."

"Oh, fuck you," I say and then lean in and kiss him, my tongue swirling around his mouth as I pull the keys from his back pocket.

He grunts and glowers at me when I dangle them before him.

"You tricked me, you fucker."

"You're easy," I say as we all pile into the car, Ben leaning against Cash and reaching between his legs to massage his dick.

I swear, a tipsy Ben is a horny one. More so than normal. Which is saying something.

"What are you doing?" I ask as I start the engine, and Ben nearly purrs.

"I'm horny. That food had an aphrodisiac in it, I think."

"What food had that in it? And did I not get any?" I ask because I don't remember that at all. But I was slightly distracted by the way Ben and Cash were licking their forks. Those tongues, those lips.

I shift in my seat and grip the steering wheel.

"You're not horny?" Ben asks. "I'm surprised to hear that."

"No, I am. Of course I am, but listen, if I don't get to take you on my part of the date, I'm gonna be pissed." Cash groans and I glance over. "Ben, take your hand off of Cash's dick."

Ben just seems to rub it harder.

Ridiculous men.

Horny bastards.

"Goddamnit," I say as I lean over and grab on to Ben's hand, pulling it onto my lap. Which was a mistake because now he's rubbing my dick.

And my dick likes it.

"Behave," I hiss, but Ben just presses his lips to the curve of my neck, making my skin break out in goosebumps.

"Make me come. I want you both to make me come," he moans, his hand moving to his own cock and rubbing through the fabric of his jeans.

He's arching into it and being completely obscene. Which, to be honest, I totally love. But Jesus fuck.

What are we supposed to do about it? We're in the middle of a fancy parking lot. People could see him getting railed. And as much as that turns me on, I don't want Ben to get arrested.

"Oh god," Ben whines and then gasps loudly. "Oh god, I need you."

Cash and I are both watching him, our breathing growing labored as Ben moans and gasps, like a horny little shit.

"Get in the back with him," I finally say, peeling my eyes off of Ben and focusing on the parking lot in front of me. There are expensive cars all around us, and I wonder if anyone is sitting behind those tinted windows, watching.

"Get in the back with him, Cash and get him off. I want to go to the goddamn fair!"

Ben stops stroking himself for a second and eyes me. "Oh shit. I love the fair."

I lean over and kiss him before reaching across the two of them and pushing the passenger side door open. They both stumble out and then fall into the backseat, the two of them moaning as their mouths meet in a clash of lust and need.

I hear a zipper being lowered and the slurp of a mouth, my eyes swiveling to the rearview mirror to see Ben's head leaning back, his mouth open in a silent cry.

Fuck, this is hot, I think as I pull carefully out of the lot and drive toward my destination. It's gonna take us about fifteen minutes to get there and Cash uses every minute of it to edge Ben into oblivion. He only comes when we're finally in line to buy tickets for parking. As soon as I come to a stop, he explodes in Cash's mouth with a strained cry, the tendons in his neck popping out.

He's breathing heavily, his eyes glazed over as Cash sits up. He swipes at his mouth, his lips puffy, his eyes watering slightly.

"You better now?" I ask Ben, and he just swallows, nodding slowly.

I press the heel of my palm to my dick as I find a spot to park. Well shit. Ben is clearly feeling better, but Cash and I are worse for wear, the two of us having to tuck our hard cocks into the waistbands of our pants before we get out, lest we traumatize the people milling about.

Ben stumbles into us and we both place our hands up to steady him, Cash's across his shoulders and mine around his waist. He tucks himself into our sides as we make our way toward the entrance of the fair. People are streaming in, and I feel excitement bubble through me.

This was a fucking genius idea.

"I haven't been to a fair in forever," Ben says softly as we get up to the ticket booth. There are a lot of people wandering around, most dressed in long flowing dresses and a few men wearing colorful joggers and eclectic shirts. I also notice there are a lot of pagan symbols hanging around necks and people wearing stones.

Hm, odd, but maybe this is a convention or something. One time I went somewhere and was surrounded by Amish people. They were on a tour.

It was pretty fucking weird, but also so damn cool.

Those fuckers don't have cars. Just use horses. Pretty damn wild.

"Is that a crown of rocks?" I ask, taking in a woman wearing a long flowing dress and a bunch of black rocks on her head. Ben chuckles, his nose nestling into my shoulder, muffling his laugh.

"Are we fucking old or what?" Cash grumbles as we walk to the entrance, handing the young girl with purple hair and nose piercings our tickets. "Everyone's sense of style is so weird these days," he adds, and then I hear Ben start to giggle.

"Oh my god, Ford," he says with a smile and a small snort. "This isn't the fair you're thinking of."

My brows meet, and I stare down at Ben who looks like he's about to start laughing. His cheeks are red and his lips are pulled between his teeth.

"What kind of fair is it?" I ask, and he points to a large banner in the distance.

"A metaphysical one."

Cash makes a face, and I scrunch up my nose. "What the fuck is that?"

"You know, like healing stones and yoni eggs... psychics..." Ben explains and my mouth drops open.

"No Ferris wheels and deep-fried Oreos?"

Ben shrugs and then smiles softly at me. "I still love it. Love it so much."

The way he says it makes my heart beat double-time in my chest, and I lean down and kiss him deeply.

"Your mom loved this shit. I mean, I didn't plan it this way, but it seems fortuitous, right? Like she's giving her blessing."

Ben blinks up at me. "Yeah. It does."

"What the fuck do you do at these fairs?" Cash asks as we start to meander, a man with some incense moving past us with a look of severe concentration in his eyes. Maybe he's trying not to poop. I've seen that look before.

"I don't know. I think probably go to a palm reader, buy some sex rocks..." Ben begins and my eyes widen.

"What now? Sex rocks?"

"Yeah, you know like ones that give off sexual energy..."

My hand wraps around his, and I pull the two of them forward.

"Let's get us some of those."

"I don't think it's possible for us to have more sex," Cash grumbles, but he's wrong. He is so fucking wrong.

"Ben could do it all fucking day long, you dick," I say, and Ben nods his head. "And since you're older than me, I think you could use some help."

Cash scoffs. "Oh fuck off. I fuck just fine. My dick is still hard."

A woman standing at a table nearby must overhear us because she smiles widely and waves us toward her. She's middle-aged and wearing several gems in her ears and around her neck. Her arms are piled with bracelets that I'm sure have some significance. Not sure what, but there's a reason she's wearing so many, I'm sure.

"I overheard you. I have just what you need."

She waves her hand over some black crystals and says, "Smoky quartz for low libido."

Cash grumbles, and I snort a laugh. "We definitely need some of those for this old guy here."

She holds up some red stones. "Oh, and here are some carnelian gemstones. They help with sexual energy."

Cash grabs one and eyes it. "Think Ford needs this. His energy has been off lately."

Well, that's just not true, I think, but let him have it.

"What else do you recommend," Ben asks kindly, his eyes roaming over the table before him. The woman shows him some more stones and before we know it, we have a bag full.

"We're gonna have such good sex tonight," Ben says with a waggle of his eyebrows before pulling us along. "And I think the ladies at the senior home will like some of these too."

"I don't think old people need to be having sex," Cash says, and Ben rolls his eyes.

"I know, but they do it so much. They make me look like a nun."

We end up at another booth where a woman fawns all over Ben, remarking on his aura and energy, before persuading us to buy a crown of clear quartz and obsidian for him.

"For your prince's balance and vitality," she says as Ben places it on his head and winks at us.

Yeah, okay, he looks hot like that. I could see him wearing that as he rides us. The thought gets me hard just standing here, which is a problem. Perhaps these rocks are working their magic through the plastic bag slung around my arm.

Jesus. If they are working, I may have a hard dick the rest of the night. Not preferable.

"Oh, let's go over here!" Ben pulls us forward again, and we follow him through the entire fair, leaving after a couple hours with bags full of creams and gemstones and a new pack of Tarot cards.

"Jesus, that was... something else," Cash says lowly, and I roll my eyes at him before pulling him into me. I press my lips to his jaw and then lick my way to his mouth. He moans against me and mutters, "Damn rocks."

Damn rocks indeed.

"Come on, let's go home. Unless you have something else planned?" Ben asks, and I shake my head, already feeling the need to get inside of him.

"The nice psychic lady did tell us we have a wild ride ahead of us," Ben says as I unlock the door to the car and touch his butt as he gets in.

His crown shifts slightly as he looks back at me. His eyelids are glittering with eyeshadow and he's wearing a citrine necklace around his neck.

He looks so fucking good. But he'd look even better naked.

"I think my wild ride will be you two and your cocks," he says as I start up the car and drive us home. Yeah, I'm down with that. I've been aching since I watched him get sucked off in the back of the car.

But more than that, I want to hold him, to listen to him talk and laugh. Tonight made my heart feel light—watching him wander around the stalls, rubbing oils on his arms and sipping on some calming tea we bought him. I can't help but smile when I look at him. And I can tell Cash feels the same way.

He's even wearing his moon necklace that Ben bought each of us. *Partnership*, he'd said it meant. That's what we are. Partners.

And I like that a whole hell of a lot.

———

"Oh god," Ben groans as he slides down on my wet dick. He's wearing nothing but that crown, his cock straining up from his groin, his head thrown back as he rides me. He looks witchy, ethereal. Like a goddess.

Cash is lying next to me, running a smooth rock over my chest and kissing my neck.

"Think these rocks work," I say as Ben slams down on me, taking me harder than I thought was possible. That ass is pure magic. A miracle worker.

"Fuck," I groan as Ben leans down and kisses Cash, pulling his bottom lip between his teeth and sucking. Cash grunts, reaching out and rubbing that rock right over Ben's dick.

Ben gasps and then starts to rut against me, my cock dragging in and out of his tight hole as he moves.

"I'm gonna do you next. I'm gonna do you both all night," Ben pants as he pulls off of me. He pushes Cash onto his back and grabs on to the rock, sliding it over his own balls while he sinks down on Cash's dick.

"Oh fuck," Cash says as he grabs on to Ben's waist to help him bounce.

It's hot. It's so fucking sexy. I lean over and pull Ben's dick right into my mouth, sucking on it until he's chanting my name.

"I want you both. Both at the same time."

Cash and I both groan at the thought as Ben continues to ride him.

"Those big cocks, stretching me. At the same time. Oh god," Ben says as I sit up and start to jack him, my mouth latching on to his. I'm sucking his tongue into my mouth as he moans his need but before he comes, he switches dicks again, pushing me onto my back and slamming down on me.

It's wild, chaotic, just a slash of tongues and dicks and sweat. I don't know how he's got us in this chokehold, but the two of us are living for it.

"Fuck, Ford," Ben murmurs as he sinks down on me again and again. "Cash. Fuck him while he's fucking me."

Cash doesn't hesitate, just moves in between my legs, pushing my knees up as far as they can go, Ben still taking my dick. He's not even slowing down, just a frantic glide over my cock again and again.

"You want this?" Cash asks, and I nod, letting him slip a lubed finger into my ass. I groan at the feeling of being stuffed, but easily adapt as he sticks two and then three fingers inside of me.

Ben is watching us both and then leans forward to give Cash better access to my hole. I should be nervous, should be afraid that it will hurt, but I only find myself begging for it. Without warning, I feel the head of Cash's dick push inside of me, a gentle sting before he slams home.

I cry out, and Ben does too as the three of us connect in a way we haven't before. It's unearthly, it's heavenly. It's sinful. Completely hedonistic.

My cock being ridden, my ass shoved full of dick.

It's the perfect way to die.

We're just hands and bodies and slapping skin, until Ben twists his upper body and starts to kiss Cash, my hand wrapping around his cock as I start to pump him. He cries out as jets of cum splash across my abdomen and the sight of it has me releasing into his ass. Cash is the final hold out, his low groan echoing around the room as he empties himself into me. And then it's just a mix of heavy breathing and grunts as we collapse onto the bed in exhaustion.

"God, that was so hot," Ben says as he snuggles into our sides. None of us bother cleaning up, just let the cum sit on us and in our bodies.

"I was being serious about double penetration. Just for the record," he adds, and Cash peeks his eyes open and meets my stare.

"I don't think so, Ben."

"I think so," he retorts and then closes his eyes with a sigh. "I'll show you both I can take it. I promise. I want it."

And that's the thought I'm left with as I fall asleep.

CHAPTER TWENTY

BEN

"What are these?" Martha asks as I hand them each a bracelet.

"They're gemstones," I say with a smile. "Those ones are for sexual vitality."

Norma snatches it out of Martha's hand and slips it on her wrist.

"Oh, you old goose, you don't need any more sexual energy," Martha says. "You know I'm dry as a rock and need all the help I can get."

My stomach rolls at the thought, and I shoot her a glare. "Martha, I don't need to know that."

She waves my comment away. "It's the truth. Vikki, look at these. What are these for? They're so pretty."

"I don't remember, just that they all had to do with sex."

"Can we have more than one?" Vikki asks, and I shrug. Ford, Cash, and I don't really need any more help with our sex life. They keep up with me just fine. I'm more than happy with how often I'm getting it. Just this morning, they took me again in the shower. One right after the other.

It hurts to sit, but I'm not complaining. I love being reminded that I'm theirs.

When I get home tonight, they're going to cook me dinner and then sit with me in the hot tub. I can't wait to get my ass eaten again while bent over the side.

"What are *these?*" a familiar voice croons. When I look up, I see Emery and Lex stride up to my desk. If I didn't know any better, I'd think the two of them were brothers. Maybe it's the tattoos and the wild look in both of their eyes, but they're eerily similar.

"Oh, I love these colors! They're like Skittles," Emery exclaims as he starts to dig through the bag uninvited. "What are these?"

He holds up a purple bracelet and tries it on, holding out his arm and examining it in the light.

"Are these up for grabs?" he asks, and I nod.

"Sure, we have more than enough for everyone."

Emery beams at me. "August is gonna think this is so sexy. I bet I can wear this around my penis like a necklace."

Vikki snorts, and Emery flushes. "I didn't mean to say that out loud, but now that I have... think it would work?"

"I think I'd advise against putting anything around your weiner," Lex says, and Emery rolls his eyes.

"God, but that's no fun."

Lex huffs. "What if you have to get it cut off? Your dick, I mean."

Emery considers that a moment and then nods. "Fine, no necklace for my weiner, but maybe my balls."

Norma chuckles as Emery takes two more bracelets before flinging his arms around Vikki and Martha.

"Okay, we're here to eat and get our nails done. I'm thinking a bright pink..." He wanders off with them, Lex waggling his fingers at me and trailing behind. Then I watch as Norma reaches into the bag I brought and stuffs a few more bracelets into her bra.

Welp, I don't want those anymore.

"Thanks, dearie. I'm already feeling the tingle," she says as she follows her friends down the hallway toward the dining hall. I watch them go and then sigh, putting the bag of remaining gemstones under the counter and getting back to work. Over the next few hours, I check in a few people and chat with some of the staff nurses before finding some downtime to text Ford and Cash.

Well, sext is more like it.

Our messages started out innocently enough, but then quickly turned hot. I can just see them both at work, sneakily messaging me. Maybe they're in the bathroom together, jacking each other off while I send them dirty thought after dirty thought.

I shift in my seat.

Fuck, that would be so hot.

I look down at my phone and see that they've both messaged me in the group chat.

FORD:

Show me your dick.

CASH:

He's at work. He can't.

ME:

I can go to the bathroom.

FORD:

Do it. I want to see. Then when you get home,
I'm gonna make you scream.

Home. That's what Ford's house feels like to me, much more than my garage apartment. And I know Cash feels the same way too. The two of them have worked together to remodel a lot of it, and Cash's rental is really just a place for him to sleep. He hasn't been back to his place much lately, most of his clothes are stuffed in a dresser in the guest room. Mine are there too, hanging in the closet.

It feels like we moved in together without discussing it. The thought of going back to my silent apartment and sliding into my empty bed just makes me anxious. I don't want to sleep alone ever again, not after I've had them both like this.

And while the sex is fantastic, it's not the only reason I want to be with them. For the first time in my life, I feel wholly taken care of, cherished. I love how they both listen to me, how they ask me about my day, how they seek to make my life easier. My dad was always so good, so conscientious about making sure I had what I needed. He did his best, but being a single parent, things inevitably slipped through the cracks, and I often ended up feeling lonely and ignored. But Ford and Cash are different. They see me in a way my dad never did, they know me better, on a deeper level. And they give me all the attention and affection I crave.

They care about me. We've never really talked about where this is going, but I know that this is more than sex for them too.

It has to be, right?

After work is finished early afternoon, I zip to class where I hang out with Tatum, filling him in on what's been going on with my life before finally heading back to Ford's. As soon as I walk through the front door, I'm greeted by the two of them. They're in the kitchen, working on dinner, but stop what they're doing as soon as the front door snicks shut and move toward me, pulling me in for long-drawn-out kisses, turning me on in the process.

"Guys," I pant as I attempt to not ruin dinner by distracting them with my dick.

"Just one more," Ford says as he pulls me in for a bruising kiss. His tongue slides into my mouth, and he bites on my lips, making me clutch on to him and moan.

Fuck, I could be kissed by them for a hundred years and it would never grow old.

When we finally pull away, I press my fingers against my lips and then shoo them both back to the kitchen. They only do as they're told because my stomach rumbles. Loudly.

"Gotta feed my boo," Ford says with a wink as I sit down at the kitchen table, watching them work. I *could* help, but I know they like to do this for me, so I kick my legs up on the chair opposite me and relax.

Ford hands me a glass and I glance down at the orangish drink. "What is this?"

"A drink that goes with dinner. I can't pronounce it, but it's tasty," Ford says, and I sip at it and then sigh.

"Yeah, you're right, that is good. So what are you guys making?" I ask when the aroma of basil and oregano hits my nostrils.

"A caprese salad, pasta with a Bolognese sauce, and tiramisu for dessert. We aren't making the dessert," Ford clarifies. "Just bought it from the store, but everything else is all us, baby."

"I can't wait," I say, feeling my heart flutter in my chest. This is so damn romantic. These guys. My guys.

"We have wine too," Cash says. "Had it delivered from a vineyard down south."

"Oh, you guys didn't have to do that, but I love it all the same."

"Yeah, well, you deserve it," Cash says with a wink before turning and getting back to work.

I sip at my drink and smile to myself. I could happily sit here all night just watching them. I'm in heaven. There can't be anything better than this.

It's only when the doorbell rings and my dad appears on the porch as Ford opens the front door that the dream world I've been living in suddenly implodes.

This isn't real life, this can't be my real life for so many reasons.

What the fuck was I thinking?

"Hey, D-Dad," I stutter when Ford takes a step back from the entryway and rejoins Cash in the kitchen, his cheeks flushed, his throat bobbing slightly at this unexpected guest. Our bubble-wrapped reality is starting to tear.

"Oh. Hey, Ben. Sorry... I was just swinging by on my way home to return Ford's power drill when I saw your car in the driveway. Is everything okay?" my dad says, setting the drill down awkwardly and then running a hand through his hair. He looks guilty, probably for party crashing, but the thing is, he has nothing to feel bad about. If anything, I'm the one who should be apologizing to him. For what I'm doing behind his back. For what we're all doing despite knowing what this could do to him.

"Oh, yeah, I just... Cash and Ford invited me over for dinner. A celebration for acing my midterm."

My dad's face falls slightly, and I suddenly feel like shit. I should have told him about my progress in school, he should have been the first one I told, but I didn't. I didn't even *think* about it.

"I'm glad to hear it," he says, eyeing me, and I nod, standing up and moving to grab some wine from the fridge.

"Want to stay for dinner?" I ask, not really wanting him to, but also wanting to repair any damage I've done. I know my dad's feelings are hurt. I can see it in the way he fiddles with the rings on his fingers, his eyes flicking from me to the floor and then back again.

By keeping secrets like this, I've hurt his heart.

Fuck. He's been hurt enough.

Jesus, I'm a terrible son.

And don't even get me started on whether or not he's figured out what I'm up to behind his back. He can't know though. He can't. I just can't bring myself to believe it. Because as much as I know I'm a terrible son, I can convince myself I'm not by pretending this isn't that bad.

But if I ever see the hurt on his face, the disappointment when he finds out what I've done, what we've done, I might not survive it.

"Yeah, I could eat."

I nod and pour him a glass, setting it next to my dad as he makes himself at home at the kitchen table.

"Where's Avery?" I ask, trying to distract him slightly. I don't want him to overthink this situation too much. It is kind of odd that I'm here. If he really did examine it too closely, he'd start to get suspicious.

"He's out with friends." My dad eyes me again and then shrugs. "He can do what he wants."

"Of course he can," I reply when Ford and Cash set the caprese salad on the table.

"Don't eat it all, you lug," Ford says, and my dad beams up at him.

"Fancy," my dad says, reaching out and snagging some bread, plopping some mozzarella and a tomato onto it. He shoves it in his mouth sloppily, chews, and swallows, and then sits back and sighs.

"It's been a hell of a long time since we all hung out. I've missed it."

"Me too, man," Ford says, and Cash nods.

"Life keeps getting in the way, and now that you have Avery as a roommate, you've been busy." The way Cash says that makes my cheeks heat. I don't want to think about my dad doing any of that. Nope. No siree.

My dad smirks and then loads up another piece of bread with cheese, shoving it in his mouth and then sipping his wine. "Maybe after dinner, we can all go for a ride."

Cash and Ford share a look, a minuscule one that only I notice.

"Yeah, we can do that," I say, and my dad smiles as he reaches out and grabs some more food off the plate. I join in and pretty soon it's polished off.

"Good thing we made some for us," Cash says as he pulls out another plate from the fridge. The two of them join us at the table, and once more, we polish the caprese salad off before moving to the main course. We chat about the shop and my classes until we're all stuffed full.

"How about a ride and then cake?" Cash offers, and we all agree, standing up and grabbing our jackets. My dad doesn't seem to notice how I disappear into the guest room to snatch one off a hanger, and thank god for that. I don't know how I could explain that one away.

We're already walking such a thin rope.

Such a thin fucking rope.

Within minutes, the motorcycles are brought outside, the low rumble echoing down the street as they turn them on. I have the urge to hop on the back with Cash or Ford, would love to do that, but I know I should spend this ride with my dad.

"You ready?" he asks as he pats my hand, and I hold on tight.

"Just like old times," I say, and my dad chuckles.

"Like old times."

I consider telling him, just blurting it all out, but the possible repercussions of it keep my mouth shut.

"Love you, Dad," I say and he pats my hand again.

We roar off into the distance.

———

After the ride, I end up back in my own apartment, feeling like I had to leave Ford's when my dad did. It wouldn't have made sense to him if I had said I was staying.

But now I'm all alone, and while I'm trying to behave normally—and not like a crazed maniac—I'm finding it incredibly difficult. I feel their absence palpably.

"You do not need them," I say as I force myself to watch a movie alone.

"You are a strong and independent man," I tell myself as I chew on my nails.

"You are not controlled by your dick," I say when I stand up halfway through the movie and head out to my car.

My cock is literally pointing the way.

"Just for a little bit longer," I whisper to myself as I drive back to Ford's place.

He makes me park in the garage this time just in case my dad decides to stop by again. I can hide in the closet if he makes an appearance—because me spending the night we couldn't explain away.

"I don't think he knows," Ford says reassuringly as he helps me out of my sweater before starting to strip me out of my pants, his warm hands eager as he leads me to the bedroom where Cash is. He's freshly showered, his back pressed up against the headboard, wearing only tight boxer briefs, showing off his muscular hairy thighs.

I crawl up against him and straddle his lap, kissing him feverishly. His big hands grab on to my waist, pulling me even closer as Ford moves in behind us. I can feel the brush of his cock against my back, and I sigh into Cash's mouth.

This. This is where I want to be every fucking night.

Being fucked.

And then held.

"We should tell your dad soon," Ford says as he kisses his way up my neck. My lips move away from Cash's, and I shake my head.

"No. He can't know."

The two of them freeze, their hands simultaneously tightening on me.

"But he needs to know, Ben" Cash says as he looks up at me. "This isn't just fucking for us."

Ford agrees, "It's not. Is that what this is for you?"

I shake my head and swallow, feeling my eyes sting. "No, but...do we have to label it? I just know that you both feel like home."

Their hands loosen on me, my answer seeming to satisfy them, but they don't continue what they started.

"We can be your home," Ford says as he slides away from me and flops down on the bed.

Cash eyes him and then moves me off his lap.

My heart is thumping in my chest, my cock still painfully hard. Are they really not going to get me off? Is this some kind of game?

Cash sees my expression and reaches out and pulls me into his chest. "We need to get some sleep."

I should revolt, should demand I be taken care of, but I don't. I just bite my tongue as Ford crowds me in from behind, his hand sliding across my bare stomach. Their touch makes my entire body clench with need.

But neither of them makes a move, and I don't want to be rejected, so I let it go.

I can try again tomorrow.

———

"So, how long has it been since you've gotten some," Tatum asks, leaning forward and poking at my flushed cheeks with his bright purple nails.

I'm embarrassed to admit it, but it's been almost four days of nada. Zip. Motherfucking zilch. Cash and Ford have done nothing but kiss me, bringing me close to begging for release before cutting me off.

I refuse to be the one to say anything, to show them how desperate I am for it just to be rejected. But god, it's driving me crazy.

I should communicate like an adult, but I'm not thinking clearly.

"You do look a bit crazed," Tatum says as he pulls out a bag of candy and shovels some into his mouth. "I mean, you have the sex drive of a hyena."

"Do they have notoriously high sex drives?" I ask, and Tatum shrugs.

"No clue, but it sounded funny."

I roll my eyes but continue to sit with my thoughts. Are they not interested in me anymore? Do they not want me? Was my dad showing up the reason they're behaving this way? Did it scare them? Are they second-guessing everything we've done? Will they end this?

Oh god, the thought of it makes my stomach churn. I've risked so much. Made so many decisions based on the two of them. They can't give me up now. Right? I can't be so disposable.

My mom makes her appearance in my head, but I shake her off, trying to keep myself centered.

She won't care what I do, she's not even around. She loved me no matter what. I know that.

But I'm slowly losing my mind. I hate behaving. I gave in and started being bad, and I love it now. There's no going back for me. I'm all in.

"If I were you," Tatum interrupts my spiraling thoughts. "I'd get some toys and show them what they're missing. Taunt them a little bit. Make *them* beg for once."

We say goodbye, and I ponder his suggestion as I make my way back to my place. I *do* have some good toys tucked away in my closet, for emergencies only.

Seems this is a full-blown crisis.

I could make national news at this point.

Call in the National Guard. I'm going in.

I'm shoving dildos into my bag when my dad appears in my doorway, making me nearly scream. God, what if he saw what I was packing? I'd never survive the embarrassment.

"Sheesh, Dad," I say, clutching my chest. "Why are you lurking?"

He grins and looks bashful. "Just saw your car and wanted to come say hello. You've been gone a lot."

I feel terrible for that, and yet I still kick that bag of toys farther into the closet. Those damn things are coming with me whether I want them to or not. I'm committed to it now. I have a plan of action.

"Yeah, I've been super busy."

"I was thinking we could grab breakfast tomorrow at that café we like," he suggests, and I nod.

"Of course. Just let me know when and I'll be there."

He beams and then taps the door jam. "Great, is it...is it cool if Avery joins us?"

I don't even hesitate. "Of course, Dad. I really like him."

His cheeks flush and his Adam's apple bobs. "Yeah, Ben. Me too."

He disappears a moment later, and I stare down at my bag of toys lying on the ground. A dust bunny hops on by, clinging to the tip of an exposed dildo. Well, fuck. I'll have to make sure nothing weird gets shoved up my hole later.

I bend down and gather everything up once more.

And as I do, my thoughts wander. Maybe I shouldn't go over there tonight. Maybe I should stay away, give them space. They don't seem interested in me right now anyways.

Maybe I'll call Tatum and spend time with him instead. He always has a way of distracting me so I don't slowly lose my mind.

I stare down at my phone, hoping that Ford and Cash will change my mind somehow, but they haven't messaged me.

Well, okay, they have messaged, but it's just generic conversation that they could write to anyone.

And I am not anyone.

I am Ben. Their Ben.

That has to mean something.

I huff, grabbing my stuff and rushing down to my crappy car, shoving everything into the trunk.

Yeah, fuck this. My mind is made up. I'm gonna go hang out with Tatum, and *if* I have time, I'll go to Ford's later.

Maybe.

I'll teach them a lesson.

Teach them not to ignore me.

And my ass.

I call Tatum, already on my way to his place, only to find out that he's actually somewhere else, but extends the invite all the same.

"Come hang with us, bro! This house is fucking killer!"

I end up driving across town, curious at what my friend's gotten up to when I pull up to a giant mansion with a scary-looking gate. Are those gargoyles? Is that a sniper rifle?

A camera creaks as it swivels above me, and a man with a suit appears out of a guard house. He looks stern and a bit like a hitman.

I bet he's packing more than that giant dick protruding from his slacks right now.

Bet he has a big one tucked in the back of his pants.

The thought makes my lips wobble.

"ID," he barks, and I pull it out of my wallet, feeling suddenly nervous. What if they search my trunk and find the dildos?

What will they think? That I'm a dildo delivery driver? That I'm here to deliver them to the owner of this house?

Who is the owner?

For fuck's sake.

The man's eyes roam over my face, and he hands me my ID before asking me to pop my trunk.

Well, fuck.

I consider backing up and escaping, but it's too damn late now. I end up doing what I'm asked, and when the man appears before me once more, he just nods.

He probably saw that bag of dildos and felt sorry for me and has now let me through the gates because he knows I'm a sad sack who isn't getting anything anymore. That I've had to resort to all sorts of toys to get myself off.

I'm only twenty-one, and I'm in dire need of help.

"Angel is waiting for you," he announces, and for a moment, I wonder who the fuck Angel is. Not that I ask him that. No, I just drive forward slowly, trying not to give myself away.

It's only when I park my car and see an angelic guy with curly blond hair standing on the front steps with Tatum by his side that I realize I've seen him before.

This is Anthony Costello's son. That man has two cars in the shop that are there to be refurbished. And every time he shows up to check in, I feel my butthole clench.

And not in a good way.

"Hi!" Angel says softly with a genuine smile and a blush to his cheeks. "I remember you. I'm Angel."

"Hi, yeah, I remember you too. I'm Ben."

"I know," he says and then Tatum slings an arm around Angel's shoulders and jostles him slightly. Angel peers up at Tatum and rolls his eyes, but Tatum ignores him, reaching out his other arm and forcing me to schlep over to him.

He pulls me into his side and kisses my temple with a loud *mwah*.

"Alright, you fuckers. Time to finally be friends so we can hang out together. You know, when Ben isn't getting his ass pounded."

Angel looks at Tatum and then shakes his head. "Tatum, really. You need to watch your mouth, I swear. My dad isn't going to let you visit if he thinks you're corrupting me."

"But corruption is so fun and your dad knows that full well."

I follow them up the exterior marble steps and into a lavish interior. Everything is white and gray and silver. Even the paint looks rich. I can't believe people live like this. How much money does this guy have?

I've heard whisperings that Anthony is in the mafia, but who the fuck is in the mafia these days? That's not a real thing. Right? Or maybe it's the mob. Jesus. Fuck.

"What's your dad do?" I ask, and Angel shrugs.

"I don't know. Something to do with shipping."

"Yeah, shipping drugs," Tatum snorts, his voice echoing off the pristine walls. I swear, my friend has no sense of self-preservation.

"Shush," Angel says with a laugh but it dies off when an imposing man appears on the stairs leading up to the second level. He's wearing a suit and tie, looking impeccable.

Anthony.

I recognize him from the shop, and even from a distance, I feel like I'm going to poop my pants.

He glowers down at Tatum who only waggles his fingers at him, completely unbothered by this man. "Hello, hottie."

Anthony's jaw ticks and Angel bites his lip to stifle a giggle, pulling the two of us forward quickly.

"God. You make him so mad," Angel says quietly. "I swear."

"It's too fun," Tatum says, his pink hair awry, his cheeks flushed as Angel pulls us down a long hallway and into some kind of conservatory. It's enormous with tropical plants covering every inch of the space. It's like a veritable Garden of Eden.

"God, this is so cool," I say, and Angel nods.

"My dad built it for me. He knows how much I love nature."

I mean, I would think someone could just go for a hike, but then again, Anthony doesn't seem like he lets Angel out of his sight.

"I'm telling you. You have to go on a camping trip with me and the guys," Tatum suggests.

Angel flushes and shakes his head. "My dad wouldn't let me. I'm really not supposed to leave the house without him or a bodyguard."

"Pfft. He's such a controlling boob. Maybe he'll come with us. He could share my tent."

Angel giggles again and then settles down on a lush chair, gesturing for us to sit too.

"No, he's not gay. Sorry to burst your bubble."

"Trust me. I can get anyone to turn."

I doubt that he'd be able to turn someone like Anthony, but who the fuck knows? Tatum has his ways.

"Well, good luck. And I hope you're both hungry. I'm having the cook bring us some snacks," he says and then turns toward me. "I hope that's okay. I know this can all be a little much."

"Oh, it's fine. It's just different. But different isn't bad," I pipe up, wanting to make sure he's comfortable. He seems like he's in need of friends. I can't imagine how lonely it must be for him to be trapped in this mansion all fucking day long. Although he has a jungle at his disposal and a cook.

"You're right. Different isn't bad," Angel says, his blue eyes flashing. "I heard all about your love for different things."

I eye Tatum, and he shrugs. Well, apparently my secrets aren't as safe with him as I thought, but really, who's Angel going to tell? The plants? Anthony?

I doubt he'd give a fuck.

"Yeah, well, it might all be over," I say with a shrug.

Tatum rolls his eyes, but Angel leans forward. "Why?" He looks so serious and so goddamn sweet that I spill the beans. The entirety of the can. Right out here in the open. It's a full on barbecue. I obviously can't be trusted. They should lock me away for safe-keeping.

Halfway through my blathering about my guilt and my mom and my insatiable horniness, Tatum wandered off, stating he needed to use the bathroom, but he's been gone now for at least thirty minutes. He's either taking the biggest shit in history or he's gotten lost.

"I think he's riling up my dad," Angel suggests, and I shift in my seat. Because isn't that dangerous? I mean, seriously, only Tatum would do something so stupid. "It's easy to do. Diablo does it all the time."

I've heard that name before, but I can't remember where. "Who's Diablo?"

"My twin brother," he says and then shakes his head. "Anyways, don't worry. My dad knows we're friends. He won't take him to the shed out back."

My face falls, and Angel sputters. "Really, he'd never do that. It was a poor joke. Oh god, this is why I don't have friends."

"No, no, you're fine," I lie and then reach out and pluck some more grapes from the charcuterie board the cook made us. The cucumber sandwiches he supplied are also delicious and don't get me started on the salami.

God, I miss salami. Specifically the human kind.

"I've never seen a human salami," Angel says, and my eyes widen at that.

"Excuse me?" I ask, not believing this—both the fact that I said any of that out loud and that Angel is a virgin. Well, I mean, I *can* believe it because look at who his dad is. But my god, he has to be at least twenty-something, and he's absolutely gorgeous. If he went to a club with me, he'd be propositioned immediately. I'd have to bat them all away.

"My dad's a bit overprotective."

I lean forward, fiddling with my cup. "Would your dad let you go out if you're with friends?"

"I don't know, but I sure would like to be fucked."

The way he says it, so honest and innocent makes me nearly choke. "Yeah, I mean, you're missing out, man."

He nods and sighs. "One day. One day, I'll take it in both ends at the same time. Like you."

I stare at him and lean back with a smile. "It is really fucking nice. Getting your brains fucked out of you."

He sighs, a dreamy look in his eyes. "I can't wait."

I pause and then lick my lips. "Have Tatum take you out, bring a bodyguard or whatever, but live your life."

Angel considers it for a minute. "I don't know. I'll have to weigh my options. I'd hate for my dad to find out who fucked me and then cut them to pieces."

The way those words settle over me makes a mortified laugh escape my lips. "Jesus."

"You're telling me. Even Jesus isn't safe here," he says softly and then smiles at me.

"Wanna go see something cool?" he asks, suddenly standing up.

"As long as it's not dead bodies, yeah, let's go."

CHAPTER TWENTY-ONE

FORD

Cash is about to blow a gasket, and not in a good way. Ben isn't answering his phone, and we have no clue where he is.

"Told you I wanted to put a tracker on his goddamn phone."

"Yeah, and I told you to go for it and then you said it was too insane. You literally contradicted yourself and talked your way out of it."

Cash folds his arms across his chest and glowers at me as I sip noisily on my grape soda. I mean, we both decided to calm down on the fucking because we knew that we needed to give Ben some time to figure out what he really wants out of this. We need him to be all in, to tell his father the truth, if this is going to continue. And honestly, Dean showing up scared us a bit. What if we'd been in the middle of bending him over the table? How could we have explained that away?

I don't fucking know, and now we're both trying to play it cool.

Much to my disappointment. I don't play anything cool.

"We both decided to chill and now he's out there probably getting it from someone else."

I roll my eyes. "He wouldn't do that. He's not like that."

"He's young and horny. We didn't give it to him, and now he's discarded us."

"Yeah, well, we will give it to him. We just wanted to cool it for a bit and give him some time," I say and then frown at Cash, who looks like he's about to explode.

"Yeah, we cooled it and gave him too much time, and now he's gone."

I sigh and then pull him into me, feeling him relax against my body the longer I hold him.

"Come on, let's...I don't know, let's fix up the sex shed while we wait for him to get here. We can plan all the things we want to do in it."

Cash snorts. "Jesus, I thought that was a joke when you called it that."

"Well, it was, but now I'm seriously considering the validity of having one. Plus, I think Ben would like to have one too. A nice little kinky room."

Cash considers it and then sighs. "Fine, yeah, let's go rip shit up. It will make me feel better."

And it does, for the both of us. We're knee-deep in sawdust, creating a table in the shed when Ben appears in the yard, looking plastered off his ass and slightly wobbly.

"What the hell?" Cash mutters as he moves toward him, pulling him into his arms. "How much did you drink?"

"I had an entire wine cellar full of wine. And it was good wine. Expensive," Ben slurs, wobbling slightly. "Also, I took an Uber here and the guy smelled like weed."

He giggles slightly, and I frown. I can almost feel Cash's entire body rumble with rage at this information.

"Where were you?"

"At a mob boss's house. He has sheds out back too. But he cuts people up... Angel told me."

"What mob boss?" I ask, thinking he's joking, but it's only when he utters the name Anthony that my blood runs cold.

"You're not to go there again," Cash says, picking him up and bringing him inside the house. I follow closely, watching as Ben wraps his legs around Cash's back and starts to lick his way up his neck.

"You guys are so filthy. I want you to fuck me, just like this."

"You're drunk," I say, and Ben stares at me, those pretty fucking eyes meeting mine.

"You don't want me sober, so might as well fuck me while I'm wasted."

Cash and I exchange a look, and I sigh. Yeah, we fucked this up. Didn't handle it the right way. At all.

But it's too late now. We have to deal with the consequences.

Cash throws him onto the bed, and Ben bounces, his legs spreading in the process.

"Is that why you went out?" Cash asks, and Ben just leans up, eyeing the two of us.

"Well, you weren't interested. Had to find a way to entertain myself."

The way he says it, so bratty, turns me the fuck on. I like this side of Ben. Talking back. Makes me want to do things to his ass that make him cry.

But Cash just looks like he wants to give Ben a lecture.

"Come on," I suggest. "Let's just get him off so he can sleep this off."

Ben nods as he starts stroking his cock through his pants.

"Yes, please. Get me off. I've missed you."

Cash's stern demeanor cracks a bit, and he sighs. He turns toward me and shakes his head.

"We can't. Not when he's like this."

I peer over at Ben who is pouting.

"We have to do something," I hiss, and Cash sighs.

"Fine. A shower and then we let him sober up. And if he can manage that, we can fuck him."

Ben stumbles out of bed, nearly falling on his ass as he runs to the bathroom. We follow along, stripping out of our clothes as we go.

"Hurry," he says as he tries to get out of his jeans, only ending up with his hand in the toilet instead.

He stares down at it and then looks up at us, his pants pulled down his thighs, his shirt riding up his torso.

He's never looked hotter.

"I really do need a shower now," he says and then stands up and attempts to shuck the rest of his clothes, but fails miserably. We have to help him, putting him gently in the shower and then crowding around him.

His hands slap against our skin as he drags his fingers across our chests, his head tilted back, his chest rising and falling as he struggles to breathe.

"It's been four days," he slurs. "Four. Days."

I meet Cash's eyes, and he nods, falling to his knees and taking Ben's cock into his mouth, making him moan loudly as I lower my mouth to his.

His hand grasps on to Cash's hair as the other threads through mine.

I kiss him deeply, my tongue slashing into his mouth until he's coming, his entire body shaking with the force of it. He slumps against me as Cash stands up, wiping his hand across the back of his mouth.

"I have dildos at the front door," Ben says, almost asleep. "Lots of dildos."

I eye Cash, and his lips twitch.

"Need to get them. Hide them."

"Hide them from who?" I ask, and Ben shrugs.

"From you. It's a surprise."

I chuckle at that as I pull him from the shower and we dry him off. Then we dress and walk to the bed, climbing under the covers, Ben sprawled out between us.

"When I sober up, your dicks better be in me," he says and then waggles a finger at me.

"Both of yours. I won't stand for this... sexual manipulation."

"We aren't talking about this while you're drunk," Cash says, and I see Ben open his mouth to shoot a retort, but I distract him instead. Two of my fingers slide into his mouth and he sucks on them, his eyes shutting in bliss.

He's probably imagining that this is a dick, my dick. Or Cash's.

Either way, it's made him happy.

I glance over at Cash and see his heated expression. He wants more and so do I. The past four days were torture, and the shower didn't help.

Our dicks are both hard and straining against our sweatpants, but neither of us are going to do anything about it until he wakes up sober.

And even then, he may not feel like it. He'll probably have a massive hangover.

Fucking Anthony.

"We need to have a serious talk about going to that man's house," Cash whispers, and I nod.

I couldn't lose Ben.

Couldn't lose Cash either.

The thought of anything happening to either of them makes my stomach churn. I've known Cash for ages but Ben has inserted himself into our lives seamlessly.

I'm already planning for the future.

It's silly, but my mind still goes there. Of weddings, and rings, and kids.

Fuck, I know I'm older, but I've always wanted kids. I think maybe I always wanted them with Cash, but now that Ben is here, I can't imagine raising them without the two of them by my side.

"Think Ben wants kids?" I blurt when I hear his soft snores.

Cash eyes me and then props his head up with his hand, his fingers sliding across Ben's stomach.

"He's young."

I nod and then eye my best friend, my lover. "Do you want kids?"

"Yeah. I do."

The finality of it, the assuredness.

"So do I," I whisper, looking down at the guy who's brought us all together. The lynchpin between the two of us.

"We have to tell Dean."

Ben seems to hear us even in his sleep because he whimpers. I slide closer to him and rest my hand against Ben's ass, a nice touch that nestles my hand right next to Cash's cock too.

Win. Win.

"We do, but we need Ben to be okay with it."

Cash nods, and then I meet his stare. "Let's just focus on getting you through your parents' anniversary tomorrow night and then we can work on Dean. We can do this. Together."

Cash nestles his face in Ben's neck.

"Yeah."

It's just a whisper, but I know that it holds weight.

We can.

We can do this.

The three of us.

————

"Come here," Cash hisses.

I blink my eyes open and notice that Ben is huddled under the blankets. He's snoring slightly and seems to be completely dead to the world. Alcohol will do that to a person.

Cash is standing above me, and he nods toward the door.

As nimbly as I can, I follow Cash out into the other room, adjusting my morning wood as I go.

"What is it?" I ask as I rub the sleep from my eyes.

Cash leans down and holds up a duffle bag. He sets it on the kitchen table with a clunk and then unzips it.

"Look."

I peer inside and find my lips turning up at the corners.

"He wasn't joking about the dildos."

"No, he wasn't."

"Why does he have so many?" I ask as I start to sift through them. It's an impressive collection, one that even I could envy. And it's not just dildos. It's all sorts of toys.

Seems Ben has always been a horny little fucker.

No wonder he needs two dicks to keep him satisfied. One just wouldn't do.

"I don't know, but what the fuck do we do with all these?"

He picks one up and jiggles it in front of his face. It's enormous and my cock twitches in my pants when I envision Ben sliding that up his butt.

"I mean, we use them on him," I say with a shrug, and Cash glowers at me.

"Is he not happy with our dicks?" he asks, and I roll my eyes, knowing that Cash is feeling insecure.

"No. He's happy with them. I guarantee it. He's probably just pissed at us for making him wait. For taking it slow. I mean, he barreled into our sex lives."

"He did. How did it happen for you?" Cash asks, setting the dildo down on the table with a thunk.

I feel suddenly nervous for some reason. Guess this is something we haven't discussed before.

"A couple months ago I drove him home. Dean was out and uh... well, he had been dropping all these hints at work. Flirting, you know," I rub the back of my neck. "And it just kind of happened. We sucked each other's dicks on his bed."

Cash stares at me for a minute. "Just like that?"

"Yeah, well, I mean, he invited me up. And I went. He'd been tempting me for weeks."

"Did you feel guilty after?" Cash asks, and I nod.

"Of course I did. He's Dean's son. But fuck, he's hot."

Cash nods and then says, "He sucked my cock after we'd both been drinking. I didn't even know I wanted him until he had me down his throat."

I run a hand through my hair and sigh. "Fuck, he's so irresistible."

"I know."

We shift on our feet, not quite sure what to do now, when we hear a rustling in the bedroom.

Ben appears in the hallway, his hair sideways, a crease down his forehead from the pillow.

His eyes slide from us to the bag on the table, and his cheeks flush.

"Oh shit."

"Yeah," I say, picking up the huge dildo and pointing it at him. "And we plan on using them too. Our cocks not good enough?"

I ask it in a teasing voice but he takes it much too seriously. He shakes his head.

"No. No, I just..."

He strides forward and grabs on to the duffle bag before turning around and disappearing back into the bedroom. Of course, we follow, crowding him in the bathroom as he brushes his teeth. The bag is at his feet, and I can't help but eye it.

"I feel like death," he murmurs, and Cash and I smirk as we move to scrub at our teeth as well.

"Maybe next time," Cash says, spitting out his toothpaste. "Don't go to a mobster's house and drink all his wine."

Ben flushes and then rinses out his mouth, moving to the shower and turning it on.

"I can do what I want," he says sassily as he strips out of his clothes.

He bends down, shifting through the bag and pulling out a suction cup dildo and a Fleshlight.

"You're not the boss of me. I don't need you."

We watch as he angrily sticks the dildo to the wall of the shower and then fumbles with the lube we left on the shelf.

"I think he's mad," I whisper to Cash, who just glowers at me.

"No shit." Then he turns to Ben and says roughly, "You have five minutes and then we're coming in."

He rolls his eyes as he slides his fingers up inside of him.

"I don't need five minutes."

He removes his fingers and then bends slightly and slides back onto the dildo with a gasp, his cock jumping. When he's firmly pressed against the wall, he slides the Fleshlight over his cock as he stares at us.

He's teasing us. I know it. And Cash is losing his patience.

"Fuck this," Cash says, but I stop him, grabbing on to his neck and holding him in place.

"Give him his time."

Cash rolls his eyes, pushing my arm off and moving toward the shower. Ben's movements falter when Cash enters, grabbing the cock sleeve and tossing it aside. His hand grabs on to Ben's chin and tilts his head slightly, crashing his mouth into his.

Ben moans into his mouth as Cash helps him fuck against the dildo, lifting him slightly and pegging him repeatedly.

I don't waste any more time watching. I strip and join them, kissing them both as Ben takes that silicone dick up his ass over and over until he's begging, his cock leaking.

"You're ours," Cash says as he wraps his arms around Ben and pulls him against his chest, dragging the dick out of him and replacing it with his own. Ben's head knocks against the wall as Cash fucks into him, my hand wrapped around my dick as I watch them fuck. The way Cash's hips move, the way his ass flexes with each forward thrust sets my entire body on fire.

It's all power and need. And he channels it all into Ben who is moaning loudly.

"Oh god! Oh fuck! Yes!"

Cash is grunting with the force of it, the power to restrain himself from emptying his entire load into Ben's ass.

No, he's drawing it out. A punishment of sorts.

And Ben is taking it so damn good.

"Yes. Ours. You're. Ours."

"Yours!" Ben cries out as Cash lifts him into his arms and turns toward me. I step forward just as Ben's back falls against my chest, his arms wrapping around my neck as Cash uses my body for leverage.

Ben is splayed out between us as Cash continues wrecking his ass. The slap of wet skin, the smell of sex, the sounds coming from Ben are all making the will to resist coming difficult.

Ben is jacking his dick frantically now, wanting to come, but I smack his hand away, wanting my turn with him when he's this wild. It's been a long four days.

"No you're coming untouched," I growl into Ben's ear and his eyes roll back into his head as his lips seek mine. I give him my mouth, licking into him over and over until Cash finally explodes.

The orgasm seems to go on forever, probably from the lack of sex since we both held out for the days we were denying Ben. As Cash gives one last thrust, I shift Ben in our arms, and it's my turn. His back is pressed against Cash, the same way he was pressed against me as I slide into him. Cash's cum eases the way in, and I am balls deep in seconds.

Ben groans as I tilt my hips up, rocking into him. Fuck, he's tight and hot. Always so goddamn ready for us.

"Untouched," I grunt as I work my dick in and out of him, wanting to see him explode before I find my own release.

He's moaning loudly, our names a chant on his lips. Cash is twisting his nipples, playing with his balls, teasing him with each touch until Ben is nearly crying in frustration. His cock is an angry purple, the tip leaking profusely as we continue to fuck him, kiss him, bring him so close to the edge only to slap his hand away when he seeks release.

"Please. Please. I'll be good," he groans, arching back and gasping as I hit his prostate.

I do it again and again until he's nearly screaming, his head thrown back, his cock spurting endlessly as I work him through his orgasm. And then I let myself go, exploding into his ass and filling him up.

"Get a plug," I pant as I lift Ben up and press him against the wall, my cock still inside of him.

Ben is languidly sucking on my neck as Cash returns with a plug. I pull out of him gently, and Cash works it inside of him. Ben sighs happily as he slides to his feet.

He's holding on to us tightly as we all wash, almost as if he can't bear to be parted from us. And when we finally exit and dry off, he looks sheepish.

"I lost my mind a bit back there," he says.

Cash pulls him into a slow kiss and then says, "That's fine. Just lose it with us."

He nods and then his eyes widen.

"Oh shit. Oh fuck," he suddenly rushes out to the other room and swears. "I need to go meet my dad for breakfast. I'm late."

We help him dress, my dick twitching in my pants when I see that the plug is still inside of him.

He doesn't have time to take it out though, and before we can say anything, he's out the door, zipping up his pants and brushing his hair back with his fingers.

"Well fuck." Cash folds his arms across his chest and sighs.

"Sex shed?" I ask, and Cash grumbles his agreement.

CHAPTER TWENTY-TWO

BEN

Well, I forgot to take the damn plug out, and it's making me squirm in my seat. I mean, realistically, I could take it out in the bathroom and dump it in the trash, but I do really like this plug.

I don't want to toss it.

So I leave it in. A firm reminder of who I belong to.

A firm reminder that I'm betraying my dad in the worst way.

We all are.

"Sorry I was late," I say as I stare at the menu before me in the small café across town. There's a smudge of ketchup on the side and when I lifted it from the table it stuck slightly, but they do have the best French toast.

I try not to look at the kitchen whenever I walk back to the bathroom—makes me slightly disgusted.

"I was just... I slept in."

It's a lie. I was busy getting fucked, but I can't say that.

"You okay?" my dad asks. "You feeling alright?"

I nod and peek up. I worry if I look up for too long, he'll see the guilt in my eyes. Or Avery will. He's very astute, and I'm afraid he may say something to my dad.

"Yeah, just tired and a little frazzled, but I'm glad I'm here."

"I am too."

I glance at Avery, seeing him in a pink top and matching lipstick. He looks so pretty in such a natural way. It's no wonder my dad is infatuated with him.

"You look really nice today, Avery."

"So do you."

He smirks at me, and I roll my eyes with a laugh. I look wrecked, but I did the best I could on such little notice. I'm pretty sure my hair is looking a little worse for wear and I think my shirt is on inside out.

But it's too late now.

I doubt my dad even notices anyways.

The waitress appears, bringing me a coffee and creamer, and we place our orders. As soon as she's gone, I force myself to look at my dad, the spoon swiveling around in my coffee mug, clinking softly against the ceramic as it goes.

"So, what are your plans today?" I ask, looking at both Avery and my dad. "Something wild and fun?"

I see the way my dad peeks over at Avery and how Avery's cheeks flush slightly. I'm almost certain they're messing around. Not that I want to think about them messing around, but still. I can see the way they look at each other. How much they seem to want one another. It's how I look at Cash and Ford. It's how they look at me.

I'm surprised no one's noticed.

"Yeah, Dean. We doing anything *wild?*" The way Avery teases my dad makes his cheeks flush under all that scruff.

"Yeah, you know me," he says, clearing his throat.

Fuck. He looks so gone. So fucking happy. My dad deserves someone who loves him. Someone to bring him out of his shell. Someone to help him live again. Someone to make him wild.

"I was going to take Avery to the farmer's market and then go for a ride. Is that wild enough for you?"

"Sounds about right," I say with a smile.

"What about you? What do you have going on today?" my dad asks.

I shift in my seat and bite my lip. Well, I was planning on going home after this and spending time with Cash and Ford. And then tonight we are going to Cash's parents' anniversary party. But I don't say any of that. I wish I could. But I just can't.

"Probably just studying with some friends."

My dad eyes me for a little too long, and I glance away, messing with the salt and pepper shakers. I touch a bit of something gooey on the side and quickly let go of them, fiddling with my napkin instead.

"Yeah, makes sense. It's your last semester. Fuck, where did the time go? Your mom would be so proud."

My chest clenches. "Yeah. I think she would be."

Avery reaches out and threads his fingers with my dad's, and I stare at their connected bodies for a little too long. It should be weird, but it's not. It's perfect, actually.

The two of them make sense.

Like the aligning of the stars.

Two people so different and yet so right for one another.

"So um… you guys together?" I ask softly, and Avery wets his lips, looking at my dad before responding.

"We're seeing where this goes," Dad says after a long pause.

Avery rolls his lips between his teeth, nudging my dad softly. "We're serious about one another. That's what he means to say."

My dad clears his throat, and Avery rolls his eyes. "He knows what he wants. He just doesn't want to admit it."

I roll my eyes a bit. "Dad, you can admit it. I don't mind. I'm really happy for you two."

It's silent for a long minute, and then my dad sighs. "Yeah. Okay. Avery's right. He's it for me, Ben. I… it took me a while to come to terms with it, but he's who I want."

I grin at him. "Good. I'm glad. You deserve it."

Avery smirks at my dad and says, "Told you so."

"Yeah, whatever. I know. You're usually right. It's a problem."

I watch as he leans over and places a kiss on Avery's temple and my heartbeat triples. For a second, I envision Ford and Cash here with me too. What would that look like, the two of them surrounding me, pressing kisses to my face as I sit across from my dad?

The thought is so overwhelming, I almost lose the ability to breathe.

My mind suddenly shifts to a day in the future, where I'm walked down the aisle, my dad at my side, Ford and Cash waiting for me at the end.

My mom's face flashes in my line of sight, and I feel my eyes well up with tears.

Fuck.

I swipe at them and take a long sip of my coffee. It burns my tongue, but distracts me enough from the sting in my throat and eyes.

"You okay?" my dad asks, and I nod, gulping roughly.

"Just... I had a thought. I'm fine."

He looks concerned, and I wave my hand around. "Just thought about Mom. You know..."

"Yeah," he says, and Avery puts his arm around Dean.

"It's fine. Just... thought about my wedding day."

The words blurt out before I can stop them and my dad stares at me hard.

"You thinking about getting married?"

I shake my head and then nod and then shake my head again. "One day. I'd like to."

"I'd like that too," my dad says and then swipes at his eyes. "But enough of this silly crying, tell me about the old ladies in the home. What have they been up to?"

I regale them with tales as the food comes and we dig in, my stomach slightly churning from all the lies I've been telling. Part of me just wants to lay everything out. My dad has always been so supportive of me, has been there for everything I've wanted to do. But now I'm doing his two best friends, and I worry it would ruin everything. They own a business together, have been friends since college.

I'm his son.

He doesn't need to know.

Not yet. Not ever.

I'm not sure how that will all work out in the end, but I can't think about it now.

No, I'm just focused on my French toast and eggs.

For the rest of breakfast we chat about everything and nothing, but I suddenly start to squirm when my dad asks me if I'm seeing anyone. It's a random question thrown in there between asking me what I plan on doing this summer and if I still like pumpkin pie. As soon as that question leaves his lips, I grow flustered and stuff my mouth full of food until I can't answer, and Avery, bless him, changes the subject, remarking on the very boring decor lining the walls.

When it's time to leave, I give my dad and Avery a hug and then scurry off, looking in my rearview mirror as I pull out of the parking lot. I see Avery touching my dad's face and speaking to him gently.

My dad looks over at my car with a strange expression, and I force my gaze forward.

I don't want to know what they're talking about. I just don't. Ignorance is bliss.

Ignorance is my friend.

It's probably not about me anyways. It's probably about their plans for later.

Instead of going to Ford's, I head back to my apartment, jogging up the stairs and into my bathroom. It's there that I pull the plug out, clean myself up, and change my clothes. I do need to get ready for tonight, but my suit is at Ford's house.

They're probably wondering when I'm coming back home, but I just toss my phone on the bed and flop down, staring at the wall.

The image that filtered through my mind earlier. The three of us at our wedding makes my eyes sting once more.

That can't ever happen right?

Impossible.

That's what this is.

I groan and dig my fists into my cheeks.

Goddamnit.

———

My mom was never buried. Having died so young, my dad did not have the funds for a lavish funeral. So, she was cremated and her ashes were spread out on the banks of a small river she and my dad used to frequent. Lavender bushes line the shore, and I sit by them, leaning back and listening to the rush of water. It's usually so hot here in California that oftentimes the river dries up, the bed visible beneath. But it's been a rainy season and the water is wild.

I don't come here that often. But sometimes I do—just to be close to her.

I don't subscribe to the belief that she communicates with me somehow, but I do wonder what she would say to me if she were here. What she would do. How she would be.

How different I'd be too.

I stare at the wet rocks and then turn my gaze up to the clouds and blue sky. The sun peeks out at me, and I feel my eyelids flutter closed.

"What the fuck do I do, Mom?"

I hear nothing but the rush of water and then a bird flutters near me. My eyes pop open and for a stupid second I think that it's a sign from above, until the damn thing poops on the rock next to me.

"For fuck's sake," I murmur with a small laugh. I knew my mom had a sense of humor, but that went a little too far.

"Ben?" a familiar voice says, and I look over my shoulder at Ford and Cash standing behind me. My heart gallops in my chest.

"Hey," I whisper. "How did you find me?"

Ford throws a thumb over at Cash. "Put a tracker on your phone."

I stare at Cash who just purses his lips and shrugs. "For the times you disappear. Like today."

I smile at them both, my lips a little wobbly. "That's really creepy, but kind of romantic. I want to track you both too."

They move toward me, pulling out their phones and telling me how to do it. I see the app they downloaded on my phone, and as much as I feel like I should revolt against the idea of them always knowing where I am, a part of me takes comfort in having them know.

I love that they cared enough to do this.

I stare down at the three small blue dots on the map, and I swallow roughly.

They came. For me.

They're on either side of me, their shoulders brushing mine, their legs pulled up to their chests, their strong, tattooed arms resting on their knees. I can see their hands, rings adorning each finger, blinking in the sun.

I want one of them, one from each of them—to wear. I want everyone to know they're mine.

"You talking to her?" Ford asks, interrupting my thoughts.

I nod. "I was and then a bird pooped on that rock over there."

Ford and Cash chuckle. "Maybe it was her, she always did have a weird sense of humor."

I swallow and then look intently at the rushing stream. "Do you think she'd be happy for us?"

They're silent.

"I think…" Cash begins. "If she knew how much…" he clears his throat, "…how much we care for you, I think she'd be thrilled."

"Yeah, over the fucking moon," Ford adds softly, and I lay my head on his shoulder, letting Cash hold my hand.

I don't know how to feel. Part of me still feels guilty for lying, for going behind my dad's back, but the other part of me…well, I was drawn to them both and them to me. All at the same time. It can't be wrong if it feels so right.

Right?

How did we come together so seamlessly, so easily? It had to be some kind of divine intervention.

Maybe my mom is out there somewhere, a bird pooping on rocks and trying to get her point across. Maybe she's trying to keep us together.

The thought makes me smile, and I sigh, my eyes closing as I bask in the sunlight peeking through the clouds.

It all still seems a little hopeless at worst and very complicated at best, but for some reason, when they're both here next to me, I feel like I can do anything.

My thumb fiddles with a ring on Cash's finger and I blurt, "I want one of your rings. One from each of you."

They both turn to look at me, and I feel my cheeks heating.

"We can do that."

They each take turns pulling one off and sliding them on my fingers. My hands are smaller than theirs, so I wear one on each thumb, deciding

I'm going to either get them fitted when I can afford it or wear them around a chain on my neck.

"They look good on you," Ford says, and I smile, leaning over to kiss him and then Cash.

And then we just sit for what feels like hours, talking, reminiscing, and lazily kissing one another until it's time to go.

For the first time today, I'm not worried about anything.

Because the two of them have me, and I have them. We can make it through anything. Together.

CHAPTER TWENTY-THREE

"God, this fucking tie," I grumble, pulling at it as the three of us make our way noisily up the long driveway to my parents' house. We borrowed the loudest car we could find, and Ford makes sure to rev it a few times, drawing several withering stares.

Good. Let them look.

I don't want to be here with these rich, stuck-up assholes. The only good thing is that Ford and Ben are both here.

Looking sexy as fuck in their tailored suits.

I want to rip their clothes off at the seams and bend them both over, taking turns in each of their asses.

That's the only thing getting me through the night—knowing what I get to do when I get home.

Ford parks the car and lets it idle, the rumble loud even inside.

"We don't have to show up. We can just fucking go," Ford says, and I run a hand down my face, feeling the scruff abrade my palm. I didn't bother shaving. I look as unkempt as I know I can get away with.

"Yeah, Cash. We can just go," Ben echoes, reaching out and grabbing on to my hand. He squeezes it gently, and I pull it up to my lips, kissing it softly. The rings Ford and I both gave him are on each thumb and fuck, they look good on him.

Real damn good.

"No, let's just go. Get it over with and then leave."

Ford shuts the engine off, but not before revving it one more time.

When he gets out, we follow, Ben's hands on both of our chests, straightening our jackets and ties.

"I'm so hard for you both right now," he whispers. "You look so goddamn hot dressed up like this."

I move closer to him, leaning down slightly and biting at his ear.

"Maybe we can sneak away and find a place to fuck. I know all the secret spots."

Ben shivers, and Ford and I both smirk, the two of us placing a hand on his back and walking us forward. The house I grew up in looms in front of us and with each step forward, I feel my chest tighten and my heart sink.

Fuck. I don't want to be here. But if I didn't show up, then I'd never hear the end of it. Ford always tells me to block them, but I'm not quite ready for that.

Although, at the moment, it seems like a pretty good idea.

Never having to do this again.

Fuck yes.

"Wow, this is a big place. How come I've never been here before?" Ben asks, and I clear my throat.

"Because your dad hates this place just as much as Ford does."

Ben nods, straightening his shoulders. "Then I hate it too. Let's raise hell."

I feel a flutter of something in my chest, as if the weight of this evening is slowly disintegrating, piece by piece.

People are filtering through the large wooden door as the three of us make our way up the marble steps. Columns stand on either side and large pots with colorful overflowing flowers hang from each one.

"Don't be deceived," I whisper to Ben. "This is all a fucking show."

Ben nods and clenches his jaw, almost like he's about to march into war as we finally enter the house. People are milling about, champagne flutes in their hands, all dressed formally. Women in floor-length dresses and men wearing suits like us.

Ford grabs drinks for each of us from a waiter as we make our way toward the backyard. Fairy lights line a large pergola, and I see the pool I'd spent hours in when I was a child. Over the years they've made small changes. A koi pond, an orchard with my mom's favorite fruits, a waterfall in the pool. But to me, it all feels the same.

A cold, loveless home that I couldn't wait to get away from.

"Oh, there're the assholes now," Ford murmurs and then points them out to Ben, who scowls.

I love that he's getting so protective that he almost seems to be growling, like a small lion cub.

I want to push him against the wall and fuck him, want to turn those growls of anger into something more. Into something feral. For me.

As soon as the three of us begin to approach, my parents turn to look at me. Almost as if they were waiting for me to arrive. Ford reaches out and cups the back of my neck, squeezing it gently.

"Let's give them hell," Ben says, moving forward. We follow beside him, like soldiers protecting the prince. Our prince. That's what he is.

I should have had him wear that crown he bought. It looked hot as fuck on him.

I'd fuck him like the royalty he is.

"Cash. Ford," my mom says, her voice clipped and snobby. God, I hate this. I nod at her, and Ford gives a small wave before her eyes settle on Ben.

"And who's this?"

"This is Ben," I say as Ford steps just a little closer to him.

I watch the way that my mother's eyes flick down to where our bodies connect, and my dad clears his throat. He's wearing a suit that looks fucking expensive, his graying beard trimmed neatly. I look so much like him, it's funny.

Too bad we couldn't be any more different.

"Still friends, I see?" he says to Ford, and Ford smirks.

"More than that now."

My dad's brows knit.

Before Ford can say anything else, someone appears to my right and takes over the conversation, both of my parents turning their gazes away from us. So I use that opportunity to lead them away. I've done my part. I'm here, I said hello. I'm sure they'll find me again. They haven't nearly met their quota of personal jabs for the night.

"I wanted to make out with you both in front of them," Ford says, and Ben lets out a choked laugh.

"Yeah, well, save it for later. I'm sure they'll do something we all hate and then we can fuck off."

"Sounds like a plan, now let's eat. The one good thing about these fucking snobs is they have good food."

He grabs on to Ben's hand and pulls him toward the tables of food located under a canopy. We grab plates and by the time we're seated, we have piles of food and drinks in front of us.

"God, this is delicious," Ben says, taking a dainty bite of some kind of crab cake.

"It is and it's good to see you eating normally," Ford replies, and Ben flushes.

"I don't eat much when I'm stressed. Just feel too sick, you know?"

"No, because when I'm stressed I eat like a fucking dog. But glad to know we aren't stressing you out," I say, and Ben smiles softly at me.

"No, you're not."

He takes another bite and the three of us just sit there, stuffing our faces, our ankles linked under the table. Music starts to play, and in the distance I see people start to come together to dance.

"You gonna show off your moves?" Ford asks me, and I roll my eyes.

"Fuck you."

Ben stares at me expectantly. "What do you mean? Like you know how to dance-dance?"

"My parents made me take lessons growing up."

Around a mouthful of food, Ford pipes up. "It's hot as fuck. He leads the way and makes my dick hard.

A woman passing stares at Ford who is talking a little too loudly, and I almost chastise him before remembering that I don't give a fuck. I hope he uses his megaphone voice—I hope he announces everything in great detail.

Anything to leave this shitshow earlier.

"Come on. Show me those moves," Ben says, standing up and holding out his hand to me.

I can't say no. Not to him. Moving toward him, I link my fingers with his and pull him toward the dance floor my parents set up near the koi pond. I hate all this pretentiousness, but I do give them props for making shit look nice.

"Show me," Ben says as he comes to a stop on the edge of the floor. I step toward him, placing his hand on my shoulder and mine on his waist before linking our fingers once more and stepping to my right.

Ben's cheeks are flushed as we move across the floor, drawing eyes to us. But I don't care. Let them think what they want. Let them draw their own conclusions. All I can see is him, all I can feel is him beneath my palms.

His eyes twinkle as they meet my intense gaze, and he bites his bottom lip.

"You're looking at me like you want to kiss me," he says softly.

"That's because I do."

His cheeks flush brighter, the brush of freckles across his nose darkening as that pretty pink spreads across his cheeks.

"You should."

I bring him closer to me, almost flush with my body as my hand snakes up his back and clutches the back of his neck. At this moment, I don't care who sees, don't care what kind of judgments they'll make.

Because all I care about in this moment is kissing Ben.

My mouth meets his, and he sighs into me, his hand sliding up into my hair as our tongues collide. I can feel the space between us dissipate as our bodies press together. We're so close I can feel his heart beating against my chest. I want him to be this close to me forever.

I want them both to stay with me until I draw my last breath.

As soon as the song ends, Ford taps Ben on the shoulder and takes his place. He's so much bigger than Ben, he just fits in my arms like he was always meant to be. I don't know how I didn't realize this for so long.

"We fit good together. Always have," Ford says, and I roll my lips between my teeth.

"Yeah, guess you're right."

"Always knew it, just had to bide my time. Just so happens that Ben is the one who got you to see reason."

We turn to look at Ben who is watching us with a hooded gaze. He's sipping on a glass of wine and looking so fucking delectable.

"How did we get so lucky?" Ford asks, and I shake my head.

"Don't know. Don't know if we deserve it. If we deserve him."

Ford presses his forehead to mine, and he grabs on to my shoulders with both hands.

"I deserve you both. And I plan on keeping the two of you until I die."

His lips slide across mine, and I feel my eyelashes flutter.

"We're drawing a crowd," I say.

Ford smirks. "Don't care."

"They're probably wondering what's going on."

"Let them think whatever they want."

Ford wet his lips and his eyes fall to my mouth once more and before I can even blink he's on me, his lips pressed to mine. I tilt my head and let him lick salaciously into me, our bodies pressed into each other's for a long-drawn-out minute before he finally pulls away. Ben appears at our side and he reaches up, pulling me down slightly so he can kiss me too. I moan into his mouth and am left chasing his lips as he pulls away and presses his mouth to Ford's.

Fuck, I want them. I love them.

I can't imagine my life without either of them in it.

If I could, I'd marry them both tomorrow. I know that sounds insane when several weeks ago, I wasn't sure if I was even into men, but now, after being with them the way I have, I can't imagine ever being parted from them.

When we finally all pull away, our chests heaving, our eyes glazed over with lust, I see a group of people watching us and whispering.

Well fuck.

"Think they know now," Ford says with a goofy grin.

I turn and see my parents watching us, a frown on both of their faces.

I'm sure it has less to do with me being with a man, and more to do with the fact that I took the attention off of them this evening. I caused a scene when I was raised to be not seen and not heard. I was just a trophy for them to parade around when they felt like it. The rest of the time, I went ignored. The only time I ever felt seen was when I was with Ford.

He always saw me.

And now I have Ben, who is pressing his hand against my chest, his head resting on my shoulder.

He's perfect.

The song changes and the three of us don't move away from each other. We just press in further, our bodies rocking back and forth, our heads pressed together.

"What do we do now?" Ben asks, and Ford and I both lean down and press a kiss to his cheeks at the same time.

"I say we go get another drink," Ford replies, and I nod.

"Could use another drink. And then let's go inside and see if we can find a place to make out. I just want to kiss you both for a while."

Without hesitation, we all start to move, making our way to the bar where we wait for our drinks to be made. We're still touching, as if we can't stand to be apart for too long.

I glance over and see Ford whispering something into Ben's ear, and I wonder what he's saying. But before I can ask, my mom finds us, her lips pinched in annoyance.

"Hello again," I say, moving my gaze from her to the bottles lining the shelves behind the makeshift bar.

"That's all you have to say? You could have told us you were bringing your boyfriends."

Ford smiles widely at her, like the shit he is. And I love him all the more for it.

"Didn't think to tell you," I say, and my mom narrows her eyes at me.

"Well, if you could keep those displays of affection away from guests, that would be much appreciated."

Ben's shoulders stiffen and he leans into me, nuzzling at my neck.

Her eyes move to him, but he ignores her, his hand resting on my chest, stoking the fire within me.

"So we shouldn't suck each other's fingers in public?" Ford asks, lifting my hand to his mouth and licking up my thumb.

My mom's cheeks flush and she huffs, moving away from us quickly.

Ford chuckles as he watches her leave, dropping my hand and grabbing the drink the bartender has set on the counter. He slurps half of it down in one gulp before nodding toward the house.

"Let's go show Ben your old room. Maybe give your mom a chance to cool her jets."

"Oh, yes, I'd love to see that," Ben whispers and is the first to move toward the house, his hand in mine as he nearly pulls me through the backdoor. People are still mingling inside, but they go unnoticed as we move up the stairs to the second floor.

"This house is so ridiculously big. I can't believe you grew up here," Ben says as we make our way down a long hallway. "Like this place even has wings."

"Yeah, it's dumb," I mutter, and Ford chuckles behind us.

"It's fucking cool. Too bad the people that own it are dicks."

Ford jogs ahead and then pushes open the door to my old room. Not that it resembles where I lived as a child. As soon as I moved out for college, my mom redid it. Now instead of posters lining the black walls and a rumpled queen bed in the corner of the room, the walls are a boring beige and the bed features a white comforter that's never been used.

"Erased you pretty fast," Ford says and then flops backward on the bed, sprawling out.

"Yeah. Don't much care now. It was a nice thought that maybe they'd forget about me altogether."

"Pfft, you're unforgettable," Ford says, and Ben crawls up next to Ford, kicking off his shoes and lying down next to him.

"Maybe we should break this room in," Ben suggests, and I stare at the two of them, looking delectable all dressed up and sprawled out for me. Probably shouldn't fuck them both with a party downstairs, but I still want to.

"You know we don't always have to fuck, Benjamin," Ford teases. "I'd be good with a heavy make-out session and just holding you."

Ben flushes and then swallows. "I know, but I kind of want it. I want you both. Always. But especially here, in his old room."

Ford eyes me, and I tilt my chin down slightly, giving Ford the permission he wants.

He leans over toward Ben, his hand sliding up his side as their tongues visibly tangle. Ben's hand drags down Ford's chest straight to his groin, squeezing Ford's hardening cock.

Wordlessly, I move to the door and lock it, wanting to desecrate this room, to leave evidence of our tryst, but not wanting anyone to watch.

God, I hope someone brought lube.

Just as I think it, Ford reaches into his jacket pocket and pulls out a handful of lube packets and some kind of sex toy.

"What is that?"

He waggles his eyebrows at me. "A vibrating cock sleeve."

I let out a loud laugh, and Ford just smirks at me as Ben kisses his way across his neck.

"Had to be prepared for you horny fuckers," he says as he yanks at his tie, loosening it. His hair is mussed and he looks so fucking hot that my dick aches. Ben's hips are grinding against Ford's leg, his breath coming out in short pants. The sight of the two of them makes heat flood my body. I feel like I'm combusting, like my entire body is going to ignite and explode.

The two of them continue to make out, their clothes slowly being peeled away until they're only clad in their boxers, their shirts opened, their ties hanging loosely around their necks. They looked good in the suits, but they look even better utterly wrecked.

I quickly shed my jacket, shoes, and pants, and stepping in front of Ben, I hook my fingers in his boxers, yanking them down and exposing him to me. His cock springs out and smacks against his abdomen. My hand wraps around his dick, stroking it as I rip open a lube packet with my teeth.

Ben sees it and starts groaning loudly as I liberally coat him in the liquid, letting it drip across his balls and down his crack.

"Yes, I need this. I need you," he says, a look of pure adoration moving across his face.

"You do," Ford says. "And we need you just as much."

He grabs on to Ben's face and forces him to look into his eyes. "This is more than just sex, Benjamin. This is your future, right here. The three of us. Together."

Ben swallows and nods, his eyes watering, and to be honest, Ford got me choked up as well.

I know what this is for me. I'm so fucking glad that they feel the same.

"Alright, now let's have some more fun," Ford says as he grabs on to the cock sleeve, sliding it over Ben's hard dick. He bucks up and groans, his hands reaching out for the two of us. He grabs on to both of our biceps and squeezes hard as Ford continues to dial up the vibrations.

"I can't!"

"You can," I say as a I slide my fingers into his ass.

He gasps at the sensation, a gasp that turns into a long, loud moan, his hands clenching the comforter beneath him.

"Oh my god!" He's whining now, his cock stiff and leaking as he ruts into the air.

"Turn him over," Ford grunts and we both flip Ben onto his hands and knees. His ass is out, his body trembling as Ford palms his cheeks. I waste no time, my fingers moving back into his hole, curling them inside of him and making him nearly sob in need.

"Love that sound," I say, and Ford nods, pouring lube over his straining dick.

"Gimme," he says, pulling my hand away from Ben and slotting his cock at Ben's hole.

"Breathe, baby," he says and then slams his hips forward.

Ben cries out, his eyes screwed shut, his entire body arching up as Ford takes him over and over. The sounds of their bodies meeting, the smell of sex in the air nearly throws me over the edge. It's too much. These two men who I'm crazy about, finding pleasure with each other...

They're mine. All fucking mine.

I reach out and cup Ford's ass, feeling it clench with each forward thrust.

"You gonna let me in that ass, Ford?" I ask, my hands sliding up his back, his shirt bunching around his neck. I take in that strong, muscular back, all those tattoos. Some I saw him get, some I've only seen in passing. But I remember all of them because they're a part of him.

My best friend. My lover.

"Stick that tattooed cock up me right this instant," Ford grunts. "Fucking tease."

"Yeah, that what you want?" I grumble back as I grab a lube packet. I pull out my dick, tucking the waistband of my briefs under my balls, slather it up and press it to his hole.

"Fuck me, Cash. Fuck me so Ben can feel you thrusting in me."

I push myself into him roughly, not even prepping him and Ford gasps, his body bent over Ben's.

"Jesus," Ford says, huffing. "I mean, take it slow, why don't you."

"You said *this instant* so I did what you asked."

"Fucker."

"Yeah, more like fuck you."

His muted laughs become moans as I kiss my way across his shoulders. He tastes like soap and sweat and something so uniquely Ford. So uniquely mine.

"Damn, you're tight."

I shift my hips, dragging my cock out of him only to slide it right back in. Ford's hole clenches around me and he gasps as my balls hit his.

Ben is looking behind him, wanting to see, wanting to experience what we're doing. He's such a fucking slut for it.

For us.

"Like what you see, Ben?" I ask and he nods, his eyes hooded, his entire face flushed.

"I do. I love watching you both fuck."

"Hm," I say as I pull my cock out of Ford once more and thrust it back in, hard. Ford groans, his hips slamming into Ben.

"Your ass is incredible."

"I fucking know it," Ford says as we all start to move in tandem. My hips hit Ford's ass as Ford slams into Ben, each of us taking turns with one another. Each of us finding a way to get what we need. It's fluid movements, almost as if we know what the other is going to do, as if we're becoming one moving machine. It makes the three of us slowly lose track of time. We're just souls finding pleasure in one another.

The party is still going on outside. I can hear the music filtering through the panes of the glass, but the sounds which are music to my ears are the groans and grunts from Ford and Ben, mingling with mine to create such a beautiful symphony.

"I'm gonna come!" Ben cries out, his body jerking, his cries filling the space.

Ford's body clenches, his movements frantic as he follows him over. The sight of it, the way the two of them moan their release has me filling Ford's hole with so much cum I know he's going to be dripping with my release the rest of the night.

"Oh fuck," Ben says, twitching on the bed, the cock sleeve still vibrating around his dick.

"Turn it off. Oh my god," he groans, his cheeks flushed, his hair standing straight up.

I pull out of Ford as he reaches for the controller, and the hum of the vibration dies down. Ben sighs, his entire body going lax as he breathes in deeply.

"I got cum all over your mom's bed."

"Good, leave it," Ford says, reaching down and using the corner of the comforter to wipe Ben's ass. It's ridiculous and so fucking rude, and yet I can't help but smile. It's perfect. The two of them leaving their mark in this room.

A laugh slips out of my mouth, and before I can stop myself I say, "God, I fucking love you."

The words linger between us and the two of them freeze and stare up at me. Ben is up on his elbows and Ford has his leg up on the bed, his hand still clutching the comforter.

"You for real?" Ford asks, and I shake my head, feeling my cheeks heat.

I run a hand down my face.

"He doesn't love us," Ben says, and Ford rolls his eyes, moving toward me and pulling me into a filthy kiss.

"He does, just doesn't want to admit it."

"I do. I want to admit it," I say when we finally pull apart. "But I didn't mean to say that right now."

"He loves us," Ben says with a growing smile.

Ford laughs and then kisses my cheek.

"He loves us."

I stare at the two of them, feeling my heart beating a little too fast.

"Well, do you two fuckers love me?" I ask and Ben's smile splits his face nearly in half.

"That's for you to find out," Ford says. "Seems we need to give some clues."

"I love clues," Ben says.

"We could do a scavenger hunt."

"I love scavenger hunts."

"Fuck you both," I grumble as I yank on my pants and start to fix my tie. They're both laughing at me, and I swear, I should be mad, but instead, I just feel light.

This night should have been so fucking awful, a strain on my mind, but they're here with me and everything just seems right.

"Let's get you both put back together," I say. "I worked up an appetite."

———

We eventually make our way back to the party. None of us are in a hurry, except our stomachs signaling to each of us that we want to eat.

It's amazing how much energy fucking takes out of a person. I should have a six-pack by now with all this thrusting.

"Really, what is wrong with you?" my mom asks when we finally make our way back to a table, our plates full once more. "You disappear and then show up looking..." She waves her hand around, looking flustered.

"Had some fun," I say and then plop down on my chair and shove a crab cake into my mouth. I don't know why I'm feeling defiant, but then again, I'm forty-two years old. I can do whatever the fuck I want. If she doesn't like how I'm behaving, she can just not invite me next time.

"Well, get up. I have someone I want you to meet. A very important client."

I don't know why the fuck she wants me to meet a client, but I get up anyways, wiping my mouth with the back of my hand. I hope I have something stuck in my teeth. I hope I'm an embarrassment.

I glance back at Ford and Ben, and Ford blows me a kiss causing me to smirk.

That fucker.

"So who's this important client?" I ask and my mom doesn't answer, just continues walking until I see my dad speaking with a man in a dark suit. As soon as he turns, my heart rate doubles.

"Anthony," I say, and my mom's eyebrows rise.

"You know each other?"

"Yeah. We do."

Anthony takes a sip of his drink and says, "I've had the pleasure of Cash working on a few of my cars."

"Ah," my dad says.

"Nice to see you here," I say, hoping like hell Anthony doesn't say anything to Dean if he sees Ben and Ford in attendance. Although they're on the other side of the yard, so I doubt he will. But then, Anthony seems to see everything. There's a reason he's so powerful and rich. A lesser, more distracted man wouldn't last this long in his position.

"I didn't know you were in business together," I tell my dad, who just nods.

"Have been for years."

I frown at that. I knew my father dealt in some shady business, but I didn't realize how far it went. Although, technically we're in business with Anthony, too. Dean seems perfectly fine with continuing to work on Anthony's pet projects.

I glance over my shoulder, hoping that Ford and Ben stay away, but of course neither of them do. They're walking hand in hand toward us, concern in both of their gazes. They're probably looking at my face and thinking something is wrong. Well, there is. Something is terribly wrong.

I should have never brought them here. Ben isn't ready for Dean to know about us and we need to be the ones to tell him. He can't find out from any of these fuckers. It will destroy him.

Hell.

I turn my gaze back to my parents, and I see Anthony's lips twitch. Oh, he so fucking knows.

"I see you have a secret hobby of your own," he says before adding, "Hobbies."

My gaze darkens, and Anthony takes a slow sip of his drink.

"If I'd known, I wouldn't have invited him," Anthony says slowly.

Looking more amused than anything. My heart stops as my gaze shifts up and I see Dean making his way through the crowd, his hair a mess, his hand fiddling with the tie around his neck. He looks like he got dressed in the car. I have no earthly idea why he'd be here. He's never come before. The only reason Ford has ever been to my parents' place is because he forced his way in.

Dean never cared to entertain my parents. He always stayed away.

But now he's here.

Anthony. That fuck.

Dean looks up and catches my gaze, looking almost relieved when he sees me and then his eyes swoop to Ford and Ben who are approaching. His gaze drops to their entwined hands and his brow furrows.

Fuck.

Fuck.

I watch as Ben and Ford quickly pull away, Ben's cheeks flushed, his chest moving up and down frantically. He looks pale and close to passing out.

Anthony holds his drink out and shrugs. "I invited him here to discuss an anniversary gift I've commissioned for your parents. If I'd known you'd be here, I would have just deferred to your expertise."

But I'm barely listening, the rush of blood in my ears a little too loud. Dean's gaze is moving between us, and I swallow roughly.

Perhaps we can still salvage it. Perhaps we can make this right.

Fuck, we should have told him sooner.

We shouldn't have kept this a secret.

We should have been more careful.

"I'll let you have your time," Anthony says and moves away, disappearing into the crowd, leaving my eyes to ping-pong between Ben, Ford, and Dean.

"What's going on?" my mom hisses, but no one answers her. She's just white noise at this point.

Dean cocks his head and then runs a hand down his face, stepping forward and placing his hand on his son's trembling shoulder. "This has gone on long enough. I think you have something to tell me."

Ben's eyes fall to the ground, and he swipes at his eyes before turning and bolting.

He's running, slipping slightly on the grass as his legs carry him farther and farther away.

Ford moves to go after him, but I grab on to him.

"Wait. Give him a second."

Ford looks at me, his eyes watery. "But he's upset. He doesn't need a second."

Dean sighs and then reaches out and tugs us a little farther away from my parents, who are glowering at us for making a scene.

That's all they've ever cared about. Appearances.

Dean shakes his head. "No. Let me. I'll go find him and talk to him."

"Shit, Dean," I murmur, and he shakes his head.

"We can all talk about this later. Just know that I know. I've known for a while. I might be an idiot sometimes, but I'm not that dumb."

I swallow loudly, and Ford curses under his breath.

"We didn't mean for it to happen..."

"I know."

"And it was all above board. We weren't creeping on him. It's still new," Ford interjects.

"I know that too."

"Hell, Cash wasn't even into guys until—"

His words are cut off, and he looks at me sheepishly. I run a hand over my forehead, feeling like I'm about to throw up. My entire body is vibrating with nerves. But despite it, I feel something unwavering move through me.

"We love him," I say after a moment of silence.

"We do," Ford adds. "We're fucking obsessed with him."

Dean sighs. "I figured. And I get it. I just... I need to find him to tell him that I love him. The three of you being together changes nothing. But I know my son. I know he's built this up in his head, and I don't want him to worry."

"How are you okay with this?"

"How could I not be? He's with the two best men I know."

Ford sniffles loudly and then pulls Dean into a hug. "Goddamn you. Making me cry."

Dean pats him roughly on the back and then slaps me on the shoulder.

"You always were a crybaby."

"Fuck you," Ford says with a laugh, and I pull Ford into me.

"Right. Well, it's been a few minutes. He's had time to cool off. I'll message you where we end up. You can come get him when I'm done reassuring him that this changes nothing."

Dean turns his back and walks away, leaving Ford and me to do nothing other than just stand and watch him disappear.

"That was unexpected," Ford says softly, and I let out a broken laugh.

"Yeah, but in the best way. Now Dean needs to hurry the fuck up so we can go get our guy."

CHAPTER TWENTY-FOUR

BEN

My lungs are screaming at me, reminding me for a second that I need to do more cardio or else I may die trying to escape the disappointed look on my father's face. I'm gonna be running for years over this.

I may keel over dead sooner rather than later.

Could I run all the way to the city without stopping?

I may attempt it.

Because he knows. He saw and he knows.

My eyes are stinging, and it's when I skid into the driveway that I let the first tear fall.

Fuck, I've ruined everything. Hands on my knees, I bend over to catch my breath. But it's fucking hard to inhale when you're in the middle of an emotional breakdown.

How am I ever going to face him again?

I can't.

I'm going to have to move.

To Maine.

An island in Maine. With no way to get there except a boat.

"Seems you need an escape," a deep voice says behind me, and I turn and see Anthony Costello staring at me, his hands in his sleek suit pockets, his head cocked slightly. "I happen to have a ride."

For the first time since meeting him, the thought of getting into a car with this man doesn't terrify me. Maybe it's because I'm more afraid of seeing my dad again.

"Can you drive me to Maine?"

His lips twitch. "How about we just get out of here and then make plans."

"Yeah, okay. I can do that," I say and Anthony nods, walking forward, and I follow him to a sleek black car. I've never even heard of this one. Probably cost a million dollars.

It beeps and he opens the door for me.

I don't even hesitate, just slide inside and let him close it behind me. I take in the rich interior through swimming eyes.

Expensive leather, the smell of cigars, not a speck of dust or dirt anywhere.

"Ready?" Anthony asks as he starts up the car and pulls out of the driveway.

"Why are you helping me?" I ask.

Anthony is silent for a moment and then says lowly, "I have two sons. You remind me of them both. Sweet like Angel and yet devious like Diablo."

I shift in my seat and swipe at my eyes.

"I didn't mean to be devious. I've never done anything like this before, but I liked it... I liked them. So much."

Anthony races down the road, one hand on the wheel, the other tapping a rhythm on the console.

"You speak in the past tense. Liked?"

"It's over. It's over now that my dad knows."

Anthony's hand stops moving. "Coming from a man who's lived longer than you, it's never over until they're dead."

I let out a huff. "Jesus."

His fingers start tapping out a different beat, and I eye him.

"You're not going to kill me, are you?"

"No. Because if I did, that little friend of yours would never leave me alone."

Another laugh huffs of out me, and I swipe at my eyes again. "Yeah, Tatum is relentless."

Anthony doesn't say another word, just continues driving me to God knows where. Maine, hopefully.

"Where would you like me to take you?" Anthony asks. "Besides Maine?"

"Can I go to your place?" I ask, suddenly realizing that if I go anywhere else, they'll find me.

"Of course. Angel will be happy to see you again. He's been talking about you."

I nod and then turn my gaze out the window, watching as the trees swish past, just a blur of grays and blacks now that the sun has set. A bit like my mind at the moment, just a blur, just a fucking mess.

I don't want to lose my dad over this. He's more important than...

The thought makes me inhale sharply. I love my dad, but I'm in love with Cash and Ford. I love them, and I don't want to give them up.

There's no way my dad will be okay with this. The confusion and disappointment I saw on his face makes my heart crack a little more. If I keep this up, I'll be heartless.

When we finally turn into his long driveway and park, Anthony turns toward me.

"You're welcome to go anywhere in the house, but please avoid the sheds outside."

"Why?"

"I have...business in there that you would not want to see."

I nod quickly, getting out of his car and following him up the stairs to the house. Angel is waiting outside, almost as if he was expecting me. His hair is pulled back into a small ponytail and his blue eyes light up when they land on mine.

"Hi again," he says, pulling me into a hug. He smells like honey and sunshine. Just pure goodness. No wonder Anthony wants to protect him.

"My dad said you're sad. I know just what you need."

I don't even try and fight it, just let him lead the way.

————

"You feel better?" Angel asks as we sit in an actual movie theater in the basement. I didn't even know it was possible to have something like this in a house, but then again, I'm sure whatever Angel wants, he gets.

"I mean, I still feel like shit, but this has distracted me, yeah."

For the past hour, I've sat with Angel, a romantic comedy playing on the screen in front of us. I watched some of it, in between bouts of intense sobbing.

My phone was blowing up, so I turned it off.

I just need some time. I can't face them all yet, knowing I ruined their friendship. Knowing I broke my dad's heart and his trust by lying to him.

A beep turns my gaze to Angel's phone.

"Tatum's calling."

I let my head fall back against the plush seat and say, "Go ahead and answer. He won't stop until he gets what he wants."

Angel puts him on speaker, and I hear my best friend say, "Yo, you have him, right? Because those three guys are going crazy. I mean, not that I'm complaining. It's like super-hot. They're all grumbly and disheveled. And they're wearing suits. Like how much can a gay boy handle?"

Angel laughs softly. "Yeah. He's here."

"Thank fuck. Yo, hotties. Ben's with my friend. I'll show you the way."

"We don't need you to—" I hear Cash say, but then the phone call ends.

I stare at Angel. "I guess I have to face it, don't I?"

"Sadly, yeah."

Angel sits up and reaches over and fiddles with my hair.

"You look like a hot mess though. Let's fix you up before they get here. You need to go out with dignity. At least that's what my dad tells me."

I let him lead me upstairs, passing a few guards milling around. I avoid eye contact with all of them. I don't want them to see me as a threat and accidentally shoot me.

But we make it safely up to the bathroom, and Angel proceeds to fuss over me until I look presentable. Or at least as presentable as I can be with my red-rimmed eyes and puffy nose. I am not a pretty crier.

Suddenly, Angel freezes and then smiles at me. I hear shouting and a crash downstairs, and I sit up straight, my heart thumping in my chest.

"Oh, it's like a real-life movie. They're here to get you, babe."

I shake my head and run a trembling hand down my throat.

"I don't want to."

"You have to," Angel says softly as we make our way down the hallway to the stairs. I slow my pace, dragging this out. Not wanting to face what I've done, what I've become.

"We just want to see him," Cash says, his voice growing angry. Oh god, I hope that Anthony doesn't have one of his men shoot him.

"He's safe. When he wants to see you, you'll be allowed to," Anthony responds, his voice made of steel.

"Oh god, that's hot. Getting me all bothered," Tatum groans as I make my way to the top of the stairs.

"No. I'm... I'm here," I manage to say as I make my way toward them.

My dad meets my stare but my gaze is pulled toward Cash and Ford who are rushing up the stairs, pulling me into their arms. I am crushed between them, the feel of them, the scent of their musk making my eyes break out in tears once more.

God, I'm never going to get over this if I have to give them up.

"You never fucking run from us again," Cash grumbles.

"Never again," Ford adds, and I swallow roughly.

"Okay," I say because I know that there probably won't be a next time.

With a strength I don't really feel, I turn toward my dad who is waiting at the bottom of the stairs. Anthony is off to the side next to Tatum, who is standing on his tiptoes and whispering something in his ear. I see Anthony's fist clenching near his side before he grabs on to Tatum's neck and walks him backward into the hallway, Tatum smirking the whole way.

Before I can think too hard about what that means, I'm in front of my dad. His lips are slightly wobbly and his eyes look a bit panicked. Fuck. I did this. I made him afraid.

"I'm so sorry," I whisper, feeling my cheeks heat.

My dad watches me intently and then sighs, pulling me into a hug. "Shit, Ben. You don't ever need to run from me. You can always tell me things. Anything. I'll always listen."

The sincerity in his voice, the way he's squeezing me to his strong chest makes sobs wrack my body. All the shame, the guilt exploding out of my eyes and onto his shoulder. I'm drenching him with my tears.

"I'm so fucking sorry," I choke out. "I should have done better...I know you're so disappointed in me."

"No. No."

I can't hear him though and continue blubbering. "Mom would be so ashamed. Please don't hate me. Please don't hate Cash and Ford. It's not their fault..."

My words are incoherent, but being around for his fair share of my breakdowns, my dad just squeezes me tighter.

"No. No, Benjamin. Don't be sorry. Don't be ashamed for falling in love with two incredible men."

I freeze and pull back, swiping at my running nose and eyes.

"What?"

"You fell in love with two men who I love like brothers. How could I be upset with you for that? I've had some time to think about it and I'm happy for you three."

Those words make me sob even harder, my entire body shaking as I let him pull me into him again.

"Can I speak with my son privately," my dad says. "Please. Just a minute."

Ford and Cash seem reluctant to let me go, but eventually let my dad lead me into a secluded hallway. We stare at each other awkwardly for a minute, and then I swipe at my eyes, asking with a shaky voice, "How long have you known?"

"I had suspicions for weeks. But it was solidified when I showed up at Ford's and you were there."

I huff a laugh and groan. "Fuck. I'm sorry. I didn't mean to lie to you, I just couldn't..."

My dad rests his hands on my shoulders and shakes his head. "It's okay. As long as you're happy..."

I nod vigorously. "I am. I have been."

"Good. Then, I'm glad."

We just stare at each other and my dad pats my shoulders, squeezing them gently.

"I'll always be your dad. But I know as your partners, that Cash and Ford will be the ones you usually go to, but please know you can always come to me. And now that you know I know, can we do things together again?"

I swallow and nod.

"I'd love that."

He grins. "Now listen, when you ran, Cash and Ford almost died. They're worried about you. You should go to them. Reassure them that everything is going to be alright."

"Will it, Dad?"

He nods and then presses a kiss to my forehead. "I guarantee it will. They just want you to be happy, and that's enough for me."

"How did you get to be so awesome?" I ask and my dad looks smug.

"I've always been awesome."

I let out a laugh and then grow serious when he adds, "And it's also Avery. I think, well, I've changed a lot about the way I think since him."

I nod and then pull him into a quick hug before moving back out to the foyer. Cash and Ford are standing there, shoulder to shoulder, their eyes narrowed, worry lining their faces as I approach.

"Welp, I think I'll leave you three to it." My dad grabs his keys out of his pocket, jangles them and then disappears out the front door.

Ford and Cash are staring at me, looking angry and relieved as I shift before them, feeling like a child in trouble.

"Should we go home?" I ask.

"Yeah. And then we're gonna talk."

———

They're mad. I can tell. And yet the relief I'm feeling that my dad doesn't hate me has made me less upset. I mean, I don't want them mad at me either, but the intense relief has me slightly giddy.

And nauseous.

I stare at their glowering faces. They're so handsome, so perfect in every way. I don't want them to be upset with me right now. I want them to kiss me, to hold me, to tell me that my freak out didn't ruin anything.

That I'm still theirs.

Can you imagine if after all of this, they break up with me over how stupid I was?

God, I'd fight them for another chance.

I'd have to prove that I'm worth it.

The car shuts off and Ford and Cash get out without a backward glance, and I scamper after them, trying like hell to keep it together.

I want to blurt it all out, to beg them for forgiveness, but I don't think now is the time. They're both so quiet, so stoic. I thought they were relieved when they ran up the stairs to hug me at Anthony's house, but now they're cold and distant.

Did we go through all of that just to end it here?

Please tell me that it's not over.

I follow them back to the bedroom where I watch them strip off their clothes, tossing their suits onto the ground and climbing in bed.

It's like an out-of-body experience. I'm watching them move about their life without me.

Maybe I should leave.

"Don't even think about it," Cash grumbles and then points to the spot between them. "Get undressed and get your ass over here."

"Are you sure?"

Ford snorts. "We're fucking sure, Benjamin. Get your hot ass over here before I make you."

I don't even hesitate, just do as they say, crawling between them in only my boxers and nestling between their two big bodies with a sigh. Their hands instantly land on me, stroking, touching, soothing. In seconds, I already feel my heart lighten.

They wouldn't touch me like this if it was over.

It's not over.

"Are you mad at me?" I ask after gathering the courage.

Cash huffs. "I'm pissed."

I feel my eyes sting and swallow loudly just as Ford jumps in. "What he means to say, is we're both upset you ran away, but we're glad you're here now."

I blink up at him and nod. "I am too. I just... I panicked when I saw my dad. I thought he'd hate me forever."

"He could never," Ford says. "He'd never hate you, baby."

I blink at that, trying not to cry. I don't want to start that again. My eyes already hurt from earlier. They need a break.

Cash shifts behind me, his groin connecting with my ass. "But we have things we need to discuss. You went with Anthony."

My throat clicks. "I didn't know what else to do at the time. I wasn't thinking rationally. And he offered."

"I don't like you going over there. He's dangerous," Cash says, his hand tightening on me. "He's a bad guy."

"I know, but I really like Angel. He can't be that bad when he's made such a beautiful, kind human."

Ford and Cash seem to silently communicate because Cash's hand softens against me and he nuzzles his face into my neck, his scruff tickling my skin.

"Fine. Just don't run from us again. We were worried."

"So fucking worried," Ford chimes in and then presses a kiss to my forehead.

"Next time, you stay and you tell us what you're thinking. We will communicate. Like adults."

"Yeah. I can do that."

Ford runs a hand across my cheek, and I meet his stare. "But now things are good, yeah? Your dad knows and he approves, so we can stop hiding. We can stop sneaking around and even do shit like family barbecues."

"I'd like that."

"We can basically get married now," Ford says and my heart jumps in my chest.

"Oh," I gasp as I pull Ford even closer to me. His chest presses to mine and my head rests against his shoulder. The feeling of both their bodies pressed up against mine is slowly lulling my tired eyes to sleep.

"I could marry you both. If you'd want me."

"He says that like he's unsure," Ford scoffs, and Cash chuckles.

"We'll prove it to him. He'll see."

I reach out and rest my hands on them, bringing them even closer to me.

"I love you both. So much," I say, and I hear them hold their breath before each of them repeat it back to me.

"*I love you, too.*"

———

I wake up with a need inside of me. The dream I just had, where I was walking down an aisle toward Cash and Ford, has left me almost panting with the need to have them both. I want them both at the same time. Inside of me. I want to feel complete, like the entirety of me begins and ends with them both.

It's almost symbolic.

But today's a busy day. I have work and then class.

But after.

After I get home, I'm going to take them both. I'm going to have them spill inside of me, marking me as theirs.

All day I'm nervous, planning, plotting. I worry Cash won't go through with it, worried that he'll hurt me. Worry that Ford will go along with what Cash says. What if they reject me?

I'll be crushed.

Tatum sees through me almost instantly, teasing me about it relentlessly.

"You're gonna do it, huh? Gonna convince them to give you a nice double P?"

I roll my eyes and then narrow them. "Serious question though, have you ever done that?"

Tatum sighs. "Nope, haven't been so lucky. So I want all the details."

I lean back in my chair in the school cafeteria, fiddling with my drink as I watch Tatum destroy a sub.

"You have lettuce on your chin," I say when he comes up for air.

He waggles his eyebrows at me. "It's called an accessory."

A laugh bursts out of me as he swipes it off his chin and then slurps it into his mouth.

"God, you're the nastiest eater."

"Got a big mouth, can put lots of things in it."

Another laugh bursts out of me, and when it finally dies down, I lean forward, suddenly so curious.

"What happened with you and Anthony the other night?" I ask, and Tatum shrugs.

"Nothing. I wish, but that man is so fucking straight. I just like to annoy him. Makes my dick hard."

I smile at that and he grins goofily. "He really hates me though. He said he was gonna cut my tongue out."

"Jesus."

"It was after I licked him."

My eyes widen, and he grins at me. "I like to think he secretly loved it."

I doubt that, but then realize that Tatum might behave like a barbarian, but he knows what he's doing. I don't think Anthony would hurt a friend of Angel's.

But what the fuck do I know?

"Be careful, Tatum. Don't make him so angry that he actually follows through with those threats."

"Pfft, I will. Don't worry, but get this. I'm going over tonight, gonna wear something really revealing. Gonna make him really pissed."

"Why would he be pissed?"

He shrugs again. "Don't know, but when I told him what I was gonna wear, he got all quiet. Did that hot jaw-clenching thing. God, it's fun to get him all riled up."

Well, I think it's a bad idea to taunt someone like that. But telling Tatum not to do something will only make him more determined. So I don't say anything, just turn my mind to other things, like how it will feel to have both Cash and Ford stretching me wide open later.

After watching Tatum eat the rest of his sandwich and then gorge himself on a bagel, we sit through a long lecture that seems to never end. When I finally make it back to Ford's place, my heart is nearly galloping in anticipation of what's to come.

The two of them are out back, their bodies sweaty and dirty from working on a project. They're always working like this. At the shop, at home. No wonder their bodies are amazing.

Fuck, they're so hot.

My cock instantly perks up.

Well, that's a lie. My cock has been perked up all day, just waiting. Now it positively aches.

"There he is," Ford says, and I roll my lips between my teeth as I adjust my dick.

Cash's eyes swivel down to it, but he doesn't comment on it.

"What have you been working on?" I ask, and Cash and Ford look at each other from their seats. Their strong legs are spread out, and I wet my lips. I want to grind against them, want to come across their pants.

"We're working on a little something for you," Ford says and my cheeks heat as he reaches over and pulls me onto his lap. His hand sneaks under my shirt and rubs against the skin there, making my already overeager body shiver with need.

"It started off as a joke, but the more we got to know you, the more we thought it would suit you," Ford continues on, pretending to be oblivious to my obvious needy state.

I glance at Cash, and he smiles softly at me.

"What is it?" I ask as I lean back, arching my hips up in the hopes that Ford's hand slips down to my waiting cock. Not that he gives that to me.

Fucking tease.

"A sex shed," Cash replies, and I freeze.

"What?"

"You heard us. A sex shed. We're gonna put all sorts of fun stuff in there. Gonna make you scream," Ford says with a laugh. "Cash has already been researching some fun furniture. There's some freaky shit out there, Benjamin."

I'm panting now, not sure what the hell they're talking about, but whatever they have planned, I'm game. I'm ready for any of it. Freaky furniture and all.

"It's not done yet, but when it is, you'll be the first to know."

I squirm on Ford's lap and then groan when his finger slides across my waist. He's teasing me, the two of them are, telling me about sex sheds and kinky furniture all while not touching my dick.

"Stop teasing me," I murmur. "You're both cock teases."

Cash lets out a low chuckle. "Seems you deserve it."

My head rolls back, and I arch my hips up once more. "For what? What did I do now?"

"Cash is still grumpy about yesterday."

Oh god, I think as I slide off Ford's lap and crawl to Cash. I settle between his legs and paw at his jeans.

He stares down at me and touches my face gently.

"So fucking pretty," he says lowly.

I nearly purr at the compliment. "I'll stay here on my knees, sucking your cock until your mood improves. I'll be such a good boy."

His hand slides through my hair and tightens, pulling my face down against his crotch. I rub my cheek against his hardening cock, my own leaking in my jeans.

Fuck. I want them. Need them. Yesterday I thought it would all come crashing to an end, and yet here I am, with the two of them, talking about the future.

Our future.

"I want you both," I groan as I start to work Cash's pants open. "I want you both in me, together. Tonight."

Cash stops moving, his hand tightening in my hair. I know he's thinking about it, about me taking the two of them.

I know what he's about to say, that he's going to turn me down, so I shut him up by pulling his cock out and stuffing it down my throat. He grunts, his hips arching up as he tugs his pants down a little lower, letting me have better access to his dick and balls.

I slurp at him, my tongue snaking up underneath his dick, following the vein there before sucking on his cockhead.

He's lost the ability to speak, which is fine with me. I don't want him to think too hard about double penetration. I want him to just do it.

I dip my head once more and swallow around him before bobbing my head, loving that Ford is watching us. I groan around his length, my hand moving to unbutton my pants and slide inside, jerking my aching dick.

"Look at him, so fucking needy," Cash groans. "Can't keep his own hand off his dick."

He pushes me down on his length, forcing me to hold my breath. My eyes water, my face turning red as he holds me there before pulling me off of him and staring at my mouth.

"Good boy."

"Fuck, yeah he is. It's my turn," Ford says.

I take a lungful of air and crawl to Ford, not wasting any time. I take his dick into my mouth, hollowing out my cheeks and sucking him into my throat, gagging slightly on his length before pulling off and taking him all over again. Ford is just as rough with me, making me choke and gasp, but I love it. Love being used by the two of them.

Back and forth I go between them, like an animal, crawling on all fours and just sucking them off, bringing them close to the edge only to move to the other to do the same thing.

We edge ourselves into oblivion for what seems like hours until Cash finally stands and picks me up without a word, settling me in his arms and striding into the house. His pants are hanging loosely around his hips, and I palm his ass, loving the feel of it. My hooded, watery eyes flick up to see Ford following us, holding his jeans up around his waist as we move into the bedroom.

I'm dumped onto the bed and before I even come to a rest, they're undressing me, unwrapping me like a present before they discard all of their own clothes. They look so good, sweaty and flushed. They're going to utterly wreck me. They're going to turn me inside out and make me scream.

I grab on to my dick, holding it tightly so I don't burst before they're inside of me. I don't want to ruin it. Not when I've been waiting all this time.

"I want you both. In me. Now."

Cash is so far gone that he doesn't even hesitate, just grabs the lube and pushes my legs to my chest.

"If that's what you want. You slut."

"I am. I'm a slut for you both."

Ford leans down and kisses me roughly, his tongue licking across my cheek to my ear where he whispers, "We'll both work you open, fist you, and then we'll take you."

I groan as their fingers slide down my taint and then move inside of me—one, two, three, four. I feel the stretch of it, the burn. Lube trickles down my crack onto the bed, making such a mess, but I need it. I need all of it to make sure that I can do this.

I want to do this.

"Fuck, look at him," Ford says, and I move onto my elbows to see both of them watching as my ass takes their fingers. All of them. I'm split wide open and I want more.

"I can take more. I can take it all."

"I know you can. You're doing so good," Cash says as he adds more lube and the two of them press into me further. I fall back and arch up, my cock jumping as they work into me, knuckle deep. And then Cash is beside me, pulling me on top of him, kissing me deeply as Ford slowly works his fist into my ass. It's thick and the sting of it aches, but I'm patient, feeling my body loosen for him so that he can press farther into me.

"Fuck, he's doing it. Shit, Cash," Ford says as he leans forward and kisses my lower back. I groan at the feel of it, biting my bottom lip to keep myself from screaming.

"Good boy. You're doing so good," Cash says, reaching up and pulling me down for a tender kiss. He kisses me softly, gently as Ford continues to work me open. Farther and farther until I feel the slip of his hand press inside of me with a pop.

And then he's in.

"He did it. Shit, he did it," Ford says as he lazily pumps his fist into me.

I groan at the sensation, loving that Cash is reaching down to feel it, feel how good I am.

"Fuck, Ben," he says and then kisses me once more, his tongue tangling with mine. "You're so perfect."

I groan as Ford continues to fist me before finally removing his hand from me. I groan at the absence of it, but it's not long before he takes Cash's cock and slides it easily inside of my hole. My open, eager hole. Cash bends his knees and thrusts his length gently into me until he's balls deep and then he pulls me down against him, his lips on mine as Ford lines his own dick up with my hole and pushes in.

I cry out at the feel of it, but I've been stretched open and Ford's cock pushes in without too much work. He's slow and careful, his groans mixing with ours until they're both seated deep inside of me.

"Shit, Ford. I can feel your dick against mine. So hot."

"Feels so damn good," Ford moans.

"Yes," I gasp. "Yes. Yes."

Ford reaches around me and pumps my cock, making it positively ache with the need to release.

"Move. I want you both moving," I groan, arching back and feeling them both slide into me even more.

Ford is panting above me and Cash is positively on fire below.

"That what you want, Benjamin? You want us to wreck you," Ford rasps into my ear.

"Yes. Make me yours. Make me...."

It's Ford who moves first. He pulls out and presses back into me, making Cash moan into my mouth as I bend down and kiss him fiercely, loving the feel of being so split open.

"Shit. Shit," Ford mutters as Cash starts to buck his hips, both fucking into me, gently, slowly, but enough to make me nearly scream in pleasure.

I feel their hands on me—rubbing, squeezing, holding me in place as they take what they want from me. Ford is biting his way across my shoulder before lifting me slightly, turning my head and kissing me.

Cash gazes up at Ford and then their lips meet, tongues tangling as they moan into each other.

When they finally pull apart, I beg. I'm nearly crying from the need to come.

"Please. Please!"

"Fuck, it's too much!" Cash groans. "I can't last. Shit."

Ford grunts as they both start railing into me, leaving me nearly mindless with the pain and pleasure of it, of being used. But still, they think only of me. Cash grabs on to my dick and pumps it, and it only takes a few seconds before I explode on a scream. Cash's neck strains, and I watch as he shudders, emptying himself into me. Ford swears, his hands tightening on my hips almost painfully as he slams into me several times before falling onto my back, his cock twitching in my hole. I fall onto Cash, my entire body trembling as I try to catch my breath.

I can feel it, their cum filling me up completely. They both marked me. Claimed me. Both of my men.

Mine.

"Don't pull out. Not yet," I say as my eyes close. "Just give me a few more minutes."

And they do, they leave their softening cocks inside of me until they slip out naturally. Then they settle me on the bed between them. My ass is dripping from their release, still stretched open. But I don't care. I just know that I want to do that again.

"Can we do that again?" I ask.

"We can, but you need time to recover," Cash says, and Ford kisses my shoulder before leaning over me and kissing Cash.

I sigh and feel my eyes close. I'm so fucking happy I could die right now and regret nothing.

"Love you," I murmur as I fall asleep.

"Love you too."

"Love you both."

EPILOGUE

FORD

TWO MONTHS LATER

"How's life treating you and Avery?" I ask as I kick my feet up on the table, watching as Ben and Cash bend over the cooler to grab us all drinks. They both have mighty fine asses if I do say so. Love to feel Cash's flex when he's pounding into me.

"Good. Real fucking good, man," Dean says, and I smile at him.

"You deserve it. And he sure is pretty to look at." I glance over and see Avery inside the house, making us a salad. He's wearing a flowing, flowery dress, his blond hair pulled into a French braid, his lips a pretty pink.

Dean frowns at my comment, and I smirk at him. "I mean, he is. Look at him. It's just an objective statement. Don't worry. I've only got eyes for Ben and Cash."

His frown straightens out and he nods. "Good. Avery is mine."

"Got it, boss."

Ben makes his way back to me, looking so fucking cute in his ripped jeans, Converse, and tight blue shirt. He looks better naked, but I digress.

He hands me a grape soda and then proceeds to sit on my lap, snuggling into my chest and sighing. It's like he's been waiting to do this all day, despite having woken up on top of me this morning.

He's just the cuddliest.

Since the day Dean found out about us and the air was cleared, the three of us have been over a few times for dinner and a few motorcycle rides. It's never been uncomfortable. Dean seems happy that Ben found us, that we love him so much. That we take care of him. We make sure he eats and gets enough rest. And not that we tell his dad this, but we sexually satisfy him. All the fucking time.

I smirk at that and then my mind wanders to the future. Our future. Dean got teary-eyed last time we were over and blubbered that he can't wait for us to get married. That he can't wait to walk Ben down the aisle. It wasn't the first time he's mentioned it.

But I whole-heartedly agree with him. I can't fucking wait either.

"When are the ladies gonna be here?" Dean asks, and Ben glances at his phone.

"Soon. Lex is bringing them. He said that sometimes Norma takes a long time to get ready because she forgets where she puts her glasses and keys."

Dean smiles at that.

"Glad he's bringing them. It was a blast last time."

"It was!" Avery says as he appears at Dean's side, leaning over and kissing his cheek. Dean grins at him before pulling him in for a long-drawn-out kiss, tongue and all.

Ben grumbles under his breath, and I let out a laugh, nuzzling his neck.

"Don't be weird about it, babe."

He rolls his eyes at me before moving off of me to settle on Cash's lap. That guy just needs both of us all the time. I fucking love it. Love that I never feel like I'm competing, that Ben unequivocally wants us both.

And we feel the same about him.

It's never a fight, it never feels like one is the odd man out. We just fit perfectly.

"How does it feel to be a college grad now, Ben?" Avery asks. "Finally done. I can't believe it."

"I'm so glad it's over, but now I need to find a job."

"You don't need to rush," Cash says. "We can take care of you until you find something you love."

Ben stares lovingly at Cash, touching his face tenderly. Cash leans into it like the softie he is. "I know. But I don't want to be a leech. I don't want you to feel like I'm taking advantage of you."

"You're never a leech," I pipe up, and Ben squirms on Cash's lap. He probably wants to sit on both of us, but there aren't chairs here that would fit the three of us. So Ben just has to move from lap to lap.

He doesn't have to do that at our place though. We have a bench at my place. I built it. Fits the three of us perfectly.

"Now that Ben moved in with us, what are you gonna do with the garage apartment?" Cash asks.

Dean flips the burgers. "Probably use it as Avery's art studio."

Avery smiles widely. "I can do nudes up there. Of your dad."

Ben huffs, and I laugh.

"Avery," Dean says, blushing. "Jesus."

"What? It's hot."

Just as he says it, Lex appears with William, his fiancé, and Norma, Vikki, and Martha.

"What's hot?" Norma asks as she moves toward a chair and sits down. "Is this a sex thing? Because I've been around the block. I know a thing or two about setting fire in the bedroom."

"She does," Martha says as she walks over to the cooler and pulls out a Capri Sun. "God, I love these things. Gets my blood sugar really high."

Lex huffs, pulling it from her hands. "Not today, Satan. Behave."

Martha glowers at him. "Give me my sugar or I will condemn you."

Lex looks like he's about to lose his shit, but William comes over and presses a hand to his chest, instantly calming him.

He whispers something to Lex, and I watch as Lex hands Martha the drink with a sigh.

"One, Martha, and I mean it. No more sneaking them in your bra."

She beams and then ambles back to the porch, nearly tripping up the stairs before Dean grabs her and leads her to a seat. Lex is back to nearly having a stroke over them as Avery sets out a few appetizers. The ladies obliterate all the food in minutes, and I cackle at the way Lex glowers.

"They're going to be the death of me, William. I already have gray hair," Lex hisses behind me.

"They'll be fine. You worry too much."

He huffs and the two of them make their way inside to help Avery. Norma leans over to me and waggles her eyebrows. "So, how is it being with two other men at the same time?"

I slurp on my soda and waggle my eyebrows back at her.

"So hot. The positions are endless."

She hoots and slaps at her knee, looking delighted.

I lean back and watch as Ben feeds Cash some potato salad off a fork, his eyes catching on mine. Fuck, he's hot, so fucking perfect for us.

"You're next," he mouths, and I smirk at him. He can feed me all fucking day if he wants to. I won't stop him.

I'm a lucky fucking man.

EPILOGUE

CASH

Last week I broke my lease agreement and am officially moved in with Ben and Ford. Not that I wasn't living there already, but now it feels official. We all have a place to come home to now. My place never really felt like much, and Ben wasn't attached to his garage apartment. Ford's house has always been home to me, so it just made sense that this is where we'd end up.

"I told you, I was going to pay the electric, water, and gas. That's the deal."

"Not water. I never agreed to that," Ford says, and Ben rolls his eyes, his hand on his hips.

"I have to contribute. I won't be a freeloader."

I stare at them, Ford's eyes darkening and a smirk teasing his lips. "You're not, baby. You're free use, which means you pay with your ass."

Ben huffs and then rolls his eyes. "I'm not your rent boy."

But he likes it—he pretends to be irritated with the thought, but his dick is growing hard in his pants.

Ford sees it, reaching down and sliding his hand up Ben's hard length.

"You pay gas and electric. The rest is on us until you get a job that you love."

Ben frowns but arches up into Ford's touch, needing more. He already got more this morning, taking us both at the same time. Again.

He needs to be careful with that ass of his. I don't want him to ever get hurt.

Suddenly, the doorbell rings, interrupting Ford's plans and he sighs and moves to open the front door as Ben adjusts himself.

"Fuck," Ben murmurs and then glowers at me. "I know you were in on the water thing. Don't think you can use my dick to distract me from the bigger issue."

I stand up and bring him into my arms, kissing him roughly.

"But it's so easy," I say with a pat on his ass.

"Oh please, don't mind me!" Ford's mom chimes in loudly. "I love seeing people young and in love."

"Jesus, Mom. You need to give us some warning before you just stop on by."

"But I just came from my quilting class, and I have a present for Benjamin."

Ben flushes and pulls away from me, moving toward Ford's mom. She's basically adopted him. When she found out that the three of us were together, she nearly fainted from joy.

"I get not one but two son-in-laws!"

She'd shrieked it and couldn't stop smiling for hours.

Not that we're engaged. Not yet. But I have something up my sleeve. Neither Ben nor Ford know. But it's happening. Not soon, but soon enough.

"I love it," Ben says. In his hands is a brightly colored quilt that I know Ford's mom spent hours on. And probably hundreds of dollars. Quilting ain't cheap. "It's beautiful."

"I made it for your bed. I thought you needed a little more color in your life. Those bed sheets probably show everything."

I chuckle and Ford sighs as Ben oohs and aahs over the intricate pattern of fabrics, making Ford's mom beam.

"You got the colors just right. I love it."

Ben moves to the bedroom and we follow, watching as he places the quilt over the mattress, smoothing it out.

"God, it's wonderful. Thank you."

Ben sniffles and Ford's mom pulls him into a hug.

"You're welcome, love. Also, I made you all something."

She reaches into her bag and pulls out matching shirts. Ford groans and Ben chuckles, pulling his shirt off and tugging on the button-up Ford's mom made.

"It's perfect. I can't wait to match with my guys."

Ford and I pull ours on, and Ford's mom takes a picture of us together, looking like losers with matching shirts that say *"Sharing is Caring"*. But it makes Ford's mom happy and Ben is almost crying with happiness, so I let it go.

If this makes him happy, I'll do it.

I'll do whatever he wants to make him smile.

BEN

Cash proposed! The three of us drove the motorcycles up to a hilltop among the stars and the moonlight. I sat on the back of Cash's bike, clinging to him for dear life, loving the feel of him against me, loving how carefully he maneuvered in and out of traffic.

And when we finally arrived, he got down on one knee and held out rings to us.

I wept, and Ford sniffled a bit, and we both said yes.

We got Cash a ring too, later that week. We all went and picked it out together so we all match. Ford and Cash's are thicker black titanium bands while mine is a bit thinner and daintier. They're perfect.

And now, I'm curled up beside them, the TV playing in the background as we lounge on the couch after a long day of work. I still haven't found a full-time job in social work, but I'm hoping that the senior living facility I currently work reception at will hire me for a higher position. But that's yet to be seen. Right now, I'm just happy to come home to Cash and Ford, to let them hold me and fuck me to sleep.

"This movie is wretched," Cash grumbles. "I'm bored as fuck."

"It's what Ben wanted to watch."

"Well, he's half asleep too."

I arch into him, nearly purring. "You guys are making me too sleepy, rubbing me like this."

My head is on Cash's lap, his hand in my hair, and Ford is rubbing at my legs. I'm nearly comatose.

"How about we go to bed?"

"Only if you fuck me first."

"Deal."

They pick me up and bring me out to the shed, the one they made just for me.

"I love this place," I say with a sigh as they set me down on a cushioned table. Sex toys surround us, and I feel my cock harden with need.

"We're gonna take care of you, Ben," Ford says as he starts to undress me.

"Always," Cash chimes in, leaning down to kiss me.

And that's how we spend the next few hours. They show me just how much they love me and need me, and I do the same right back.

ACKNOWLEDGMENTS

First, I would like to thank my editor, Angela O'Connell, for all of your hard work on this book. I adore you.

Thank you to my alpha readers Lark Taylor and Charity VanHuss for being so helpful. And to Nicole Dykes for all of your support.

Thanks also to Margaret Neal, Melissa Tarrington, Reading Queer All Year and sh.editsbooks for reading through this and catching all the mistakes we missed.

And last, but not least, thank you to all the readers who reached out to me with words of encouragement. They mean everything and keep me writing.

ALSO BY CORA ROSE

The Unexpected Series

Whit

Sem

Emery

Luke

Lex

Colin

Diablo

The Inevitable Series

Until Him

Always Him

Timeless Series

A Minute More

Standalone

Waiting for You

Unlucky 13

Exception

Co-writes with Nicole Dykes

Reaching Reed

Becoming Bennet

Discovering Damon